SONG OF THE SOULLESS

ATLANTIS LEGACY, BOOK 4

LINDSEY SPARKS   WRITING AS   LINDSEY FAIRLEIGH

RUBUS PRESS

Copyright © 2021 by Rubus Press
All rights reserved.

This book is a work of fiction. All characters, organizations, and events are products of the author's imaginations or are used fictitiously. No reference to any real person, living or dead, is intended or should be inferred.

Editing by Fresh as a Daisy Editing
www.freshasadaisyediting.com

Cover by We Got You Covered
www.wegotyoucoveredbookdesign.com

9781949485165

MORE BOOKS BY LINDSEY SPARKS

ECHO TRILOGY

Echo in Time

Resonance

Time Anomaly

Dissonance

Ricochet Through Time

KAT DUBOIS CHRONICLES

Ink Witch

Outcast

Underground

Soul Eater

Judgement

Afterlife

ATLANTIS LEGACY

Sacrifice of the Sinners

Legacy of the Lost

Fate of the Fallen

Dreams of the Damned

Song of the Soulless

Blood of the Broken

Rise of the Revenants

ALLWORLD ONLINE

AO: Pride & Prejudice

AO: The Wonderful Wizard of Oz

Vertigo

THE ENDING SERIES

The Ending Beginnings: Omnibus Edition

After The Ending

Into The Fire

Out Of The Ashes

Before The Dawn

World Before

THE ENDING LEGACY

World After

For more information on Lindsey and her books:

www.authorlindseysparks.com

Join Lindsey's mailing list to stay up to date on releases

AND to get a FREE copy of *Sacrifice of the Sinners*.

www.authorlindseysparks.com/sacrifice

ACKNOWLEDGMENTS

Thank you so much to my Patreon Patrons, who support my work
on a monthly basis:

Olivia Rodriguez
Carlotta Woolcock
Teri Lindley
Fred Oelrich
Allison Mayer
Gabrielle Amarosa
Conrad

[1]

"I'm so sorry." My words faded into the incessant mechanical chorus of beeps, hums, and whirs that filled the room.

It was about the hundredth time I had whispered those three words, and I didn't think I would stop until the person to whom I was apologizing was awake to hear them. Even then, I wasn't sure I could ever stop. My guilt ran bone deep, an infected wound requiring regular draining. I hugged my legs tighter and rested my chin on my knees, the toes of my boots hanging over the edge of my chair.

Selene lay in the reclined recovery chair, one of eight in this pod of the Med Sector, four on either side of the room. My guilt festered as I stared at the seven empty recovery chairs. Of the five Amazon warriors Hades and I had stranded off-world all those millennia ago when we disabled Earth's gephyra, only Selene had survived. And for a while there, even *her* survival had been uncertain.

My focus returned to Selene's face. I scanned her familiar, angular features for any change, any sign that she might wake soon. Her pale skin had regained its usual moonlit luster, which I took to be a good sign, and her gleaming auburn waves fanned out on either side of her head. I glanced at her chest, reassuring myself it continued to rise and fall with each slow breath.

Several long sessions in the asclypos had repaired the damage done to her body by the failing cryogenerator during those last few hours she spent in the cryopod. The tubes and cords connecting her to the machines in the wall behind her recovery chair no longer offered life support, but comfort. It was only a matter of time until she woke. Until I could explain why she had been stranded on that distant, frozen planet with her team of Amazons and why *I* had stranded her there. Until I could ask for her forgiveness.

My stomach knotted at the thought of how she would respond. I turned my face away from her, resting my cheek against my knee and closing my eyes. I could almost imagine I was in the ICU of a human hospital back on Earth.

Except, I wasn't on Earth, and this was about the furthest thing from a human hospital. The woman lying there, only recently having stepped back from the precipice between life and death, wasn't even human. She was Olympian. Amazon. A survivor, barely. No thanks to me. The asclypos had done all the work. All I had been able to do was stand by and watch. And wait.

Part of me felt certain that if I took my eyes off Selene for longer than a minute or two, the monitor displaying her vitals would flatline, and she would die. I had abandoned her so many thousands of years ago. I would not abandon her now. I owed her that much, at least.

Inhaling a fortifying breath, I opened my eyes and returned to staring at Selene. My back twinged with pain from sitting in the same position for too long. I slid my feet off the edge of the chair, my boots hitting the metal floor with a dull clang. I leaned forward, setting my elbows on my knees, and scrubbed my hands over my face. My skin felt greasy, my eyes gritty. I needed a shower. And sleep. But even if I were to lie down and close my eyes, I knew I wouldn't be able to drift off. Not until I was certain Selene would be all right. Not until I had said my piece.

At the sound of a throat clearing, my spine stiffened, and my stare snapped to the doorway. I gripped the armrests of my chair, my heart hammering in my throat.

Meg stood in the doorway, the channels of her snug hoplon suit glowing a subtle amber, matching the stone of the regulator dangling from the chain around her neck and indicating that, like mine, her psychic powers were suppressed.

It was a matter of courtesy. There were no enemies to fight aboard this ship. The only enemy was the Tsakali scout we had taken prisoner on the same planet where we had found Selene and the *Elysium*, and that frightful creature didn't have a hope in hell of breaking free.

I had learned long ago that the color of my regulator impacted how others behaved toward me. Even if I wasn't in their minds, so long as my regulator glowed electric blue, paranoia would consume them. They believed I was hearing their every thought, feeling their every emotion, and sneaking a peek at their deepest, darkest secrets.

Not that it mattered much where Meg and I were concerned. With our bond, we didn't need to rely on psychic gifts to tap into one another's innermost thoughts. We were connected, always aware of what the other was thinking and feeling. That I hadn't noticed her arrival proved just how distracted I was by my obsession with Selene's recovery.

"How is she?" Meg asked. Her question wasn't necessary. She already knew, thanks to our bond. But she was offering me the catharsis of talking.

My attention drifted back to Selene's serene face. If I hadn't known better, I never would have guessed she had spent the last few days fighting for her life. "The same," I said, drawing my legs up onto the chair and turning to the side as I curled up, settling in for another lengthy stretch of watching and waiting.

Meg sighed and entered the pod, the door panel sliding shut behind her. She crossed to the recliner on the opposite side of Selene and sat, perching on the edge of the chair. "Cora, you know it's not your fault she's—"

My eyes were the only part of me that moved, shifting from Selene to Meg.

Meg crossed her arms over her chest and raised one eyebrow, the seventeen-year-old Zari psychic looking every bit the snarky teen she had never really had the chance to be. "Well, it's not."

I cinched our bond as tight as I could and shifted my attention back to Selene. I didn't have the emotional bandwidth to babysit Meg's feelings right now. I wanted her to go away, to leave me alone. But even through my annoyance, I caught a hint of something unexpected trickling through our bond: fear.

Curiosity piqued, I unfurled the complicated tangle of thoughts at the root of Meg's fear.

She was afraid Selene would replace her as my right-hand woman. Even though Meg had access to all my innermost thoughts and feelings, she still feared that once Selene woke— another *true* Amazon warrior—she would take Meg's place by my side, and Meg would become redundant. Irrelevant. No longer of any use to me. Meg feared I would discard her, and in doing so, I would prove her viper of a mother right. I would prove that Meg really was useless.

Brow furrowing and heart fracturing, I tore my stare from Selene to look at Meg. I shook my head, momentarily at a loss for words. "Meg, I—" I swallowed, still shaking my head. "I could never—I *would never* replace you," I told her. "Selene is just a friend." I frowned, glancing down at Selene. "Or she *was* a friend. I don't know what she is now." I looked at Meg once more. "She's not you. You're my—" I hesitated, searching for the right word but coming up empty. No word existed to explain the bond we shared. "You're the only one I would ever want to share this bond with."

Meg sucked in a breath to argue.

"And no," I said before she could start. "I wouldn't undo our bond if I could." I gave her a moment, letting her explore the thoughts and emotions surrounding that statement. I wanted her to know I meant it. I needed her to accept what she was to me.

It might have been a strange twist of fate and circumstance that had brought us together, but even if I had the chance to rewrite the past, I wouldn't change this. Our bond. There was something to be said about another person knowing the dark, hidden parts of one's soul. It was too easy to hide from oneself. Too easy for *me* to hide from *my*self. It was much, *much* harder for me to hide from Meg.

After a tense moment, Meg nodded, then sniffled and looked away. Just like that, we were good.

The tiniest smile tugged at the corners of my lips.

Clearing her throat, Meg stood from the edge of the recovery chair and started toward the door. The panel slid open as she approached. She paused in the doorway, one hand on the frame, and looked back at me over her shoulder.

"Let me know if you want to talk." She arched her head to the side, cracking her neck. "Or not talk. I'd love to get some more practice in with a doru . . ."

Again, the corners of my mouth lifted. This was one of the things I loved the most about Meg. She didn't want to sit around and talk about our feelings. She wanted us to beat them out of each other. She may not have been a true Olympian Amazon, but she sure acted like one.

"That'd be nice," I said, thinking I could use a little doru practice myself.

We had dorus to spare these days. The four Amazons who had perished in the cryopods no longer needed theirs. Plus, the Amazons who currently resided in the *Elysium's* Vault of Souls had stashed their gear in the ship's armory. They would, of course, expect to find their things where they had left them—upon their eventual resurrection—but until then, it seemed a waste to let such powerful weapons gather dust. A war was being waged, after all, and soon enough, we might have the womanpower needed to wield all available dorus. Assuming things went well when we dropped in on the Zari, which we were planning to do as soon as we reached Earth.

Meg mirrored my faint smile, a wordless reassurance that we were good, then turned away and stepped out into the main corridor of the Med Sector. The door panel slid shut behind her.

Once again alone in the pod, I returned to my silent vigil at Selene's side. I watched her chest rise and fall, then looked at her face.

And stood, sending the chair skittering backward, as I stared wide-eyed at Selene.

Who was staring at me.

For long seconds—an eternity—I stood there suspended, my gaze locked with Selene's. Her emerald-green eyes bore into me, peeling me open. Dissecting me.

"Wa—" Selene coughed and cleared her throat, then swallowed roughly. "Water?"

"Oh!" Spell broken, I rushed to the wall behind Selene's recovery chair and fumbled with the water bottle stashed on the recessed shelf. With shaking hands, I poured water into a lidded tumbler, then snapped the lid in place and hurried back to Selene's side. "Here you go."

Selene raised her hands to grip the cup but was too weak to hold it on her own. I helped her raise the cup to her lips and tilt it back to drink. When she seemed sated, I guided her hands and the cup down to her lap, my gaze skittering over her regulator. It still glowed a steady, subtle amber, and relief washed over me. I wanted to be the one to explain what had happened, not have Selene discover it herself by skimming through my memories. The situation was complicated, and it would be far too easy for her to misunderstand what Hades and I had done all those millennia ago—and why we had done it.

I twisted and pulled the chair closer, then sat, my back ramrod straight.

Selene managed to raise the cup on her own, taking another long drink of water.

"How do you feel?" I asked as the silence stretched uncomfortably. "For a while there, we weren't sure if you'd wake up after—" I rubbed my clammy hands on my thighs. "We weren't sure if you'd wake up."

Selene lowered the cup to her lap once more, her brow furrowing. "What—" She cleared her throat again, her gaze searching mine. "What happened?"

I opened my mouth but found I wasn't sure what to say, so I pressed my lips back together.

"The last thing I can remember is climbing into a cryopod," Selene said, answering her own question as best she could. She looked around, scanning the seven empty recovery chairs, then returned her attention to me. "Where are the others?"

I froze, a deer in headlights. For all of my wanting to explain, I had no idea how to actually do it.

Selene narrowed her eyes. In my moment of hesitation, she deactivated her regulator. A sunny topaz glow overtook the subtle amber of the pendant's stone, and she dipped into my temporarily unguarded mind.

Normally, she never would have made it past my mental barriers. But normally, I wasn't so twisted up by my tangled emotions. The guilt, more than anything else, prevented me from booting her out of my mind. I sensed her searching, digging. I knew what memories she was watching, but in that moment of weakness, of guilt-ridden paralysis, I could not stop her. The very thing I had feared most was happening, and I could *not* stop it.

Selene's expression transformed, morphing from curiosity to horror, then from horror to rage. "You—"

I held my breath.

"You killed them." Selene's chest heaved, rage burning in her eyes.

I shook my head, once again at a loss for words.

Selene yanked at the cords and tubes still attached to her body, sending the monitors in the wall behind her into a frenzy.

"Whoa," I said, raising my hands. "What are you doing? I don't think you should—"

Awkwardly, Selene rolled out of the recliner and set her feet on the floor. The thin blanket draped over her legs slid off, hanging from the chair, and Selene rose on shaky legs.

I stood, automatically reaching out to steady her.

Until she stumbled toward me, her outstretched hands burning with a lethal charge of golden energy.

I backpedaled, tripping over my chair and running into the next recliner over. I sidestepped around it, groping my way along, never taking my eyes off Selene or the promise of death electrifying her hands. "Selene, wait, I—"

A pulse of brilliant, golden light burst from Selene's right hand. It hit me like a Mack truck, cutting off my plea with a grunt and sending me flying backward. I slammed into the far wall, a bright starburst of pain erupting in my shoulder, and landed on the floor in a heap.

That had been a killing blow. If not for the protection of my hoplon suit, I would be dead right now. Even with it, I was in bad shape. Deep bone bruises in my shoulder blades, ribs, and hips, possibly even some fractures. It was impossible to say with the rush of adrenaline dulling the pain. I slumped over, gripping the side of my ribcage and wincing. The impact cracked a rib or two, that was for sure.

"You killed them!" Selene seethed as she stalked toward me, seeming to regain her strength and stability with each step, like her righteous anger fortified her weakened body.

I sucked in a breath to protest, but the pain in my ribcage forced it back out in an agonizing cough.

The golden glow of the psychic energy encasing Selene's hands intensified to blinding brightness.

I raised my hands, one shielding my eyes, the other touching the stone of my regulator to deactivate it. Only an energy barrier would save me from the coming blast. Without psychic protection, the energy would cook my body inside my hoplon suit.

Static charged the air a split second before a flash of violet light. Selene launched forward, surprise widening her eyes, and slammed into the wall beside me.

I cowered under the cascade of medical equipment knocked free by Selene's impact. She landed on the floor nearby, her head hitting the metal grating with a sickening thunk. Her arm flopped out to the side, limp but not lifeless. I could still sense her mind, dimmed by unconsciousness, but still there. Still alive.

"Cora!" Meg rushed in from the doorway and crouched in front of me. She curled her fingers around my arm, her grip firm as she pulled me up to sit, and raised her other hand to press against my forehead. She closed her eyes, a mask of concentration slipping over her face, and I sensed her psychic fingers combing through my body as she took inventory of my injuries.

Finally, she opened her eyes, her features taut with worry. "Are you all right?" She wasn't asking about my body, but about my heart. She searched my face, trying to untangle the snarled knot of thoughts and emotions flowing into her through our bond. Brow furrowing, she shook her head. "Why didn't you defend yourself?"

I looked away, unable to face the judgment in her stare. I could have told her I had been about to defend myself, but she and I both knew I would have had my shield up too late. If she hadn't shown up when she did, I would be dead. Not because I couldn't have defended myself against Selene. I should have deactivated my regulator the second I noticed Selene was awake. But because I *wouldn't* have.

Reluctantly, I turned my head to look at Selene's motionless body. "Is she okay?"

"Seems fine to me," Meg said without even looking at Selene. She didn't need to. She could sense Selene's mind, just as I could.

Footsteps banged in the corridor leading to the pod. The door panel slid open, and Emi rushed in, closely followed by Hades.

"What happened?" Emi asked, dropping to her knees beside Selene. She pressed her fingers to Selene's neck and lifted one of the unconscious woman's eyelids.

Hades crouched beside Meg and gazed down at me, his gentle expression telling me he had a fairly good idea of what had happened when Selene woke. Of Selene blaming me.

Of me letting her.

I set my jaw, unwilling to rehash the horrible confrontation, and looked at Emi. "She woke up."

[2]

The butt of my doru clanged against the metal grating on the floor as I wandered along a cramped corridor down on the service level of the *Elysium*. Overhead lights flared to life further up the hallway, activated by my motion.

Down here, in the bowels of the ship, the passageways were narrower, the ceilings lower. A veritable army of dormant bots of various shapes and sizes waited in their recessed homes in the walls. If the ship's AI needed maintenance of any kind, it would awaken the appropriate helper and get the job done itself. The guts of the ship functioned better without the interference of living hands.

There was little need for anyone to come down to this level, which was precisely why *I* was here. I spun my doru around lazily, fighting off imaginary foes in a slow-motion battle. My ribs ached with the movements, but a brief session in the asclypos had given the bones a jump start on mending the breaks, and it no longer hurt to breathe. At least, not physically. Guilt ate away at me, more agonizing than any physical pain.

Retreating to the lower levels of the ship served the purpose of providing me at least the appearance of privacy. It was all I really needed. Selene's reaction to learning about what Hades and I had done in our attempt to save our people all those millennia ago—stealing the chaos fragments powering the gephyra and stranding Selene and her team off-world—had shaken me to the core.

I supposed I had been holding out hope that when she woke, she would absolve me of my sins, cleansing me of my guilt. But she had done the exact opposite, solidifying my certainty that I was responsible for the deaths of the four other Amazons on her team. My choices—my actions—had caused their deaths. The correlation was clear. Because of me, they were dead—really dead, not just waiting for their next cycle in a consciousness orb. And *I* was alive. The same actions that had damned them had, eventually, saved me.

The rational part of my brain knew I had made the right call. The vast majority of our people survived. Sort of. They were dead—for now—but not gone. Yes, there had been casualties, but if I hadn't made the choice I did, *all* of my people would have died their ultimate deaths.

But guilt wasn't rational. It twisted in my gut, forming a knot of unsettling emotions that grew and grew and grew until there was no more room for rationality.

A muffled murmur floated up the corridor, tickling my ears. Someone else was down here.

I stopped, planting my doru on the floor, and narrowed my eyes. I cocked my head to the side, taking steady, shallow breaths as I listened for more. Silence greeted my ears. Had I imagined the voice?

"Butt-licking ball sack!" The curse was faint, but clear enough.

The corner of my mouth twitched, and I started forward again, following the periodic string of colorful curses like vulgar bread-crumbs. They lead me around a corner and to an open doorway ahead on the right.

When I reached the doorway, I found Fiona sitting on the floor in one corner of a large, square room. Glowing and blinking blue lights covered the walls, reminding me of the massive server farms so often featured in technothrillers. A huge robotic arm, almost as large as a person, hung down from the ceiling.

Fiona sat with one knee bent, the other leg stretched out on the floor. Her tablet was propped against her upraised thigh, a cord connecting it to a panel on the wall beside her. Her shocking orange hair was twisted up into a knot that sat askew on top of her head, held in place by her tablet's stylus. A mech glove encased her left hand, reaching all the way up to her elbow. I glanced at the oversized robotic arm hanging down from the center of the ceiling—one of three—thinking it had to be controlled by the mech glove. Using her free hand, Fiona swiped and tapped on the tablet's screen with her index finger, her motions jerky.

I also glanced at the plaque on the wall beside the door, directly beneath the display for the door panel controls, which glowed blue, showing the door panel had been locked in the *open* position. The Olympian words on the plaque translated to something like SYSTEM OPERATOR. I narrowed my eyes, not sure what that meant.

With a frown, I tapped my knuckles on the doorframe. "Hey, Fio—"

Fiona gasped and jumped, clutching at her chest with both hands. Her tablet tumbled off her leg, and she barely caught it before it hit the floor. She hugged the tablet to her chest and stared at me with wide eyes. "What the shit, Cora! Are you trying to give me a fracking heart attack?"

I snorted a laugh and held up a hand, flashing her an apologetic smile. "Sorry, Fio." I retracted my doru to its compact length of two feet and reached over my shoulder to tuck it into the sheath on my back. "I thought you heard me."

Fiona relaxed, her shoulders lowering. "No, I—" Her words cut off, her eyes scanning the surrounding floor. "Where'd that damn thing go?"

I tilted my head to the side as I watched her. "What thing?"

"The stylus," she said, now combing over the metal grating with her hand.

The corners of my mouth tensed in a suppressed smile, and I cleared my throat. When Fiona looked up at me, I tapped the top of my head. My own hair was tied back in a low, messy bun, but Fiona's was high on the crown of her head, the stylus poking out of it like a pin in a pincushion.

"Oh," Fiona said, tugging the stylus free. "Duh." As she started writing on the tablet, I moved closer, craning my neck to see what was on the screen. She was making notes over a chaotic combination of English and Olympian characters, some kind of code that was incomprehensible to me without dipping into Fiona's mind to understand.

My brow furrowed. "What are you working on?"

Fiona jotted a few more notes, then sighed and stabbed the stylus into her bun before setting the tablet by her hip on the floor. "The simulation." She closed her eyes, rubbing her eyelids with her thumb and fingertips. "The *new* simulation, I mean." She lowered her hand and opened her eyes, resting her head back against the wall. Lights blinked and flashed behind her.

"I've duplicated the core coding of the Olympian simulation," Fiona said as she glanced up at the robotic arm, twisting and raising her gloved hand. The robotic arm tucked itself back into the recess in the ceiling. "And I have the Earth simulation ready to go." She tugged the mech glove off her hand and set it down beside the tablet. "But every time I attempt to run both sims simultaneously, the Earth simulation shuts down before it can even fully boot up."

My mouth fell open. "You finished the Earth simulation?" I raised my eyebrows. "*Already?*"

We had only been on the ship for a few days. Fiona's task in our mission to save as many humans as possible from the impending Tsakali attack on Earth was to build a Matrix-level simulation to house millions—possibly billions—of humans for however long it took us to find a safe, habitable planet to settle. The task sounded insurmountable to me. And Fiona had done it in a matter of *days*?

Fiona shrugged one shoulder and glanced away. "Well, I mean, I already had the zip file for Allworld Online's root code stashed on my external," she said, downplaying what she had accomplished. "And Gertie helped me sync AO with the ship's existing simulation framework. All we had to do was—"

I held up a hand. "Wait a sec. Who's Gertie?" Because there definitely weren't any living people on board the *Elysium* who went by that name.

Fiona looked around and swept an arm out to one side. "You're looking at her."

I peered around the room, then squinted at Fiona, momentarily wondering if sleep deprivation and mental overexertion had sapped her sanity. But then I recalled the words written on the plaque beside the door to this room: SYSTEM OPERATOR. My eyes widened, my brows climbing higher. She was talking about the ship. Or rather, the Artificial Intelligence that controlled the complex operations of the ship.

I scanned the space with renewed interest, my attention finally returning to Fiona. "You named the ship's AI *Gertie*?"

A small smile curved Fiona's lips, and she gave a low portion of the wall an affectionate pat. "Aye. After my Gran. She's got the same twisted sense of humor, and she's always nagging me about taking better care of myself. It seemed fitting." Fiona's eyes met mine, her smile fading. "You think it's stupid."

Frowning, I shook my head. "Not at all. I just figured you would have gone with 'Mother'." Fiona was a big fan of the *Alien* franchise. Whenever we played a game set in space, she dressed her avatar as Ripley, without fail.

Fiona scrunched up her face like she smelled something bad.

"I tried," she said. "Gertie wouldn't accept the name. Said it was an Olympian title or some such."

I nodded my head to the side. It was a title—*in* Olympian. It surprised me that the English translation wasn't acceptable, but I figured the system must operate on meaning rather than actual language.

"I thought about going with Sigourney," Fiona continued. "But it's such a mouthful, and Siggy just doesn't feel the same . . ." She shrugged. "She likes the stories I've told her about my Gran, so I went with Gertie."

I scanned the flashing walls with renewed interest. I hadn't spent any notable time interacting with AI in any of my previous lives, and I was intrigued by how Fiona described it as being able to feel and like—and as a *she*.

Fiona pressed her palm against the wall, a faint smile touching her lips. "She wants to help us. She wants the new simulation to work, but she can't find a way to run two separate, full-blown simulations simultaneously. Too much of her processing power is taken up by running the primary systems—navigation, life support, shields—the sorts of things we *kind of* need her to give her full attention to." Fiona gave the wall another affectionate pat. "It's all right, though. She's a cunning old girl. We'll figure it out."

I chewed on the inside of my cheek as I considered what she was saying. "And you can't just stick the humans in the Olympian simulation?"

Fiona shook her head. "Not without them knowing they're in a simulation. The Olympian simulation is very surreal. It's like Inception in there—the laws of physics don't apply *at all*. And since the goal here is to trick humanity into believing their simulated world is real . . ."

I nodded to myself. We had voted on how to approach humanity with the prospect of leaving behind their physical bodies to inhabit a virtual world on board an alien ship bound for a new, Earth-like planet. It sounded nuts to me, even in my own head. Most of us agreed that if we were honest with the people of Earth—if we gave them a choice to either join us incorporeally on the *Elysium* or stay in their bodies on Earth to ride out the coming apocalypse—they would choose to stay behind. Because to most people, incorporeal life in a virtual world would feel far too much like death.

Shockingly, my mom was the lone dissenting voice, believing it was more important to preserve free will than to save lives. The rest of us agreed that the humans who joined the millions of Olympian souls already residing on the *Elysium* needed to be kept in the dark about the truth of their new reality. The greater good, and all that.

To complicate matters, there was the whole issue of consciousness suicide—when a "soul" lost the will to "live" and just sort of stopped *being.* The ribbons in the consciousness orb turned gray and settled in the bottom of the sphere like ashen remains. There was no coming back from that. And without the proper time to prepare the people of Earth for leaving their bodies behind to spend an indefinite stretch in a simulated world, we feared the results of them discovering the truth would be catastrophic to humanity's collective will to "live"—so to speak.

A close relative to consciousness suicide was consciousness atrophy, when a person slowly faded away within their consciousness orb. That was the whole reason a virtual world was needed in the first place. The constant stimulation and activity prevented atrophy, but clearly, it also complicated things. If we couldn't figure out a way to run a separate simulation for the humans, we wouldn't be able to keep them in the dark about their shocking new state of existence for long. In that case, maybe it really would be better for us to be up front with humanity. It was impossible to say.

"I don't suppose you can put limitations on the current simulation?" I said, thinking out loud. "You know, to make it seem more"—I raised one hand to make air quotes with my fingers —"real."

"Nope." Fiona let her head fall back against the wall and turned it from side to side with a slow, deliberate motion. "I already tried. Gertie can't do it." Fiona's eyes locked with mine. "Or she *won't* do it. I can't tell. She says it contradicts one of her prime directives, which is to preserve and protect her Olympian charges. Apparently placing limitations on their freedom within the simulation breaks the 'protect' directive." Fiona finished with an eye roll and a hysteria-tinged laugh. "Seems like a loose interpretation to me, but then, Gertie's a stubborn and opinionated old bat."

I studied Fiona, my brow furrowing as I wondered just how long she had been down here. "Fio, when was the last time you got some sleep?"

We had been on the ship for a little over three Earth days, en route to Earth for two of those three days, and based on the dark circles under Fiona's eyes and her apparently unraveling mental state, I was betting she hadn't slept a wink this whole time.

"Pfff . . ." Fiona swatted my question away with a flick of her hand. "Sleep is for weenies. I'll sleep when I'm dead."

"Which might be sooner than anticipated, if you keep at it," I said dryly. "When was the last time you backed yourself up?"

We had all agreed it would be smart to store daily backups of our own consciousnesses, considering the very real threat inherent to space travel through a Tsakali-infested galaxy. If one of us should suffer from an untimely death, at least a relatively recent version of ourselves could join the new simulation and eventually be reborn with the rest of the *Elysium's* disembodied residents.

Fiona rubbed her eyes with the palms of her hands, then blinked several times, staring at the far wall as if she could see through it. "Dunno. I think I made a backup yesterday." Another semi-hysterical laugh bubbled up from her chest. "Whatever 'yesterday' means here . . ."

I stepped closer to Fiona and held out my hand to her. "All right, Fio. Time to take a break." When Fiona didn't respond, I snapped my fingers and waved my hand in front of her face. "Get on up."

Fiona blinked, looking at my hand, then up at me. "Go? Why? Where are we going?"

I laughed under my breath. "Genetec Sector. I'm due for a backup, too. We'll make a quick copy of ourselves, and then *you're* going to get some sleep. We need you bringing your A game when we reach Earth."

"Fine." Fiona reached her arms over her head and arched her back in a full-body stretch. She placed her hand in mine, tucking her tablet under her other arm. "I need to pee anyway. Can you believe there aren't any bathrooms down here?"

"Well, this level wasn't built with people in mind. At least, not the living kind."

Fiona grunted her dissent. She groaned as I hoisted her up to her feet. "How close to Earth are we, anyway?"

"One more FTL jump." My eyes met hers. "We should be home tomorrow."

[3]

I stared down at the food on my tray, picking at the lasagna-like brick with my metal spork and *not* thinking about Selene. Not wondering if she was still unconscious. Not replaying her enraged words on a loop in my head.

My mom had been playing around with the ship's food generator, attempting to recreate some of her favorite dishes. Her fascination surprised me. She was a terrible cook, and she had somehow managed to avoid preparing anything in the kitchen at Blackthorn Manor that wasn't a sandwich or didn't come from a box for as long as I could remember. But then, this wasn't really cooking; it was experimenting. And here on the *Elysium*, there was no kitchen. There was a machine that would produce any food or dish programmed into it, so long as it had an adequate supply of the necessary molecular ingredients in its supply cartridges.

I pushed a chunk of imitation meat to the corner of the tray, where I had stashed the rest. It tasted like Italian sausage, but it had the texture of a rubber ball. This wasn't the worst result of her efforts. It also wasn't the best.

I scooped a bite of pseudo-noodle onto my spork and lifted it part of the way to my mouth. I had zero appetite. Exhaustion will do that to a person.

Funny, considering I had given Fiona such a hard time for letting herself become overtired. Now I was the one who was sleep deprived, while Fiona, freshly risen from an extended sleep and seated at the table in the corner of the crew dining room, looked well-rested and hyper-focused on her tablet. But how was I supposed to fall asleep when every time I closed my eyes, I saw Selene's face? Her hatred. Her rage. I couldn't shake it.

The sound of a food tray being set on the opposite side of my table startled me, and I raised tired eyes to find Raiden lowering himself down into a chair. He lifted his own spork, studying the utensil through narrowed eyes. "You know," he started, "of all the things I expected to find on an alien spaceship, I'd have to say a spork never made the list." He frowned, his focus still locked on the utensil.

The corner of my mouth tensed in an almost smile. This was the old Raiden, the one I had grown up with, not the one who had come back from battle, injured in ways that couldn't be seen. He could still brood with the best of them, but his sunnier, sillier, chattier side had been emerging more and more frequently.

"Some say it's neither a fork nor a spoon," Raiden went on, "and therefore is lacking all around. But I would counter that it's actually *both* a fork and a spoon, and is therefore *more* than either utensil on its own." He studied the spork for a few more seconds, then shrugged and dug into his mock-lasagna.

I stared at him. I was at a complete and utter loss for words.

Raiden chewed his first bite, grimaced—no doubt as he discovered the delightful texture of the wannabe sausage—and, with visible effort, swallowed the food. "Delicious," he said, flashing me a forced smile and scooping up another bite.

I coughed a laugh and shook my head. "You've given the spork situation way too much thought."

Raiden swallowed his second bite, loaded a third onto his

spork, and looked at me. "Maybe." The skin at the outer corners of his eyes crinkled as his lips curved into a genuine smile. "But it got you to laugh." He took another bite.

I chuckled and shook my head, returning to picking not-sausage out of my not-lasagna. He kind of had a point. Lifting my mood had always been a specialty of his. Less so now—post-military—than before. But apparently, he still had the knack for it.

Since leaving the frozen colony on board the *Elysium*, I hadn't seen as much of Raiden as I would have liked. He had been spending most of his time in the armory, ogling the impressive array of Olympian weapons alongside my mom, when she wasn't experimenting culinarily.

I hadn't seen much of anyone lately. Meg was busy in the Residential Sector and Training Center, arranging the accommodations for the Zari psychics, who would hopefully join us sooner rather than later. I had attempted to help her, but she had micromanaged me away. Emi was busy taking care of Selene and studying the sedated Tsakali scout in one of the research labs in the Med Sector, Fiona was all up in the AI's business, and Hades was busy scouring the ship's database for planets that would be viable for our new settlement. Everyone had something to do.

I, on the other hand, had gone from being an anxious lump at Selene's bedside to aimlessly wandering the ship, working up the nerve to return to the Med Sector to check on Selene—and to explain to her why she was wrong about me. I just had to figure out what to say.

And to convince myself she *was* wrong.

"Hey," Raiden said, his deep voice gentle. He set his spork down on his tray and rested his elbows on the table, crossing his forearms over one another.

I froze, looking at him without raising my head. "Hey?"

His expression told me it was time for some real talk.

I tensed, my shoulders hunching. So much for lifting my mood.

"I heard about what happened when your friend woke up." The compassion in his eyes was too much, and I averted my gaze to my tray, focusing on the small pile of rubbery meat. But Raiden wouldn't let me hide, and he forged on. "About what she said to you . . ."

I pressed my lips together and clenched my jaw, consciously taking even breaths through my nose. I glanced up at him, just for a fraction of a second. "Meg told you?"

"Yeah," Raiden said. "And a blind man could see that you're having a hard time with the situation."

Eyes still locked on my tray, I sat back in my chair, surrendering to the discomfort of what was coming.

Raiden sighed. "Listen, Cora. I know you don't like to talk about your feelings and all that—"

I lifted my eyes to meet his, raising my eyebrows to agree. *Don't like* was an understatement.

Raiden raised one eyebrow, letting me know he wasn't about to back down. But the challenging expression quickly faded back into nauseating compassion, and once again I averted my gaze to the tray. "I don't know all that happened in the Alpha site way back when—"

"You're right," I said quietly, crossing my arms over my chest. "You don't know." And I didn't want to think about it, let alone talk about it.

"But," Raiden continued, uncowed, "I've picked up enough from being around you and Hades to know that whatever you guys did, it was what you had to do to save your people. Greater good and all that. I mean, you sacrificed your own Goddamn life to give your people a chance to survive."

I jutted out my jaw, and my nostrils flared.

"Maybe you *did* do something that contributed to what happened to Selene and the others we found—"

I scoffed, finally raising my eyes to meet his. "That's a really tactful way to say I helped kill them."

Raiden shook his head, his earnest compassion making my chin quiver. "No, it isn't. You're just hearing what you want to hear." He was quiet for a moment, his eyes searching mine. "You want me to pass judgment on you. To make you feel like crap for sitting here, eating with a spork, and shooting the shit. You think you deserve to be punished because you're still alive. Because you survived when they didn't."

I shrank back into my chair, trying to run from the hard truths he was hurling at me.

Raiden leaned forward, not letting me flee. "Well, let me tell you something, Cora."

I gulped.

"I may not have lifetimes of experience under my belt," he said, his voice laced with quiet vehemence, "but I know a thing or two about survivor's guilt. I know what it can do to a person, eating away at them from the inside until there's nothing left but a shell. I know how hard it can be to come back from that. And I know I should thank my lucky Goddamn stars that I survived that suicide bombing when the rest of my unit didn't." He paused, collecting himself.

"But I can't," he said, his voice breaking. He swallowed, unshed tears shining in his eyes. "I don't. I know a hundred other factors contributed to what happened that night, but I *still* wonder what I could have done differently to save them." He glanced away, tapping his index finger on the table as he exhaled a shaky breath. "If I'd pulled the trigger sooner, or—" He shook his head, his stare returning to me, but his focus distant. On another time. Another place. "If I'd shouted a warning, or—or—" His Adam's apple bobbed. "Or done *something—anything* other than what I did—maybe they would still be alive."

His finger stilled on the table, and he blinked, refocusing on me. "But here's the thing: there is no going back. There's no way to return to milestone moments or whatever they call it in your games—"

I cleared my throat. "Checkpoints."

"Yeah, well, there are no *checkpoints* in real life. We make choices. Things happen. People die. We live with the consequences of our actions, regardless of whether those actions caused their deaths. We live, because they can't. We do something with our lives, because *they can't.*"

I swallowed, fighting back tears.

"We're going to save the Goddamn world, Cora," Raiden said, his voice rough with emotion. "Because *they can't.*"

I blinked, and a tear snuck over the brim of my eyelid.

Raiden leaned across the table, reaching out to brush the tear from my cheek with his thumb. "So, suck it up, buttercup." He flashed me a grin and settled back in his chair. "Because we've got a world to save."

[4]

I wound through the corridors of the Genetec Sector on my way to make my daily backup of myself, passing doors to laboratories with various purposes. The current corridor housed a string of generation labs, specifically Laboratory Epsilon through Theta. The door panels were shut, but I had seen the inside of a generation lab enough times to form a solid mental image of what I might find within. The cavernous spaces would seem to go on forever, filled with rows of incubation tubes, the large glass cylinders used in place of a mother's womb to grow new physical bodies.

One day, these labs would be an integral part of the rebirth of a new civilization, a melding of Olympians and humans. But right now, the generation labs went unused.

I took a right at the next intersection of corridors, leaving the generation labs behind. This long stretch of hallway only had door panels on the left, each leading to a nursery, where newborns would one day be cared for by android nurses.

A small smile curved my lips. This was the stuff science fiction fantasies were made of, and the gamer in me was a little giddy about traveling across the galaxy on a bonafide alien spaceship. It didn't matter that I had spent most of my first lifetime on a similar ship, that android nurses had raised and nurtured me during the first few years of *each* of my lifetimes . . . until I became Cora and gained a real, live human mother. It didn't matter that boarding this ship had felt a bit like coming home. It didn't matter that I was Peri, an ancient Olympian psychic warrior of the Order of Amazons, because I was also Cora, a reclusive gamer geek who had longed for the types of adventures I played in my games. And now I was living one.

My mood had been much improved since Raiden's tough-love pep talk this morning. I had even squeezed in a quick nap after lunch, Selene's scorn-filled eyes only haunting *some* of my dreams. The guilt was still there, buried deep beneath a renewed determination to save as many lives as possible from the destruction that was bound to follow the Tsakali's arrival on Earth. Raiden had reminded me I had a purpose—*now*—regardless of what had happened in the past. People were depending on me getting my head in the game, and their lives far outweighed those that had been lost because of my choices and actions millennia ago.

At the next intersection of corridors, I took a left, heading into the hallway lined by small labs with a singular purpose—the extraction of consciousnesses. And I nearly head-butted Selene.

She stumbled back a step, then froze.

Eyes locked with Selene's, I stood motionless for all of three seconds, then made an about-face and hurried back the way I had come. I was absolutely *not* up for another fight with her.

"Peri, wait," Selene blurted after my seventh step. "I mean, Cora—"

I stopped, not turning around, but no longer fleeing.

"That's the name you use now, isn't it—Cora?" She spoke Olympian, and it had been so long since I heard my native language that it took my brain a few seconds to comprehend what she was saying.

I stood in the corridor, my back to Selene, paralyzed by her presence. I took deep, even breaths. She wasn't attacking me. There was no need to run. At least, that's what I told myself.

"Your human friend, Emi, told me about your unique experience this cycle," Selene said, and I could tell from the sound of her voice that she was slowly closing the gap between us. "She told me you have a mother. A real mother." Wonder filled her voice. "I had a mother once, back on Olympus, but it was so long ago, I can't even remember what her voice sounded like. I have photos of her, but sometimes I'm not sure if my memories of her are real or just my mind fleshing out those images. I remember what she smelled like though." There was a smile in Selene's voice as she reminisced. "Like bread fresh out of the oven and honey. I could never forget that."

My whole body was tense, still waiting for the verbal lashing that was sure to come.

"I'm glad you had the chance to experience what it's like to have a real, living mother," Selene said, just a few steps behind me now. "The android nurses are lovely, but it's not the same." She let out a derisive snort. "And I never liked calling Demeter that—*mother*. She made a mockery of the word."

Selene fell quiet, and I waited for her to say more. When she didn't, I turned my head just enough that I could see her in my peripheral vision. "I wouldn't trade my mom for anything in the world," I admitted. And I meant it. The android nurses put our needs before their own because that's what we programmed them to do, but no amount of programming could replicate the selfless magic of a mother's love. It was priceless.

Silence stretched out between us, growing uncomfortable.

"Is there something I can do for you, Selene?" I asked, my voice low, restrained by uncertainty.

For a long moment, Selene didn't answer. "I—I'm sorry, Peri." She shook her head. "I mean, Cora." She exhaled a laugh. "That's going to take some getting used to." She inhaled deeply, then held the breath. "I acted rashly, and I'm sorry," she said, the words tumbling out in a rush. "Hades was there when I woke after the human psychic knocked me out." Selene rubbed the back of her neck, a small smile curving her lips. "She packs one hell of a punch . . ." Selene shook her head, her smile fading. "Hades—he let me dig through his memories."

She fell silent, and I held my breath in anticipation of what she would say next.

"When I was in your mind, I only saw bits and pieces of what actually happened," Selene finally said. "Hades helped me to see the whole picture, and—" She looked down at the floor, digging the toe of her boot into the metal grating. "I understand why you did what you did—stranding us off-world and all that. It wasn't about us. Not really. You sacrificed the few to save the many. In your place, I'd like to think I would have made the same choice." She sighed, smoothing her auburn hair back on top of her head. "And, well, I'm alive now." She raised her eyes to meet mine. "That's what matters, right?"

I swallowed roughly, choking on the words clawing their way up my throat. "But the others aren't." I wanted to kick myself for saying it, but the guilt had propelled the words up and out of me.

"No, they're not," Selene agreed. "I was the deciding vote on whether to enter cryosleep on this ship, and *I* survived. I'm alive, and they're not. I have to live with that, too."

The tension bled from my muscles, and compassion took over. I turned around to face Selene fully. "So, what now?"

Selene shrugged one shoulder. "Apparently there are some people to save on this little blue planet." Her eyebrows rose, and the corner of her mouth lifted in the hint of a smile. "I thought maybe we could start there, then see where things go."

I nodded slowly, my lips spreading into a relieved grin as a breathy laugh shook my chest. "We could rebuild the Order of Amazons," I proposed. "We don't need to wait for the next cycle generation. Meg—the girl who knocked you out—she's not the only human psychic."

"I heard." Selene chuckled and shook her head. "Hades and his little toys. He just can't resist meddling."

I bristled, some of my fragile good humor evaporating. "He did what had to be done."

Selene cocked her head to the side, studying me through narrowed eyes. "So it's true, then? You and Hades?" A bemused half-smile touched her lips. "I heard a rumor just before we left, but—" She shook her head. "I don't know. He's always been so reserved. So solitary. Back on Olympus—before the exodus—they called him the *Prince of Darkness* because he was always so distant and broody. So *serious*."

Heat crept up my neck, seeping into my cheeks. Selene was the first of my people to learn the truth of my relationship with Hades—if you could even call it that—besides Demeter, who had tried to kill me because of that relationship. I didn't know how to talk about this thing between Hades and me. It had been a secret for so long; I wasn't sure I *could* talk about it. Hiding my feelings for him was second nature. Among my people, because of my position as an Amazon, loving him had been a death sentence. And now, things between us were complicated for another reason entirely —Raiden.

Selene took a step toward me, leaning in like she was going to share a secret with me. "So, what's he like—you know, in bed?" She pursed her lips. "I always wondered. I mean, he *is* gorgeous in a frigid, untouchable way. Like a statue of one of the ancient gods."

My eyes bulged. I supposed I shouldn't have been surprised by this question coming from Selene. She had been one of the Amazons who liked to bend the rules when we were away from the Alpha site on missions, out from under Demeter's watchful eye. Her sexual exploits were more than rumors. Her relationships always ended before she returned to the Alpha site, which was why Demeter hadn't punished her for it.

Selene took another, tinier step toward me and reached out, wrapping her fingers around my forearm. "You *have* to tell me. He's incredible, isn't he?" Interest glittered in her eyes, and I didn't need my psychic powers to know she was imagining getting frisky with Hades. "The quiet ones always are," she added in a low, sultry murmur.

Cheeks burning, I coughed a laugh, glancing at the floor, the walls, the ceiling—anywhere but at Selene and her knowing stare. "OK, wow. I'm not talking about this with you. Or with anyone."

Selene sniffed and looked away. "Fine, don't tell me." She smirked, eyeing me sidelong. "But," she started in a sing-song voice, "you can't blame me if my wandering thoughts slip into your mind the next time I'm active . . ." She tapped her fingertip against her temple as her smirk widened into a wicked grin. "Sometimes I just can't help myself."

I set my jaw, not the least bit amused, especially after how she had reacted the last time she riffled through my mind unbidden. "Stay out of my head, Selene," I warned. "I mean it."

The teasing light faded from her eyes. "Of course." She bowed her head slightly, and when she straightened, she was all serious-ness again. "It was a jest, and a poor one at that. I would never invade your privacy like that again." She lowered her gaze. "I've learned my lesson there." The corner of her mouth twitched, and her focus returned to my face, mischief glittering in her eyes. "*But* an evening with a bottle or three of mead might loosen your tongue . . ." She shimmied her shoulders.

I snorted a laugh and shook my head.

"One way or another, Cora, I'll get you to spill."

I sucked in a breath to tell her she was wrong, but before I could get even a single word out, an alarm blared through the ship's speaker system—three low, drawn-out tones. We were about to drop out of faster-than-light travel.

Selene and I moved as one to the nearest wall and braced ourselves. A few seconds later, the floor shuddered, and then the ship lurched.

"Attention," Hades said through the speakers, that single word filled with the calm confidence that was his birthright as a prince of Olympus.

Selene and I exchanged a glance, and then I looked toward the front of the ship. Hades' next words made my heart skip a beat.

"We have reached Earth."

[5]

I leaned back against the circular pedestal of the navigation terminal, my hands gripping the curved edge, and stared at the giant viewscreen taking up the entire front wall of the Bridge. Earth stood front and center on the screen, a small blue and white marbled ball, appearing no larger than a volleyball, the moon its miniature silver companion. The planet grew slowly as we neared.

"This part is always disorienting," Selene murmured from beside me.

I nodded without taking my eyes off Earth. Home. It hurt my heart to think of abandoning the planet, but it was what had to be done.

"But *how* does it work?" Fiona asked. "Refraction? Adaptive camouflage? Redirection of light? Freaking *Magic*?"

Chuckling to myself, I looked over my shoulder. Fiona was up on the captain's dais with Hades, who sat in the captain's chair closely monitoring Earth's satellites on a navigation chart displayed on the semi-transparent holoscreen. Fiona stood in front of the holoscreen, no doubt obscuring part of Hades' view of the navigation chart and driving him nuts with all her questions.

She was like a dog with a bone. She had been pestering Hades for a solid five minutes about the ship's cloaking mechanism, and I knew she wouldn't let up until he explained exactly how it worked. He seemed to think he could put her off with vague explanations and insufferable condescension. He would learn.

"As I have already told you," Hades said, "the cloaking mechanism is a very complex system with many moving parts, and—"

Fiona planted her fists on her hips and twisted to look at Hades. "What I'm hearing is a lot of *blah blah blah*, telling me you don't actually know how it works."

I choked on a suppressed laugh.

Hades closed his eyes and inhaled deeply. Ever so slowly, he exhaled, and then he opened his eyes and stared ahead, pointedly not looking at Fiona. "I have a rough understanding of the theory behind the tech."

Fiona let out a bark of laughter and once again faced forward. Her mouth curved into a victorious grin. "You should've led with that, boyo. I would've let the matter drop."

I snorted. "Never would've happened," I said, nosing into their discussion. "Then Hades would have had to admit that he is not, in fact, all knowing." Hades' eyes locked with mine through the thin film of the holoscreen. I gasped melodramatically and covered my mouth with one hand. "How shocking!"

Beside me, Selene guffawed.

Hades narrowed his eyes to a glare, but the corner of his mouth twitched, telling me he was more amused than annoyed.

Movement drew my attention off to the side where a staircase led down from the balcony of the gephyra chamber overlooking the Bridge. My mom hurried down the stairs, one hand on the metal railing, her stare locked on the viewscreen. On Earth. Her lips were parted, her awe and wonder written across her face.

I caught her eye with a little wave and smiled in greeting.

She returned my smile, her stare already slipping back to the viewscreen. When she reached the bottom of the stairs, she made a beeline for me. "You know, it's the strangest thing," she said as she drew near, her focus locked on the planet slowly growing on the screen. "I don't think I fully accepted that we *weren't* on Earth until this very moment."

She came to stand at my other side, her face upturned toward the screen. "Part of me was holding on to the misguided belief that this is all a trick of the mind, and we're really inside some vast underground complex." She shook her head and let out a breathy laugh. "Of course, I *knew* we were on board a ship traveling through space, but it's as though my mind simply couldn't accept such an absurd reality."

I reached for my mom's hand, and she gripped my fingers tight, like I was the only thing tethering her to this absurd reality.

My mom glanced at me sidelong, her attention fleeting. "A product of my limited human brain, I suppose."

"Not at all," I said as I shook my head, my eyebrows raised. My attention returned to the viewscreen as well. Earth now took up more than half of the screen. "I felt the same way the first time I left the ship and walked on land." Demeter had taken me through the gephyra to Earth after blowing up my world by revealing that I had been living on a ship my whole life.

"Ground Adaptation Syndrome," Selene said, her translator implant helping her find the right words in English, though her Olympian accent was thick. "It hit everyone pretty hard when we first arrived on this planet."

I nodded, remembering watching my people drop to the ground after disembarking the *Tartarus*, some weeping, some retching. Some fainted outright. Only the Amazons had been immune, thanks to our frequent trips to Earth through the gephyra. But I had no such immunity my first time through.

"For the longest time, I was afraid that if I looked up at the sky, this great yawning void, I would fall into it." I laughed softly under my breath. "And then, when I finally did look up, I was struck by a dizzy spell that dropped me to my knees. And then I threw up." I looked at my mom and found her watching me. "You can know something without understanding it," I told her, giving her hand another squeeze. "Without internalizing it. Human, Olympian—in that, we're the same."

At the sound of heavy footsteps, I glanced over my shoulder to see Raiden approaching the navigation terminal. He stared up at the viewscreen, visibly awe-struck, but his focus shifted to me as he closed in on us.

He stopped on the far side of the circular console, pressing his palms down on the smooth surface. "Ready to go?"

My mom released my hand and crossed her arms over her chest, turning partway to face Raiden. She leaned her hip against the edge of the navigation console. "I'm a little jealous. I'd love to see the Beta site, just once . . ."

Ever the explorer, my mom. I touched her arm and offered her a gentle smile. "We need you up here, preparing for the meeting with the Security Council."

"I know." She sighed, her head drooping. "I just wish I had more time down there." She glanced at Earth, now taking up the entire viewscreen. "There's still so much to see. So much to discover and explore . . ." She cleared her throat. "No matter." Her focus returned to me, her eyes glassy. She leaned in close, wrapping her arms around me and squeezing me tight. "Have a good trip, sweetheart." She pressed her lips against my cheek. "Be safe." Her arms loosened, and she pulled back, gripping my upper arms. A sly grin curved her lips. "And don't do anything I wouldn't do." She winked.

I barked a laugh and shook my head. My mom hadn't exactly been cautious as an adventurer. She was more of a caution-to-the-wind kind of gal.

After one last squeeze of my arms, she released me and turned back to the viewscreen.

I nodded goodbye to Selene, then followed Raiden toward the open doorway at the back of the Bridge. As I passed the captain's station, I looked up to find Hades watching me. Our eyes locked, and time seemed to slow as something stronger than words passed between us.

Hades closed his eyes and bowed his head, and my heart stuttered with longing. I hated parting with him while this giant will-they-won't-they question mark hung over our heads. It was the same question mark that hovered over Raiden and me whenever we were together.

My romantic situation seemed impossible. The pathway to love was paved with shards of broken hearts. I loved them both equally, but differently. I yearned for them both. And I was determined to find a way to make things work—with both of them. One problem at a time, though, right? There would be plenty of time to tackle my tangled love life *after* we saved the world. Or rather, the people who lived on said world.

Raiden was quiet as we made our way to the transport hangar at the aft of the ship. I could hardly blame him. He was returning to his home planet for what could very well be the last time. It was a lot to process.

We rode the rear lift down a couple of levels to the floor of the cavernous transport hangar where our chosen ship awaited us, prepped and ready for the trip. The *Cerberus* was in the best condition of all the shuttles we had inherited with the *Elysium*, but that didn't mean it was in great shape. Or even in good shape.

Whereas the *Elysium*, a grand ark ship, had been constructed to withstand the passage of millennia relatively unscathed, the smaller ships had only been built to withstand centuries. Some were junk, good only for mining scrap materials. Some were garbage, completely unusable. But a few were in decent enough shape, in need of repairs after such a long period of inactivity, but usable.

After our inventory of all the ships at the start of our journey, we had directed the maintenance bots to focus on the *Cerberus* to get it in as good a shape as possible in the limited time we had before reaching Earth. The *Elysium* could pass through a planet's atmosphere, but not while maintaining its stealth shields. Alerting the general population of Earth to our presence—and causing mass panic—wasn't a part of our plan. We needed a reliable shuttle to carry us down to Earth's surface, at least once. Once we were down there, we could rely on the *Argo,* though two ships were better than one.

Raiden and I wound around junker after junker as we made our way to the *Cerberus*'s landing bay. We stopped at the bay's opening to survey our ship. I planted my hands on my hips while Raiden crossed his arms over his chest.

The *Cerberus* was a stealth shuttle, which basically looked like a flying saucer on steroids. A large orb made up the body of the ship, and it was surrounded by a single, ring-shaped wing that would fold back like a shuttlecock when the ship was accelerating or passing through a planet's atmosphere.

The *Cerberus* didn't look much better now than it had when we had set the bots to work on it, but a systems check had reported that it was flyable, if not in prime shape. Hades had directed the bots to prioritize stealth functionality and basic structural and mechanical viability. And that was about all they had accomplished, which meant no AI navigation, no weapons, and no protective shields. Now that we had reached Earth, we would have to make do with the *Cerberus*'s limited capabilities. But at least it wouldn't break apart during entry into Earth's atmosphere.

I chewed on the inside of my cheek. No AI navigation meant I would have to dust off my long unused piloting skills to fly this antique down to Earth, something I wasn't all that excited about.

"You sure we can't just take the gephyra down?" Raiden asked, trepidation lacing his words. Apparently, he wasn't all that excited about me flying us down to Earth, either.

I glanced at him out of the corner of my eye, then shook my head. One turn to the left, one to the right. "We're too close," I told him. "The locating system can't differentiate between the coordinates of our gephyra and those of the one in the Alpha site."

Raiden grunted his displeasure.

"Don't worry," I told him, elbowing his arm. "I've flown ships like this a bunch of times."

Raiden raised one eyebrow, looking at me sidelong. "How many times, exactly?"

"More than once," I said, flashing him a cheeky grin before stepping into the landing bay. I headed for the lowered ramp leading into the body of the ship, Raiden following close behind me.

Meg poked her head through the opening at the top of the ramp. "I thought I heard you guys out there." The rest of her appeared a moment later, and she jogged down the ramp to meet us. "What took you so long?" A steady stream of anxiety flowed from her to me through our bond. She was dreading the impending reunion with her people, and for good reason.

Meg's people had banished her for taking part in a rebellion that had nearly destroyed the Zari from within. But she hadn't acted of her own volition. She had been compelled by her manipulative and emotionally abusive mother, and she had been doing everything she could to make amends since.

We met at the base of the ramp. I reached out to grip her arm, offering her what little reassurance I could. The contact increased our connection, and one of her thoughts slipped into my mind.

Meg was afraid her people wouldn't allow her entry into their underground city at the Beta site. It would be inconvenient for us —and heartbreaking for Meg. She was to be our liaison, helping us negotiate terms with the Zari High Council. Our proposal for the Zari was complicated. Of course, we would welcome all of their people into the Vault of Souls with open arms, but we were hoping their psychic warriors would join us on the *Elysium* bodily. Meg had the best chance of navigating any cultural obstacles that could pop up during negotiations. We didn't need her there, necessarily, but she would be a tremendous help.

I glanced back at Raiden and nodded for him to go on ahead

and board the *Cerberus*, then turned my attention back to Meg. "It'll be all right," I reassured her. "They'll see in you what I see." I offered her a tight smile. "Even if it takes some convincing, we'll find a way for them to accept you again."

Meg looked like she was going to be sick.

I gave her arm a squeeze. "You don't have to come. If it's too much—"

Meg shut me up with a look.

"Never mind."

She squared her shoulders and raised her head higher. "Let's get this over with."

[6]

I gripped the armrests of my seat, the restraints digging into my shoulders, my whole body tense as the *Cerberus* free-fell through Earth's atmosphere.

The ship rattled all around us, but it was more a shiver than a shake. An intermittent knocking sound cut through the dull roar, as if someone clung to the outside of the ship, hammering on the hull. Shimmering red and orange flames covered the viewscreen, the results of the air molecules outside being literally torn apart, surrounding the *Cerberus* in a plasma fireball. The ship was cloaked, so to any observers down on the surface of the planet, we would appear to be a bit of space junk burning up in Earth's atmosphere.

Beside me, Raiden clutched his own armrests with a white-knuckled grip, the tendons in his neck bulging as he pressed his head back into his headrest. Meg sat strapped into the defunct weapons station behind us.

Raiden cranked his head my way, his eyes a little wild. "It's not as bad as I thought it would be," he said, his voice strained. He licked his lips. "Not as rough." But clearly just as terrifying.

I flashed him a quick smile. "Don't believe everything you see on TV," I teased, hoping to ease his nerves.

"Noted," Raiden said, returning my smile. The wild look in his eyes remained, making him appear slightly crazed.

The viewscreen lightened from deep crimson to red-streaked orange, then to a pale salmon-pink that continued to fade until, eventually, the blue sky was visible over a bed of fluffy white clouds. The start of a brilliant sunset stained the clouds farthest off to our left, a deep magenta that faded to the softest pink.

I let go of the armrests and reached for the navigation sphere in front of me. It was about the same size as a basketball, with a polished silver surface that reflected an image of me, comically distorted. I lightly placed my open hands on the smooth surface of the sphere.

The *Cerberus* shuddered as the wing fanned out into a disk surrounding the ship, pulling us out of our freefall. We stopped descending, hovering just above the cotton candy clouds.

I looked at Raiden, then glanced around my seatback to see Meg. "Do you guys feel that?"

Raiden cocked his head to the side, one eyebrow raised.

"Gravity," I said, grinning. It settled over me like a weighted blanket. The transition from artificial gravity created by centrifugal force to real planetary gravity was always disorienting, like leaving a boat after spending a month on the water. In the absence of motion, it would take some time to find one's land legs.

Returning my attention to the viewscreen, I gently rolled the navigation sphere forward. The viewscreen dipped downward as the body of the ship rolled in sync with the sphere, and the pink-tinted clouds were all we could see. With the faintest pressure, my hands sank into the surface of the sphere, and the ship glided forward. We dove into the clouds, cocooning the ship in an endless white fog.

A hush expanded in the cabin, as though the clouds

surrounding the ship were muffling the world. I realized I was holding my breath, and I forced myself to exhale.

We broke free of clouds suddenly, and vibrant green blanketed the ground far below. The Amazon Rainforest filled the viewscreen, a lush emerald canopy cut through by a snaking silver river, the greenery spreading as far as the eye could see in every direction.

"Wow," Raiden said.

I rolled the sphere backward, leveling off the ship, and let up on the pressure to slow our speed. The horizon cut across the center of the viewscreen, a meeting point between magenta clouds and shadowed rainforest canopy. A flock of birds rose from the canopy, silhouetted by the burgeoning sunset.

The view was mesmerizing. For long seconds, I could do nothing but stare in wonder, even as dread crept in. What would happen to this lush, vibrant place after the Tsakali arrived? Now it teemed with life. But would that change in a couple of months, after the Tsakali realized we had evaded them, taking the secrets of the chaos stones with us?

"So, forward is down, and backward is up?" Raiden's voice cut through the malaise that had settled over me.

I looked at him, my brows bunching together. "What?"

Raiden glanced at the navigation sphere. "The controls . . ."

"Oh, yeah," I said, shifting my attention to the sphere. "Think of it like this—the navigation sphere is the body of the ship. How I move the sphere is how the ship moves. Roll it forward to go down." I inched the sphere forward, and the viewscreen angled downward toward the rainforest canopy. "Roll it backward to go up," I explained, demonstrating until an ombre of pinks overtook the viewscreen. I rolled the sphere forward again, returning the ship to a level position. "Clockwise to turn right, and counterclockwise to go left," I added, once again demonstrating as I explained the way the controls worked.

"So," Raiden started, drawing out the word, "if rolling the sphere forward angles the ship down, what makes it go faster?"

I glanced at him, then looked out the viewscreen as I pressed my hands into the surface of the sphere. The ship responded immediately, accelerating until we were speeding through the air. "Pressure," I told him. "More pressure makes the ship speed up." I let up, my hands lightly resting on the sphere's surface. The ship slowed until it was barely moving. "Less pressure makes the ship slow down, and—" I removed my hands from the navigation sphere, and the ship jerked to a stop, hovering above the rainforest canopy. "No pressure makes the ship stop."

I rested my elbows on my armrests and looked at Raiden. "Of course, a ship with a fully functioning AI navigation system could easily handle a routine landing like this on its own. You would never have to touch the controls."

Raiden grunted softly, a thoughtful frown turning down the corners of his mouth.

"But," I went on, "we don't have one of those, so . . ." I placed my hands on the navigation sphere, and the ship gently accelerated. I rolled the sphere forward to continue our descent toward the rainforest.

Anxiety pulsed across the bond I shared with Meg, steadily growing. I peeked over my shoulder to study the young psychic. She had opted to wear a hoplon suit rather than her traditional Zari armor, and now that her reunion with her people was imminent, she was regretting her choice. She knew her people wouldn't welcome her with open arms after her involvement with her mother's rebel group, but it terrified her to think her people wouldn't accept her back at all, especially not when she showed up dressed in alien armor. In her mind, it was an overt display of her rejecting their ways. Why should they consider accepting her back into the fold when she had so clearly moved on?

I pressed my lips together and returned my attention to the fast-approaching rainforest canopy in the viewscreen, wishing there was something I could say to ease Meg's anxiety. But her worries were valid, and the matter was out of my hands. I couldn't control the reception she received from her people. All I could do was convince them to listen to her. And with their lives hanging in the balance, they *would* listen.

Focusing on the small holoscreen that hovered above the navigation sphere, displaying a topographical map of the ground below, I guided the ship toward the glowing marker pinpointing our chosen landing spot. Ahead, the rainforest ended abruptly, giving way to a barren crater that was several miles in diameter.

I swallowed my disgust. I had done this. Not by choice, but the devastating explosion of psychic energy had still come from me.

A tear snuck over the brim of my eye and streaked down my cheek. I wiped it away with my shoulder and guided the *Cerberus* down toward the edge of the crater. It would place us just a couple of miles out from the masked cliffside entrance to the Beta site, the closest cleared landing spot, according to a survey of the local terrain.

I released the pressure on the navigation sphere, slowing the ship as we neared the ground. I scanned the trees along the edge of the crater, searching for movement. The ship's cloak meant our presence should have been undetectable, but the Zari had access to a whole bevy of Olympian tech down in the Beta site. From my previous visit, I knew an abundance of precautions prevented them from using much of the old, unfamiliar tech. Mostly, if they didn't know something's purpose, they stayed away from it.

But I hadn't spent enough time in the underground settlement to know what pieces of Olympian tech they *were* familiar with. Tech like the asclypos, they used regularly, so it was entirely possible they had discovered Olympian radar, which would allow them to detect a cloaked ship. Hades hadn't shared that tech with them, but it didn't mean they hadn't stumbled upon it during the millennia plus they had been dwelling in the ancient Olympian site.

The *Cerberus* touched down on the ground, and I took a deep breath, exhaling some of the nervousness funneling into me through the bond I shared with Meg. She was a live wire. The air around her practically crackling with tension.

I took another fortifying deep breath. This would work. We needed the Zari, but they also needed us. They just didn't know how badly they needed us *yet*. But they would discover the truth soon enough.

I unfastened my seat restraints and stood, plastering a bright smile on my face before turning around. Beside me, Raiden also stood.

Meg was still seated, still strapped in. Her wide-eyed stare was locked on the edge of the rainforest. Her eyes flicked to me for a fraction of a second, then returned to the viewscreen. "Please don't do that," she said, her voice quiet and pitched higher than normal, like that of a little girl, not of a hardened warrior.

My smile wilted. "Do what?"

"Pretend everything is normal." She licked her lips, and her fingers curled around the edges of her armrests so tightly that the color had drained from her nail beds. "Nothing about this situation is normal." She wasn't talking about the big picture situation, the impending Tsakali invasion. She was talking about returning home a penitent traitor.

I closed my eyes and inhaled, soaking up as much of the anxiety flowing through our bond as I could. Tension seeped into my muscles, buzzing through my veins. When I opened my eyes again, I let my expression show that I didn't just understand how she was feeling. I felt it too.

"We're in this together." I deactivated my regulator and reached over my shoulder to draw my doru. With barely a thought, I extended the golden staff weapon to its full length until it was nearly as long as I was tall. My stare locked with Meg's. "Whatever happens, I've got your back," I promised.

Raiden gripped the plasma rifle he had taken from the *Elysium's* armory across his body. With a flick of his thumb, he flipped a switch on the side of the gun, and a high-pitched hum filled the cabin as the weapon charged in preparation to fire. "We both do."

I glanced at him, my heart filling with love at the sight of him standing at my side, ready to defend Meg. She was bound to me. And in his mind—his heart—that bound her to him, as well.

Eyes shining with unshed tears, Meg squared her shoulders and unfastened her seat restraints. She deactivated her regulator with a flick of her finger, then drew her doru. "All right," she said, setting the butt of her extended doru on the floor with a dull clang. "I'm ready."

And on the outside, she looked ready to take on anything. Even her own people. But inside, she was nervous as hell.

I nodded to her once, then marched past her and slapped my palm against the button on the wall to lower the ramp. Raiden and Meg moved quietly, and I felt more than heard them flank me as we waited for the ramp to finish lowering. The oppressive humidity of the rainforest oozed into the ship through the opening, making me grateful for my hoplon suit's built-in climate regulator.

When the ramp touched the ground, I descended, pausing at the edge to survey the devastated terrain. Recent rain had turned the thick layer of ash covering the scorched earth into sludge. I lifted my foot and stepped off the ramp, my boot sinking into the sticky muck. In the sky above the tree line, the brilliant pinks of the sunset were fading to purple as twilight settled in.

The rainforest was a wall of trees and shadows. Zari warriors could be out there, undetected by my psychic senses, watching us. The orichalcum alloy skullcaps they wore shielded their minds from psychic detection.

A shiver ran up my spine. I embraced the unease. Paranoia

would sharpen my mundane senses, which I would need to rely on more than ever during this mission.

The ground sucked at my boots, marking each step with a *squelch* as I trudged away from the *Cerberus*. I could hear the others following. Once we were several yards away, I turned and raised my bent arm in front of me so I could use the holoband on my forearm. The ramp and interior of the *Cerberus* were all that was visible of the ship.

A tap of my fingertip activated the mini holoscreen, and I pulled up the remote ship controls. A moment later, the ramp started to rise.

We waited until the ramp shut and the *Cerberus* was once again completely invisible, then turned and headed for the tree line. Meg took the lead as soon as we reached the edge of the rainforest, finding a trail within minutes. Raiden followed her, and I brought up the rear.

Both Meg and I decreased the flow of psychic energy running through our dorus and hoplon suits until the channels barely glowed. Our eyes adjusted as the light continued to fade, but soon enough, Raiden and I were stumbling over every obstacle that crossed our path. Meg seemed unaffected by the darkness. But then, this was her home turf.

"Shit!" Raiden hissed, tripping over something—I couldn't see what—and tumbling to the ground. He caught himself on hands and knees.

I hurried forward to help him up.

"We could have timed this better," he grumbled, gripping my proffered hand. "Maybe waited until daylight."

I hoisted him up to his feet, and we both wiped our muddy hands on our pants. "We didn't have time to wait for—"

"Shhhh!" Meg hissed, dropping to a crouch.

Raiden and I froze. My heart hammered against my sternum. I reached out with my psychic senses like I was trying to use my eyes to see in absolute darkness. I knew I wouldn't sense any minds, even if the Zari were there. But I couldn't *not* try. It was instinct.

At the snap of a twig, I spun around, my eyes straining to see movement in the shadows of the midnight forest. My back touched Raiden's, and we slowly turned together. Shapes took form, darting among the trees. Surrounding us. Closing in.

I heard the snick of a bowstring and spun to face the oncoming arrow, raising my hand to erect an energy barrier. My hand burned with unspent electric-blue energy, but I was too late.

Or I would have been.

The arrow froze in mid-flight, inches from my eyeball. Vibrant pink energy sizzled along the shaft, and it dissolved into ash.

[7]

"Stand down! Please!"

I snapped my head to the right. My eyes opened wide as I searched the shadows for the source of the voice. It was familiar, speaking in the native Zari tongue, and easily understandable even without having access to the speaker's mind, thanks to my new translator implant. It was an interesting language, similar to ancient Greek in that it was a derivative of Olympian, but unique enough that I wouldn't have been able to understand it on my own.

Meg placed the voice before I could, and I plucked a name from her mind: Caly. She was the daughter of the Zari's head psychic, Ilyana, and someone both Meg and I considered a friend. I couldn't say the same for her accompanying warriors.

My hand still burned with electric-blue energy, and I was ready to erect a shield at the first whiff that this stalemate was over. Raiden's back pressed against my shoulder blades, rising and falling with each of his steady, controlled breaths.

"They're friends," Caly added, her tone beseeching. "They're not a threat."

"They are outsiders." This new voice was gruff and male,

dripping with hostility. It seemed to come from roughly the same place as Caly's. "They don't belong here."

I didn't move. I barely breathed.

"I take full responsibility for whatever happens while they are here," Caly said. "Their consequences are my consequences."

I narrowed my eyes, intrigued by Caly's subordinate behavior toward this man, whoever he was. From Meg, I could sense confusion and concern, but this time her worry wasn't for herself. It was for Caly—for Caly and for all the Zari's psychic warriors, because this power dynamic was *wrong*. Like the Amazons among my people, the Zari's psychic warriors held rank above all others, certainly above all men, who were incapable of storing psychic energy within their bodies. Zari psychics did not ask. They told. So why was Caly practically begging this *man* to stand down?

The man must have agreed to Caly's request, because a glowing orb of rose-pink psychic energy flared to life over my head, just out of arm's reach, illuminating the dense underbrush on either side of the trail.

At least a dozen Zari warriors surrounded us, some bearing bows, some bearing spears. All were dressed in hide loincloths and nothing else, save for the golden orichalcum alloy skullcaps protecting their minds. A red band of paint marked each warrior's face, stretching from temple to temple, and black tattoos covered their arms and torsos, each body displaying a unique and intricate array of ancient Zari designs. So far as I could tell, Caly was the only woman—and therefore the only psychic—among them.

Caly stepped out from the shadows between two large trees, dodging a vine hanging from a branch above her, as she picked her way through the underbrush. She wore the traditional Xena-esque armor of a Zari psychic warrior, the tight-fitting leather cuirass hugging her torso and short skirt of strappy pteruges providing more mobility than protection.

I slowly lowered my raised hand, redirecting the psychic energy spooled in my palm to my doru until the focus crystal blazed with a blinding electric-blue light. It made me appear less threatening, even if the inverse was true. An energy shield or blast from my doru would be far more precise and effective than one from my bare hand.

Caly reached the trail several paces ahead of Meg. She stopped, facing us, her hands on her hips and her expression pinched. She studied Meg for a moment, her eyes troubled, then moved her attention to me. Something in her stare made me think she was afraid. Of us? Or for us?

"Sorry about that." The corners of Caly's mouth tensed. "We weren't expecting visitors." She looked around, her gaze searching, and tilted her head to the side as she refocused on me. "How did you come to be here? I sensed no one," she said, shaking her head slightly. "But then, suddenly—" She tapped her first two fingertips against her temple. "I could feel you."

I eyed the warriors watching from the trees. Their silence couldn't hush the hostility in their mistrustful stares. I certainly wasn't about to tell this group about the cloaked ship parked in the crater a mile or so behind us. Clearly, something had changed among the Zari in the three weeks since we had fled. I wasn't willing to redirect any focus from the warriors surrounding us—or their bows or spears—to break through Caly's mental barriers and skim her mind for answers. But I didn't need to rely on my psychic powers to test the emotional temperature of this group to know the Zari people had sunk into a deep discordance.

"Sorry about just dropping in like this." I returned my attention to Caly, flashing her a tight smile. "I need to speak with Ilyana," I told her. "It's urgent. The fate of your people—of *all* people—hangs in the balance."

In my peripheral vision, I watched the warriors surrounding us exchange wary glances. A few spoke to their nearest companions in hushed voices, too quiet for my ears to pick up.

Caly's stare intensified, and I felt her testing my mental barriers. Her psychic touch was gentle, like she was knocking on the door to my mind, requesting permission to enter.

Intrigued, I lowered my barriers and let her in. I had my doubts about the intentions of the other warriors, but I felt certain I could trust Caly.

She skimmed my surface thoughts, then dug a little deeper, bringing herself up to speed on the Tsakali threat to Earth and what we were planning on doing about it. Within seconds, she finished and withdrew from my mind. She held my stare for a moment longer, a deep sadness shining in her eyes. Her whole life, she had dreamed of the day Hades would lift the curse he had lain upon the Zari to ensure their loyalty across generations, and she would finally be able to explore the world. But now that the cure—and her freedom—were within reach, the world she had dreamed of exploring was on the verge of annihilation.

Caly inhaled deeply, visibly sucking up and squashing her devastation, then turned toward a warrior lurking in the deepest, darkest shadows of the nearby trees. "We must take them down to the city to speak with the High Council."

The warrior stepped forward, moving into the edge of the pool of rose-pink light emanating from the glowing energy orb hovering above us. He was tall and powerfully built. His tattooed chest was adorned by a broad collar of silver and gold beads, like something stolen from the neck of a pharaoh's mummy, and gold cuffs wrapped around his muscular forearms.

I fished his name out of Meg's mind: Oryon. He was a leader among the Zari warriors. No real surprise there. *And* he was Caly's father. Interesting.

Distrust hardened Oryon's stare. He studied me for a long moment, then shifted his focus to Meg, his distrust turning to hatred. "The *prodotis* cannot come," he ordered, the Zari term for a traitor dripping with disgust.

Though she showed no outward reaction, the word—prodotis—struck Meg like a kick to the gut.

"And the *dolo* must abide by the new laws," Oryon added.

Meg was too wrapped up in the devastation caused by Oryon's immediate rejection of her to notice what he had said. But I hadn't missed it. The new laws were obviously related to psychics, and even without Meg's silent insight, I was pretty sure *dolo* wasn't a nice name for a psychic. I glanced at Raiden, noting his narrowed eyes and the hint of a frown touching his lips. He had noticed it, too.

Caly bowed her head. "Of course, Father."

I nearly choked on the abhorrent display of meekness. It grated on my bones, antithetical to my internalized world order. I clenched my jaw to stay silent and was prepared to give Caly and her dad—a real peach, that one—the benefit of the doubt that this was more of a father-daughter dynamic than a psychics-norms thing, but Meg was just as horrified. This uncomfortable interplay wasn't about Caly and her dad; it was about all the Zari psychics and what appeared to be an epic fall from grace in the eyes of the rest of their people.

Caly straightened and turned her back to Oryon. She approached Meg, stopping just out of arm's reach. Embarrassment colored her cheeks, and she flashed Meg an apologetic smile. "I'm sorry, but you'll have to wait outside. The hollow will provide shelter from the sun."

Meg took a single step toward Caly and raised one hand, resting it on her friend's shoulder in a silent show of support. "There's no need for that," she said. She withdrew her hand and turned on her heel, not once acknowledging Oryon or any of the other Zari warriors. She strode past Raiden and me, her fingers gripping mine for the briefest moment, and then she was off, running back along the path we had already traveled.

Oryon barked an order, and several of the Zari warriors rushed out of the underbrush to follow her.

I sensed Meg's intent before I felt the surge of psychic energy. Just before reaching the edge of the pool of light, she vanished.

The warriors trailing her stopped in their tracks, shouting to one another, clearly disturbed by her disappearing act.

She could have waited until she was hidden under the cover of darkness to activate her hoplon suit's stealth mode, but she had chosen to let them see her disappear. She wanted them to know she was capable of invisibility, to always wonder if she was nearby, watching. Waiting to pounce.

The corner of my mouth lifted in a bitter smile. Served them right.

"We should not take them," Oryon hissed. "We cannot trust them."

I schooled my features before turning to face the warrior leader. I caught the flare of irritation in Caly's eyes and wondered if Oryon had noticed it as well.

"Meg—the *prodotis*—already knows the way to Vytopoli," she said evenly, calmly. I was impressed by the force of will it must have taken her to keep the annoyance she surely felt from reaching her voice. "If they wanted to attack the city, they would have snuck in and ambushed us *before* they revealed their stealth capabilities. We have nothing to fear from these people, but much to fear if we turn them away."

Oryon's eyes narrowed, like he was trying to come up with some reason to disagree. But Caly's logic was sound, even if he didn't like the result. "Very well," he said, nodding once. "But do not forget that their consequences are yours, as well." His cheeks tensed in a half-assed attempt at a smile. "I will make sure the High Council knows this."

Caly raised her chin. "Do what you must, Father, and *I* will do what I must."

Raiden and I exchanged a look. Those words concealed layers of meaning hidden to us, but we had heard its promise nonetheless.

Oryon stomped the rest of the way through the underbrush until he reached the trail, stepping onto the stretch between Caly and Raiden and me. He stalked toward us, his eyes locked on me.

Raiden stepped in front of me and raised his plasma rifle, not aiming it at the warrior, but making sure Oryon knew he was prepared to use it.

Oryon stopped a couple of paces away, eyeing Raiden up and down, assessing his potential opponent. He stepped to the side, intending to go around Raiden.

Raiden mirrored his movement, not letting the warrior pass.

I placed my hand on Raiden's arm. "It's fine," I said, sidestepping to stand beside him. I glanced up at his stony face. "I'll be fine." I withdrew my hand and turned to Oryon.

His eyes were dark pools in the dim lighting. He stared me down like he could bash his way into my mind with the force of his stare alone.

"Clearly you have something to say," I said and raised my eyebrows. "Well? What is it?"

Oryon's cheek twitched. "No powers," he said, his stare dropping to the regulator hanging around my neck.

A humorless laugh shook my chest, and I rolled my eyes. "Fine." I retracted my doru and sheathed it on my back, then raised my hand and swept my fingertip around the stone in my regulator, activating the device and suppressing my psychic gifts. The electric-blue glow drained out of the focus crystal atop my doru, and the channels running the length of my weapon and armor alike faded from vibrant blue to subtle amber.

Oryon sneered, then turned his back to me and marched up the trail, barking orders to the other warriors. The underbrush rustled as the men funneled onto the trail, both ahead of and behind us.

Caly waited until Oryon had passed her before stepping closer, her cheeks burning and her eyes not quite meeting mine. "I—" Her lips twitched into another of those apologetic smiles. "I'm sorry about all of this. Much has changed since you left."

I raised my eyebrows, sending a pointed look past Caly at

Oryon, who was in a loose huddle with five of his warriors. "I can see that." My focus returned to Caly.

Finally, she met my eyes. Fear and shame haunted her gaze. "Once you speak with the High Council, you'll understand." She licked her lips, peeking over her shoulder at Oryon. "And I must warn you—"

"Calysto!" Oryon shouted. "With me!"

Caly pressed her lips together, her nostrils flaring in annoyance, and darted another glance over her shoulder. "Just do what he says," she said, the words tumbling out in a low whisper. "He won't hurt you. My father—he just—he fears you. They all do, and they need to believe they're in control." She spun away and jogged up the trail to reach Oryon.

I snorted a derisive laugh and shook my head. "Typical."

Raiden glanced at me sidelong. "Of men?"

One of the warriors motioned for us to get moving, and I stepped in front of Raiden to start up the trail. He followed close on my heel. Caly's glowing orb of rose-pink energy floated along, moving with us.

"Of people who covet power they don't have," I told him, speaking over my shoulder, my voice hushed. I shrugged that same shoulder and looked ahead. "But yeah, usually it's men."

"Correct me if I'm wrong here—and I'm not saying this is the way it should be—but aren't men usually the ones who already hold most of the power?"

"There are different kinds of power," I said, once again speaking over my shoulder. "There is the stone, which directs the course of the water with its rigid strength. And there is the water, which slowly, subtly wears away the stone, forging its own path and forever altering the stone, while the stone is helpless against the change." I glanced back at him before returning my attention to the way ahead. "Which is more powerful?"

Raiden grunted thoughtfully. "So, in this situation, we're the water, right? I feel like we're the water. But I'm also not great with metaphors."

I flashed him a slight smile. "Yeah, we're the water."

I just wasn't sure what path we would forge. What we would change. But I had the sneaking suspicion it wouldn't be a slow, subtle erosion. We didn't have time for that.

[8]

Tensions were high as Caly, Oryon, and the troop of Zari warriors escorted us down the tunnel to the Beta site. Motion-activated lights flared to life overhead as we delved deeper into the cliff-side. Caly and Oryon lead the way, while the Zari warriors spread out ahead of and behind us, shooting suspicious, even fearful glances my way. They had frisked Raiden, removing all his weapons, and now carried them spread out among them.

The first time I walked through this tunnel, I had been equal parts guest and prisoner, escorted down to the underground city by Caly's mother, Ilyana. Now, Caly walked in her mother's place, and I once again toed the line between prisoner and guest. But I had the unsettling suspicion that this time, my psychic escort was just as much a prisoner as I was.

When Oryon and Caly reached the wide lift platform at the end of the tunnel, Oryon motioned to the only other person on the platform, telling her to step forward with a condescending flick of his fingers. The woman wore a loose-fitting white shift and a golden collar around her neck. She gripped another identical collar in her hands.

My stare hardened. My jaw clenched. My nostrils flared.

Those were Amazon collars, designed to override a regulator and indefinitely suppress a psychic's gifts.

Raiden and I stopped at the edge of the tunnel, our boots still touching chiseled stone rather than the ridged metal of the lift platform. The mouth of the tunnel opened to an enormous cavern, and the underground city spread out far below, like a field of stone towers grown from the earth itself.

The Zari warriors again fanned out around and behind us. Oryon turned his hard, watchful gaze on me.

The collared woman approached Oryon, stopping to stand directly in front of him and arching her head back, like she was offering her neck to the warrior. I hadn't noticed at first, but her collar was different from any Amazon collar that had been used on me in the past. It bore a quarter-sized crystal directly in line with her throat, with the stone glowing a subtle amber.

Oryon raised his left arm, drawing my attention to a matching crystal embedded in the golden cuff wrapped around his wrist, and touched the stone to its mate in the collar. The collar's crystal flared with a sapphire light as Oryon gave the collared woman access to her powers.

The woman lowered her chin and turned toward Caly, lifting the second collar to fit it around Caly's neck. Caly stared down at the metal grating of the platform, barely flinching as the orichalcum clasp snicked shut.

I stood ramrod straight, my shoulders squared. I had been collared three times before, and it wasn't an experience I had any interest in repeating.

The collared woman turned away from Caly and headed back to her corner of the platform.

My stare darted from the collar snug around Caly's neck to the one around the retreating woman's. They really were prisoners. For the life of me, I couldn't figure out *why* they would ever let themselves be collared like this. Controlled like this. I recalled Caly's warning.

Just do what they say . . .. They need to believe they're in control.

Except, if Oryon and those like him were collaring psychics, they didn't just believe they were in control. They *were* in control. Not only because they were using the collars to suppress the psychics' gifts. But because the psychics were letting them.

The collared woman crouched, opening a box stowed in the corner of the platform and reaching inside. When she stood and turned to face us once more, she carried a third Amazon collar, the golden metal gleaming in her hands.

I could feel Oryon's challenging stare on my face, but I refused to look at him.

Tension coiled in my muscles as the collared woman approached me. My heart beat in time with her steps. Adrenaline surged, and I fought the urge to flee. To fight. To kill Oryon and the rest of these *men* who dared to subdue me.

"Is there a problem?" Oryon asked, his words a smooth, slithering boa constricting around me. He wore a poorly concealed smirk, spiteful mirth glittering in his dark gaze.

I glared at him, then glanced at Caly. Her eyes bore a plea, begging me to cooperate. I turned my attention to the collared woman standing before me, noting her faint tremble. She was clearly terrified. No psychic powers were needed to sense that. But was she afraid of Oryon, or of me? Of what I would do to her if she tried to close that golden ring around my neck?

I swallowed convulsively. If I really needed to, I could break free of the collar. I knew that now. It would take time and concentration, but I had done it twice before. It *was* possible.

Taking a deep breath, I relaxed my jaw and blanked my expression, then looked at Oryon. I refused to back down from his taunting stare, instead letting him see how little he scared me. I would let them collar me, but I would not—not for one second— let Oryon believe he could control me.

"No," I said, tensing the corners of my mouth in the approximation of a smile. "No problem."

Raiden's stare burned into the side of my face, but he didn't say a word. He trusted me, trusted that whatever I chose to do here would be the right choice. His silence—his trust—fortified my resolve. We had come here for a reason, and I would not turn back because of a little unexpected discomfort.

When I returned my attention to the woman waiting to collar me, my smile turned genuine. This wasn't her fault, and I wanted her to know that I didn't blame her. I reached out, slowly so as not to frighten her further, and wrapped my fingers around the collar. I opened it wide with a jerk of my hands, then raised it to my neck and snapped it shut.

Awareness of my psychic gifts vanished. When my regulator was activated, suppressing my psychic abilities, I could still feel their potential, like eyelids blocking the light from my eyes. But the collar was like having my eyes removed, the potential to see stolen from me.

Oryon turned to the side, sweeping one muscled arm out, inviting us to join him on the lift platform.

Head held high, I stepped onto the platform, Raiden at my side, strong, steady, silent. I reached for his hand, needing to feel connected to him. His fingers slid between mine, and calm washed over me.

As the lift carried us down to the floor of the massive cavern, we stood hand in hand, surrounded by a half-dozen of the warriors who had escorted us here. When the platform settled on the ground, Oryon stepped off first, Caly trailing dutifully behind him.

"Come," Oryon ordered, staring back at me.

Raiden gave my hand a squeeze, then released it.

I stepped ahead of him, following Oryon and Caly down the pathway that led to a stone bridge crossing the canal encircling the settlement. I had seen little of the Beta site—Vytopoli, to the Zari people—during my first visit, and I didn't have to feign interest in my surroundings as Oryon lead us through the underground city. The faux sun affixed to the apex of the cavern ceiling shone dimmer than before, the pale silver glow more akin to a full moon than the brighter sun.

We followed pathways that wound around buildings that looked so much like giant stalagmites that I genuinely believed the settlement had somehow been grown from the earth itself rather than built from quarried stone and orichalcum-reinforced metal, like the Alpha site. Infrastructure technology was about as far out of my range of expertise as anything, so it was entirely possible my people had created equipment capable of such a thing without my knowledge.

The city appeared to be a ghost town, vacant of all life. It was early enough in the night that there should still have been some life to the place. I caught the odd glimpse here or there of people —a sliver of a face peeking through some shutters, the flutter of movement out of the corner of my eye—enough to know that the appearance of abandonment was just that. An appearance. What-ever had happened here since my brief visit had frightened these people into hiding. And once again I was left to wonder—were they hiding from Oryon and those like him, or were they hiding from those like me, from the psychics?

Oryon led us through the city to the far side, where we approached another bridge crossing the canal, heading for the towering, ornately carved facade of a structure dug into the cavern wall. The facade displayed tiered columns made to look like palm trees, complete with hanging vines and decorated with depictions of nearly every rainforest creature imaginable, and some that were pure imagination, like winged serpents and something that looked a lot like a mer-monkey. The style of the designs reminded me of the ruins of Zaritcha, the Zari's ancient capital city, which Raiden and I had stumbled upon during our previous visit to the rainforest above.

I surveyed the facade as I crossed the bridge. The Zari must have added this structure during the centuries they had spent effectively trapped down here. It made sense that they would have wanted to make this place their own, to feel less like squatters in someone else's abandoned home.

Once across the bridge, Oryon marched straight toward the stairs leading to the huge wooden door set into the stone facade. It appeared to be carved from one massive slab of wood, bound to the stone doorframe by hinges made from what looked like more of the orichalcum-gold alloy they used in their skullcaps. The face of the doors displayed an intricate carving that depicted a great flood, and I wondered if it was the flood that had nearly destroyed them. The same flood that had left them vulnerable for Hades to sweep in and offer them a veritable Faustian bargain—he would save them, but only if they agreed to serve him.

Oryon held up a hand when we reached the foot of the stairs. "Wait here," he ordered. "I will announce your arrival and see if the council will grant you an audience." His tone suggested he didn't think they should.

I crossed my arms over my chest and arched an eyebrow.

Oryon's lip curled, and he turned around to march up the stairs. He raised a fist and banged on the right-hand door, three loud knocks that reverberated off the cavern walls in a booming echo.

A moment later, a smaller door hidden in the design of the larger swung outward, and another male Zari warrior emerged, slightly older than Oryon, but no less formidable. And if his hard expression was any indication, no less cranky. He spoke to Oryon, their words too quiet for me to overhear, no matter how hard I strained my ears.

When Oryon turned and gestured to Raiden and me, the other warrior looked at us—at my golden collar—and scowled. Looked like he wasn't any fonder of unexpected visitors than Oryon, especially not the *dolo* kind. The older warrior said a few more words to Oryon, then retreated through the door, shutting it tight.

I glanced at Raiden and raised my eyebrows. This somewhat hostile reception wasn't making me feel overly optimistic about our proposal. What if the Zari refused? We needed their psychics' help, and offering the rest of their people safe harbor from the coming Tsakali storm within the *Elysium's* simulation was our high-value bargaining chip. But I hadn't been counting on the Zari psychics losing their status among their people, which, so far as I could tell, was exactly what had happened.

Raiden shrugged, crossing his arms over his chest, his expression unreadable. "Stay the course," he murmured, his words for me alone.

I nodded once, then returned my attention to Oryon, who was watching us from the top of the stairs. I raised one hand to offer him a friendly little finger wave.

His eyes narrowed, his lip curling.

I flashed him a venomous smile.

Raiden covered my hand with his and forced it down. "Cora . . ."

I recrossed my arms over my chest and returned to my staring match with Oryon. He looked away first. I smirked.

The older warrior reemerged a few minutes later and nodded to Oryon before retreating through the door but leaving it open.

Oryon waved us forward.

"Here we go," I said to Raiden, then started up the steps.

I passed through the doorway first, Raiden a towering shadow close behind me, and entered a vast circular chamber. I could only imagine how long it had taken the Zari to carve out such a large space. But then, they'd had plenty of time on their hands—centuries—while they waited to fulfill their bargain with Hades and assist with the resurrection of our people.

A raised stone platform curved around the perimeter of the chamber. Thirteen thrones stood at equal intervals along the dais, appearing to have been carved out of the very bedrock. Each throne was occupied by an aged and dignified member of the Zari High Council. Save for one. Ilyana stood in front of her designated throne, younger than all the others in the room, hurtling heated words at the man seated directly across from her, all gray hair and lined, leathery skin.

Ilyana fell silent as I stepped through the doorway, staring at me with eyes widened in surprise. She should have known I was the unexpected visitor. She should have known we were on our way long before we even entered the tunnels. But she, too, wore a golden Amazon collar around her neck, blocking her access to her psychic gifts.

My steps faltered as I stared at her collar. The sight of it shook me to my core. Ilyana. Collared.

Ilyana's eyes met mine, and shame flashed across her face. The expression vanished almost as soon as it appeared, hidden behind a placid mask.

The chamber was silent, vibrating with tense expectation.

Ilyana lowered her eyes and gracefully stepped backward to settle on her throne. She folded her hands one over the other on her lap, her mask of calm never cracking.

The council member Ilyana was shouting at only a moment ago stood, revealing a large frame that suggested he had been a warrior once. His attention locked on Oryon, his expression stern. "What were you thinking, Oryon, bringing these outsiders into our city?" His voice carried the grit and gravel of age. His attention shifted to Raiden and me, and his stare lingered on my collar. He sniffed in disgust, returning his focus to Oryon. "And *that one* is a psychic?" He jutted his chin toward me without actually looking at me.

Some of the other council members exchanged glances, others hushed whispers.

I stepped forward, moving closer to the center of the chamber, my expression mirroring Ilyana's—calm, peaceful. Not a threat.

"Yes, I'm a psychic." I offered the hostile council member a tight-lipped smile. "I think you may have heard of me. My name is Persephone, but you can call me Peri," I said, figuring it was smartest to lean on the identity they knew best. The one they were most likely to respect.

The affronted council member's eyes widened, flashing with recognition. And with fear.

My smile broadened. "I don't think we met the last time I was here," I said. "You are . . .?"

He squared his shoulders and held his head higher. "I am Kosmos."

I held his stare for a full, drawn-out inhale and exhale, then dismissed him and turned away from him to address the council as a whole. "I'm here to deliver a message on behalf of Hades."

I ejected a tiny holodisk from the storage compartment in my holoband, activating it with my touch. I tossed the holodisk on the floor in front of me, and it slid forward a few feet. When it came to a stop, a life-size hologram of Hades appeared hovering directly above the disk, as statuesque and dignified as ever.

A collective gasp filled the chamber.

"You have fulfilled your end of our bargain," the holographic recording of Hades said. "Persephone is reborn, and I am revived."

I studied the faces of the council members, noting their widened eyes and dropped jaws. Tears wet a few cheeks. Perfect.

"And now," Hades announced, "I shall set you free."

[9]

"And then," the hologram of Hades said, "when you are reborn on our new planet, you will be free to walk safely under the light of our new sun."

Silence hovered in the chamber as the hologram of Hades clasped his hands behind his back and bowed his head. The council seemed to hold their breath, waiting to see if he would say more.

In the recording, Hades had given a thorough but succinct rundown of the situation, telling the Zari Council about the impending Tsakali invasion, the impossibility of fighting our ancient foe, and the threat to the entire universe should the Tsakali finally gain the ability to create chaos energy. He finished by offering the Zari people sanctuary aboard the *Elysium*—physically for the psychics, and within the Vault of Souls for everyone else.

I picked at the corner of my thumbnail with the nail of my index finger. Of course, he hadn't known about the tangled power dynamics down here when he recorded this. My gut told me this would be fuel on an already roaring fire.

The hologram flickered, then winked out. Thirteen pairs of lungs took a collective inhale. Thirteen pairs of eyes shifted to me.

Kosmos sprang out of his throne, surprisingly spry for such an elderly man, especially one of such large stature. He threw his sinewy arms wide, his chest rising and falling rapidly. "So we are expected to give up our bodies *willingly*—to abandon the physical world and submit ourselves to some—some *incorporeal* existence?" A vein bulged in his forehead.

"While they—" Kosmos glared at Ilyana. "*They* may *walk* onto the ship?" He was spitting mad. "How is this fair? It was not only the *dolos* who devoted their lives to Hades' mission. It was all of us." Kosmos' chest heaved with each breath. "It was *all* of us!"

I moved forward to collect the holodisk, remaining silent as I crouched to pick it up and as I stood and tucked it back into the storage compartment in my holoband. I glanced at Kosmos, fuming at the edge of the dais, but made a purposeful show of dismissing him. Instead, I turned to the eldest member of the Zari Council. She was an ancient woman, her skin like brown crepe paper and her hair like fine silver threads woven into a thin braid she wore slung over one shoulder. Her white linen robe hung loosely on her frail frame. But her hawkish stare belied a sharp mind honed by nearly a century of wisdom and experience.

"As Hades explained," I said, addressing her directly, "the *Elysium* has limited resources for physical passengers. While it could easily carry all the Zari people across a shorter distance, we're looking at a journey that could last far longer than a single lifetime. The ship is only equipped with enough cryopods for its crew."

That was a lie. There were tens of thousands of cryopods aboard the *Elysium*, but we didn't have the raw resources to sustain more than a couple hundred bodies in cryosleep. Any more than that, and we would have to run side missions in search of necessary resources, something we couldn't afford to do. Every time the *Elysium* stopped moving, the odds that the Tsakali would track us down increased tenfold.

"You would live out your life and die aboard the ship," I said, turning a blunt stare on Kosmos. "Is that what you want? To rob your people of the chance to live their lives out in the open? To condemn them to an existence more limited than the one they already know? Is your ego so inflated that you can't admit it benefits *us all* to have the Zari psychics on board that ship, protecting us from potential threats? Can you not see that *they* are your best chance at survival?"

Kosmos scoffed, red-faced and shaking with righteous outrage. I didn't need to hear what he would say next to know his anger had blinded him to logic. The second I walked into this chamber, he had made his mind up about me. Against me. But I listened anyway, knowing he would say his piece sooner or later. Might as well get it over with now.

"I won't stand for such outright prejudice!" he hollered. "This preferential treatment for the *enhanced* cannot be tolerated. If this is the way we leave Earth, imagine how much worse it will be for the rest of us when we reach this supposedly safe new planet when the *dolos* are the only ones alive to establish the settlement." Spittle flew from his lips as he worked himself into a frenzy. "We would be completely at their whim. At their mercy. How could we ever ensure they won't decide to leave us in this 'simulation'? Or worse yet, shut it off?"

I planted my hands on my hips, consciously attempting to keep my voice from raising. "Why would we go to all the trouble of uploading you to the Vault of Souls if we weren't planning on resurrecting you when we reached our new home?"

A manic light flared in Kosmos' eyes. "Because you need our psychics' help, and you know they won't help you if you leave the rest of us behind!"

I glanced sidelong at Ilyana, then touched my fingertips to the golden collar locked around my neck and returned my hard stare to Kosmos. "Are you so sure about that?" The words came out low and cold, more of a warning than a question.

Raiden rested his hand on my shoulder, a silent reminder to calm down.

I closed my eyes and inhaled deeply. Slowly. I opened my eyes and turned away from Kosmos. He was a lost cause, and attempting to reason with him was a wasted effort. I locked eyes with the eldest council member. "We need your psychics' help to upload *more* people to the Vault of Souls," I said evenly. "I hope you can see that we are trying to save as many people as possible."

I didn't wait for a response. I was done with begging these people to *let me* save them. Instead, I turned to Ilyana. "The offer stands to the psychics, regardless of what the council chooses for the rest of your people," I told her. "We would be honored to have you and your sisters on board the *Elysium* with us as the new generation of Amazon warriors."

I looked at the eldest council member one last time. "We need your decision by dawn."

The statement was like a stasis bomb, momentarily freezing everyone in the room. Nobody moved. Nobody spoke. Nobody even breathed.

Kosmos spat in my direction, breaking the spell. The council members erupted in a thunderous argument, eleven voices attempting to shout over one another. Only two on the dais remained silent—the eldest council member and Ilyana.

I caught the latter's eye and raised my eyebrows.

Ilyana glanced at the entrance, still guarded by the grizzled older warrior who had let us in and another Zari warrior I didn't recognize. Oryon was nowhere to be seen. Small mercies.

I turned my back on the raging council and hurried toward the door, Raiden and Caly close on my heels. Ilyana dropped from the dais with a graceful leap and rushed to meet us, her path converging with ours mere steps from the warriors guarding the door. I expected the warriors to cross their spears and block our exit, and I prepared a lineup of grappling moves in my head to disable them.

But they stepped aside as we approached, then followed us out and slammed the door shut behind them.

Shocking the hell out of me, Ilyana pressed her palm to the grizzled warrior's cheek. "Thank you, *Agapyte*."

He turned his face into her hand, pressing his lips to her palm. "We knew this day was coming. I'll guard your trail. May our paths cross again, *Krysion*."

Ilyana closed her eyes, and a tear slid down her cheek. She withdrew her hand and opened her eyes, turning toward me. "Come," she said, reaching for my arm. "It isn't safe for you here." She pulled me into motion, running toward the bridge that crossed the canal. "I know a place you can hide until we can sneak you out of the city."

We raced through the winding streets, deep into the heart of the subterranean city, where the pointed towers loomed over the shorter structures surrounding them. The shadows were our friends, concealing us from prying eyes. Ilyana led us to a shuttered tower, heading straight for the sealed front entrance. She didn't slow as she approached the solid slab of stone.

Or when she ran through it. A hologram concealed the open doorway, exactly like the one that hid the cliffside entrance to the tunnel leading down here.

My steps didn't falter as I followed her through the holographic barrier. Static electricity tingled over my body, making my hair crackle for a fraction of a second, and then I was through, surrounded by unrelenting darkness.

Light banished the immediate darkness, and Ilyana held up an antiquated oil lantern, looking like something a turn of the century explorer might have used. I thought of Charles Blackthorn, my pseudo-great-great-grandfather, who had stumbled upon the Zari during an expedition well over a century ago, and wondered if that's exactly what this lantern was.

"Come," Ilyana said, turning away and forging deeper into the building. "You'll be safer at the top."

As Raiden and I followed her, I looked around, picking up what details I could in the dim pool of light cast by the oil lantern. We were in a wide open space, fairly normal for the lobbies of our larger towers. Ilyana led us to the base of a spiral staircase that wrapped around the clear tube of a lift and hurried up the first few steps.

"What is this place?" I asked, following her up the stairs.

"The Genetec tower," Ilyana said, answering over her shoulder as she hurried onward and upward.

Understanding dawned. No wonder this building was locked up—or made to appear as though it was. Hades hadn't shared this genetic manipulation and cloning tech with the Zari, and they were smart enough to know that experimenting with it could have disastrous results, so they had shut it away. I wondered how long it had been used as a secret hiding place, and if it was a secret of the Zari psychics alone, or if others knew about it.

By the time we reached the top of the tower, at least twenty stories up, all three of us were breathing hard. The top floor was so narrow, there was only enough space for a pair of rooms, the open doorways leading off from either side of the final landing. Ilyana headed for the rightmost doorway, snuffing the flame in the lantern before she reached the opening. We followed her through.

The dim moon-like light filtering in through a broad, asymmetrical window was all that illuminated the space, but it was enough for me to make out a desk—purposely grown stone, like the buildings, from the looks of it—and the rusted steel skeleton of a desk chair that had been eroded by time. I trailed my fingertip through the thick blanket of dust on top of the desk, drawing a straight line.

This had been someone's office millennia ago. It had probably belonged to whoever had been in charge of Genetecs here in the Beta site. Hades would have been their direct superior.

Ilyana crossed to the window and stared down at her city, only her profile visible in the silver light. "Their coerced psychics won't sense you all the way up here," she said, her voice hushed. "You will be safe . . . for a while."

I joined her at the window and stared into her shadowed eyes. "What exactly is going on here, Ilyana?" I looked down at the golden collar locked around her neck and shook my head, my brows bunching together. My eyes met hers again. "Why are you letting them do this to you?"

A hysteria-tinged laugh bubbled up from Ilyana's chest, and she averted her gaze to the window. "We would not fight them," she said, her voice hollow. "We did not want to hurt our own people, and in so doing, we allowed them to imprison us. In a matter of weeks, we have become their pets. Their slaves." She laughed again, the sound harsh, bitter.

"It started with the uprising." She glanced at me. "When you were kidnapped."

I narrowed my eyes.

"They don't trust us anymore," she said. "They gave us an ultimatum—to leave our sanctuary free of will, or to stay, but to surrender control of our *enhancements* to them. They said our gifts are not natural and therefore should be treated as weapons, guarded under lock and key when not needed." Ilyana touched her fingertips to the front of her collar. "But how could we leave?" She lowered her hand. "Where could we go? The sun is every-where out there. Nowhere else is safe for us."

I pressed my lips together, attempting and failing to hold my tongue. "But you easily could have overpowered them and taken over the city yourselves."

Ilyana flashed me a sad smile. "To attack our own—that is not our way. At least, not the way of our psychics." She was quiet for a moment, staring through the window, her focus a thousand yards away. She tapped on the stone windowsill with the nails of her index and middle fingers. "Many of my sisters will want to accept your offer and join you, with or without the council's approval, but I don't know how we'll get them all out of here without having access to their powers." She looked at me. "If they weren't collared . . ." She sighed, her shoulders slumping.

"These people—" Ilyana shook her head and hugged her middle. "They are still my people. I will not spill their blood, not even to save my own life."

I touched her arm with gentle fingers. "What about to save Caly's?" I asked, invoking her daughter's name to shake her out of her funk and spur her into action.

Ilyana's eyes met mine, a familiar, hard glint returning to her stare. "If you know of a way to remove the collars ourselves . . ." She raised her hands to her neck, curling her fingers around the unbroken golden band of orichalcum. "Please, tell me."

I was quiet for a long moment, searching Ilyana's eyes, weighing her resolve to abandon her people. "There's a way," I finally admitted. "But it will take some time."

[10]

With a *snick*, the golden collar popped open, then slid off my neck
and dropped into my lap. I opened my eyes and grinned at Raiden,
who leaned back against the edge of the desk, his arms crossed
over his chest. I deactivated my regulator, savoring the rush of
psychic energy flooding my cells, then placed a palm on the floor
to leverage myself up to my feet. My legs felt like deadweight
from sitting for so long, and almost immediately, they tingled as
the blood rushed down to my feet.

At the sound of my movement, Ilyana and Caly turned away
from the asymmetric window. Ilyana's eyes sought my bare neck,
her lips parting in surprise. She shook her head, bringing her hand
up to curl around the front of her own collar. "I didn't think it
would work," she said, her voice breathy.

I hobbled toward them, trying my hardest not to trip over my
own feet while I waited for them to wake fully. "Move your
hand," I told Ilyana, reaching for her collar with both of mine. I
placed my hands over the smooth, golden orichalcum and closed
my eyes.

A moment later, her collar clicked open.

When I removed my hands, Ilyana jerked the collar off her

neck and chucked it into the corner, like she couldn't get it away from her fast enough.

I turned toward Caly and made quick work of removing her collar as well.

"Now what?" Ilyana asked, rubbing her bare neck.

I shifted my attention to the window behind her, staring down at the shadowed underground city, illuminated only by the dim silvery light of the faux moon. "Now, we wait."

Meg was out there, moving through the city with the supplies we needed, invisible to the naked eye. I had reached out to her as soon as we settled on a plan. I couldn't have pinpointed her location on a map, but I could feel her closing in, like the sound of an approaching engine. She was close. Very close.

I told Meg of the hidden holographic entrance to the tower and closed my eyes to follow her progress. I was with her as she passed through the hologram and as she crossed the lobby. I was with her as she climbed the spiraling stairs. And when she reached the landing at the top, I turned away from the window to greet her.

Ilyana and Caly looked toward the doorway, following my line of sight.

Meg appeared in the opening, literally out of thin air, a supply pack strapped to her back.

Ilyana gasped. "Megyra?" Her psychic shields slipped, allowing me to sense the joy and disapproval warring within her.

I hadn't been sure of the reception Meg would receive from Ilyana, which was why I hadn't told Ilyana *who* would deliver the supplies. Meg was supposed to pop in, remaining invisible, drop off the suits, and leave. But now that she was here, face to face with her onetime leader and idol, I could see—and feel—why that had been a flawed plan. Meg needed to face Ilyana. She needed to receive Ilyana's judgment. To be forgiven or condemned. She needed closure, one way or the other. The limbo of her existence was tearing her apart.

Meg flashed Ilyana a tight smile, nodding once in greeting.

Her smile to Caly was fuller, warmer. She crossed the floor of the dilapidated office, heading straight for me. She shrugged out of the pack and lowered it to the floor, crouching as she unclasped and unrolled the top to open it. She pulled out a couple of bundled hoplon suits, handing them to me without looking up.

I took them and passed one to Ilyana and one to Caly. Meg dug out two pairs of hoplon boots next, handing them to me one at a time. I would have offered Ilyana and Caly dorus as well if arming them with the high-powered weapons without any training wouldn't have been as dangerous to them as to their opponents.

Meg slid the empty bag off to the side and stood. She approached Ilyana slowly, woodenly, her gaze lowered to the floor. She dropped to her knees in front of Ilyana and bowed her head. "I submit myself to you," she said, speaking in the Zari tongue, the words a hushed murmur.

I held my breath, time seeming to stand still as Meg awaited Ilyana's response.

Ilyana's brow furrowed, and she tucked the hoplon suit and boots under her arm, then raised one hand, resting it on Meg's bowed head. "You should not be here, child." The faintest smile touched her lips. "But I'm glad you are."

Hope for redemption soared within Meg, so strong it brought tears to my eyes. Meg raised her face to Ilyana, peering up at her former leader.

Ilyana slid her hand down to cup the side of Meg's face, the gesture loving and maternal. "We need all the help we can get."

I peeked at Caly, but there was no hint of jealousy on her face. She had grown so much in the few weeks I had been gone. She no longer stood in Meg's shadow, vying for her mother's attention. She had come into her own, and she was ready to take on the world. But first, she had to take on her own people.

Ilyana glanced at Caly, then returned her attention to Meg. "Caly helped me to understand the impossible position your mother put you in." Ilyana's smile turned sad, and her hand fell away from Meg's face. "I'm heartbroken that our people reacted to the rebellion the way they have, but the tensions between the gifted and the rest of our people have been escalating for some time, and I believe it was inevitable that we would reach this place." She sighed and shook her head. "It is what it is."

Ilyana's smile brightened, her eyes glittering. "You must have had quite the adventure since leaving. I look forward to hearing all about it."

"There will be plenty of time for that later," I told them. Once we were on board the *Elysium*, en route to our new home planet, we would have nothing but idle time. "First," I continued, "we need to get you—" I glanced out the window. "*All* of you—out of here." I pointed with my chin to the hoplon suit and boots tucked under Ilyana's arm. "Suit up."

Ilyana set the boots on the floor and shook out the rolled-up hoplon suit. Caly did the same.

I looked at Meg. "You're probably the best one to teach them how to cloak themselves." After all, she was far more familiar with their training and ways. She would know how to convey the concepts of the cloak better than I could have done it, and hopefully, she would have them functionally invisible in a fraction of the time it had taken me to teach her.

Meg regained her feet, her tumultuous emotions of a moment ago settling into a wave of deep peace. "Yes, of course," she said, bowing her head to me in a quick nod before turning to Caly to help her out of her Zari armor.

Within minutes, Ilyana and Caly were changed, the channels running the lengths of their hoplon suits glowing peridot and rose pink, respectively. Raiden and I stood on either side of the window, hidden in the shadows of the dark office, while we stared down at the sleeping city. Behind us, the three Zari psychics sat on the floor, Meg teaching the other two how to activate their suits' cloaking mechanism.

"They're ready," Meg said, after not even an hour of coaching.

I turned my upper body to look at her, watching as she rose from the floor. To my eyes, she appeared to be alone. But my psychic senses told me otherwise. Ilyana and Caly still sat on the floor where they had been, only now they were invisible. They winked back into sight, Caly grinning broadly and her mother wearing a pleased smile.

"Good," I said, turning away from the window. I approached Meg. "Thank you." I stopped in front of her, placing a hand on her upper arm and giving a grateful squeeze. "Head back to the ship," I told her and let go of her arm. "Get ready to launch. We're taking off as soon as we get everyone on board."

Meg's brows drew together. "Can we really fit that many people on the *Cerberus*?"

I laughed through my nose. The Zari had well over a hundred psychic warriors. The *Cerberus* had seats and safety restraints for two dozen people. "It'll be a tight squeeze," I told her, "but if everyone sits on the floor and holds onto something, we should all be able to make it to the *Elysium* unscathed."

Meg nodded once, accepting my risk analysis, then vanished. I sensed her running out of the office and down the stairs.

I turned to face Ilyana and Caly. Both now stood, their expressions set to display their determination. "Only use your suits' cloaking function when strictly necessary. It will deplete your stores of psychic energy faster than you think."

"Understood," Ilyana said. "Once we have freed enough of our sisters, we won't need it anymore." She reached out to me, gripping my hands tightly in hers. "Thank you. We couldn't have escaped without you."

I quirked my mouth to the side, squinting my eyes. "I don't know if I believe that."

The corner of Ilyana's mouth rose in a sly smile. "Well then, we *wouldn't* have escaped without you. Thank you for lending us your courage." She squeezed my hands, then released them. "You know where to go?"

"Cross the bridge to the lift," I said, repeating her directions to the place where Raiden and I planned to wait for them. "Take a left when the path splits. There's a small pump house near the wall, little more than a stone hut. It has a single door with a small, round window. No other windows."

Raiden and I were to wait in the pump house until Ilyana reached the Beta site's mainframe and overloaded the central fuse with psychic energy, triggering a complete blackout. We would then power the lift with psychic energy, and it was hoped the outage would allow us to get out of the Beta site with enough of a head start to reach the *Cerberus* before Oryon and his warriors could even replace the burned-out central fuse and get the lift working again, minimizing loss of life for the Zari people we would leave behind. Ilyana still hoped to convince the rest of her people to accept our offer to upload them to the *Elysium's* Vault of Souls.

Ilyana nodded. "We'll see you at the lift." She brushed past me, hurrying toward the doorway, Caly close on her heels.

"Be safe," I murmured, watching the darkness of the stairwell swallow them up. I turned to Raiden, who still stood at the window. "Ready?"

Raiden took a step toward me. "Ready."

[11]

As Raiden and I snuck through the underground city, working our way toward the bridge that crossed the canal leading to the lift, I kept close psychic tabs on Ilyana and Caly. They had split up as soon as they left the Genetec tower, and now they moved throughout the city, freeing their enslaved sisters far more quickly than I had imagined was possible. The collars had made their oppressors complacent, leading them to believe it was safe to store all the subdued psychics in a pair of neighboring dormitories when the women weren't being used. They were wrong.

Caly was already in one of the dormitories, moving from room to room, freeing her sisters and locking away their guards in the chambers that had previously been their own prisons. Her mother's targets were less centralized.

A half-dozen teams of guards combed the streets for us, each with an uncollared psychic in tow. Ilyana stalked them, laying in wait to ambush each team and convince their pet psychic to join us. It didn't take much in the way of convincing.

Raiden and I reached the pump house without incident. We snuck inside and shut the door. It was warm and humid within the cramped space, lit only by the blinking blue lights on the complex water pump humming in the center of the hut. Every few seconds, a beep sounded, followed by a hiss as a pressure valve released a puff of steam.

Raiden made a slow circuit around the pump while I crouched by the door and shut my eyes, concentrating on masking our mental signatures from any psychics who had yet to join our rebellion.

"What do you think this pump's for?" Raiden asked, his voice a low rumble. "The hydroponic system? The canal? Plumbing?"

"All of it, I'm sure," I said without opening my eyes. "Olympian infrastructure strives for maximum efficiency."

"That makes sense." He fell quiet then, neither of us speaking as we settled in to wait.

"They're tripling the guard at the lift," I told him some time later. Those orichalcum skullcaps guarded the warriors' minds, but I could sense the frightened psychics with them and was able to skim the relevant information from their surface thoughts. Any deeper, and they would sense my intrusion. "Twelve men and three psychics."

"Are they onto us?"

I narrowed my eyes and chewed on my bottom lip. The mental barricades in the psychics' minds were too formidable for me to glean more. "I don't think so, but I can't say for sure."

"What about the three psychics? Has Ilyana reached out to them?"

I pressed my lips together and raised one shoulder in a shrug. "I can't tell without piercing their mental shields, and if I do that, they'll know I'm here. We'll just have to hope Ilyana has already reached them. Or that I'll be enough to convince them." Otherwise, it was unlikely all the Zari psychics would make it out alive. Some of the other Zari warriors would fall as well, an outcome Ilyana desperately wanted to avoid.

The hum filling the room faded as the pump suddenly powered down. My eyes popped open, and the only light in the space came from the ambient glow of the psychic energy charging my hoplon suit. I could feel, more than see, Raiden standing in front of the door, peering out the small, circular window.

"Wow," Raiden said, his voice hushed. "There's dark, and then there's this."

I stood and joined him at the little window, confirming that the power really was down. Careful to keep our minds concealed, I activated my hoplon suit's cloak, then opened the door and stepped out into a darkness so dense that it seemed to take on substance and weight. I blinked as though I might clear my vision. My eyes opened wider, instinctively attempting to let in more light. But there was no more light to let in. There was no light at all.

I reached behind me, fumbling around for Raiden's hand. When I found it, I clasped it tight and gave a gentle tug. "Let's move." We needed to clear the way to the lift before the rest of the psychics arrived.

I closed my eyes as I snuck forward, amping up my psychic radar to perceive the ambient energy present in all things. I was able to form an image in my mind of our immediate surroundings, which I used to guide our way. We moved slowly, taking our time, silence more of a necessity than speed.

A handful of Zari warriors were stationed along the path leading to the lift. The three psychics I had sensed earlier were on the lift itself with the rest of the warriors.

I paused where the path split, giving me a direct line of sight —so to speak—to the lift. The dim glow of the three psychics' regulators allowed me to see the outlines of the warriors blocking our way out. Four on the path, eight on the broad platform of the lift itself.

I gave Raiden's hand a squeeze to let him know to stay put. Then I released his hand and took a single step forward, reaching out with my mind for the three psychics. As soon as the connection formed between us, I spoke to them in their minds.

"This is Persephone of the Olympians," I told them. "I don't want to hurt you. Quite the opposite, in fact. I am working with Ilyana to free you. I can offer you freedom and sanctuary outside of this place. All you must do is stand down. Stand down and join us."

I held my breath as the three psychics wavered in a moment of uncertainty. It was a brief moment.

"What can we do to help?" one asked in my mind.

The ghost of a smile touched my lips as I let out the breath. "Distract your guards. And when I say, disable them."

I sensed the psychics' agreement with the plan. Voices floated to my ears, louder than they would have seemed in the light. One of the psychics was feigning illness.

I moved forward on silent feet. When I reached the first warrior stationed on the path, I raised my arms, hovering my hands around his neck like I was preparing to strangle him. Without ever touching him, I zapped him with a small charge of psychic energy, instantly knocking him unconscious. His knees gave out, and I caught him under the armpits, easing his limp body down to the ground. The commotion on the lift covered the noise of the ambush, and I moved on to the next warrior blocking the path. When the fourth warrior was down and I was stepping onto the lift, I told the three psychics to strike.

The struggle was brief, each of us taking out two of the warriors. By the time our second targets realized they were under attack, it was too late for them.

I released my cloak, becoming visible again. "Thank you," I told the three Zari psychics, reaching out to touch the arm of the nearest woman. Hope filled her face, and I was more determined than ever to free these women. "Can you clear them from the lift?" I asked, pointing to the unconscious warriors.

I could sense Caly drawing near, an army of psychics fanning out behind her. Farther out, shouts echoed off the stone walls of the city's towers as the rest of the Zari warriors gathered, hunting the fleeing psychics. Ilyana cut a path through the city, still invisible, but running dangerously low on psychic energy.

I grasped the bar guarding the front of the lift, the grips of my gloves creaking against the metal. Tension seeped into my body as I psychically followed Ilyana's progress. She was ahead of the mob of warriors, but just barely. Her psychic energy reserves were so low that her cloak could fall at any moment, making her visible to all.

"Come on," I chanted under my breath. "Come on . . ."

Raiden's arm brushed mine as he joined me at the front of the lift. "She'll make it. This'll work. I've got a good feeling about—"

Raiden and I both jerked our heads back to look up as the orb of light at the apex of the cavern's ceiling lit up like a miniature sun. I squinted, raising a hand to shield my eyes from the bright glow. They had restored power far quicker than we had hoped.

I looked at Raiden, my eyes bugging out, and smacked his arm with the back of my hand. "You just *had* to say something."

Raiden pressed his lips together.

"Look!" one of the three psychics on the platform with us said, pointing across the canal.

Caly and the army of psychics emerged from the cover of the shorter buildings at the edge of the city and ran toward the bridge, slowing as the crowd bottlenecked at the narrow passage.

I gripped the railing tighter. They weren't moving fast enough. The mob of Zari warriors was closing in, knocking arrows as they chased the psychics. Bloodshed was imminent.

The first arrow flew.

In a quick, smooth motion, I reached over my shoulder and drew my doru, extending it to its full length by the time the butt of the staff clanged against the lift's platform. The focus crystal flared with electric-blue light as I charged it with psychic energy. I willed the energy out of the doru, directing it to form a protective barrier behind the fleeing psychics. Dozens of arrows crashed against the barrier, sizzling to ash. The first wave of Zari warriors slowed to a walk, then stopped, staring at the shimmering wall of energy. They were trapped on the far side.

And so was Ilyana.

I sensed it the moment Ilyana ran out of psychic energy and her cloak fell. As she flickered in and out of sight, she slunk into the nearest building, a small home housing a terrified family of five. I slipped into the youngest child's mind, glimpsing the situation through her eyes. Her mother and father hugged the little girl and her two older brothers close, watching Ilyana with wide eyes. The little girl's fear lodged in my throat.

Ilyana touched her finger to her lips, asking them for the gift of their silence. The parents exchanged a look, and then the mother nodded. Ilyana peeked through the shutters over a window as Zari warriors streamed past the house.

The first few psychics reached the platform of the lift, their footsteps pounding on the metal grating as they ran to the far side, making as much room as possible for their sisters.

I closed my eyes, forming a psychic battering ram, and then I slammed it into Ilyana's mental shields. A crack formed, and I rammed her shields again. A third time, and I was through.

"Ilyana!" I said in her head. "If you can get to the edge of the city, I can shield you. You just have to get here."

There was a long moment of quiet from Ilyana. Through the little girl's eyes, I could see Ilyana leaning back against the wall beside the window, breathing hard as she considered her options. Finally, she nodded. "Very well."

Ilyana activated her regulator, cutting off access to her depleted gifts. They were of no use to her now, anyway, other than as a show of her weakness.

She waited until the stream of warriors had slowed to a trickle, then waited a little longer until one lone straggler was all she could see in either direction. She took a deep breath and then stepped through the curtain covering the doorway to the home and stopped directly in the path of the lone warrior. The father of the girl providing my viewpoint snuck forward, holding out a hand to tell the mother and kids to stay put.

I switched points of view, so I was now watching through the father's eyes. He stayed close to the wall and peered through the doorway.

The warrior skidded to a halt and aimed his spear at Ilyana.

Ilyana raised her hands in surrender. "I submit to you," she said, bowing her head. "If you bring me to the rebels, I'm sure I can talk sense into them. Please." She raised her eyes to his and took a step toward him. "They trust me." Another step. "They'll listen to me." Another step. "I just want this to end." One last step, and she was standing before him, just out of arm's reach. "Please."

The warrior gulped, his eyes wild. "Hands behind your back," he said, his voice pitched low. When Ilyana did as he bade, he raised his spear. "Turn around." He reached for the golden Amazon collar hanging from the belt of his loincloth and unclasped it. Raising the collar with trembling hands, he took a single step closer to Ilyana and snapped the collar shut around her neck.

Secure in her apparent powerlessness, he appeared to relax, taking his time to wrap a fibrous cord around her wrists, restraining her arms behind her back. When he finished, he gripped her upper arm and pulled her forward, following the route his brethren had taken up the street.

I retreated from the father's mind.

The platform was crammed full of psychics now. Only Caly remained on the far side of the bridge, waiting for her mom. She erected her own energy barrier around herself, and I pulled my shield back, wrapping it around the platform, protecting us from all angles.

I could see the crowd of warriors parting as Ilyana was escorted through. It was going to take all of my concentration to split my will and hold two shields, especially one as large as what I had erected around the lift. But I needed a clear line of sight to Ilyana. At the moment, all I could see of her was her head. If I shielded her, I could almost guarantee I would have sliced a warrior or three in half, and Ilyana wouldn't have wanted that.

Ilyana's captor guided her forward, then stopped in front of another warrior. This one I recognized. Oryon.

I groaned. "I can shield you now," I told Ilyana, speaking in her mind. "There may be some collateral damage, but you'll be safe."

"No." Her mental voice was resolute. "We've come this far. We can finish this without bloodshed."

Ilyana held her head high and addressed Oryon. "Let me speak with them. I can talk them down. I can fix this."

Through Ilyana's eyes, I watched Oryon study her, his gaze moving down the length of her body, then back up. "You changed, Ilyana," he said, his voice a low rumble. "You're dressed like her now." He rubbed his fingers over his lips and narrowed his eyes. "This makes me think you're *with* her."

He stepped closer to her, raising one hand to brush a strand of hair that had escaped from her braid away from her face.

Fear roared within Ilyana, but she wrestled the beast into submission. She had loved this man once, but their shared history brought her no comfort now. If anything, it only amplified her fear. She knew exactly what cold brutality he was capable of, yet no hint of her inner struggle broke through her serene exterior.

Oryon rested his hand on her shoulder, then raised the other and tilted her chin up with the knuckle of his index finger. "And if you're with her. . ." He bent his neck, brushing his lips over hers. "Then you're no longer with me."

Ilyana's heart skipped a beat, her fear breaking free.

Without warning, Oryon shifted his hands, gripping either side of Ilyana's head. He jerked his arms sharply, snapping her neck. Her legs went boneless, and she dropped to the floor.

"No!" I breathed.

I could still sense Ilyana's mind, but her spark was fading.

"Mom!" Caly shrieked, stumbling toward the edge of the crowd of gathered warriors. "No!" She tripped, then dropped to her knees. "NO!" Psychic energy burst out of her like a supernova. It cut through Oryon—her father—and the other warriors crowded around Ilyana's body, slicing them clean in half at the waist.

I choked on a scream.

The nearest of the warriors untouched by the blast froze as the blood and gore of their peers splattered over them. And then all hell broke loose. They panicked and turned to flee, only to run into a wall of warriors who hadn't seen the carnage.

"Maintain a shield around the platform," I ordered to nobody in particular before dropping my own shield and leaping over the railing of the lift platform. I raced to the bridge, sprinting across, and didn't slow until I was wading through the gruesome massacre caused by Caly's psychic blast. When I reached her, she was kneeling in the center of it all, cradling her mom's body, rocking gently.

I erected a shield around us as I took my final few steps. "There's a mobile asclypos aboard the *Cerberus*," I told Caly. It was too late for that, but we needed to get moving, and hope— even false hope—could be an excellent motivator. Once the hoard of warriors realized what had happened, so many more would die. Ilyana wouldn't have wanted that to be her legacy. "We can bring her back to the ship and—"

"No." Caly raised her tear-streaked face, the pain in her voice reflected in her eyes. "It won't work. She's gone." Tears continued to stream down Caly's cheeks, and she returned to staring at her mom, smearing blood on Ilyana's cheek as she stroked it tenderly. "And she never even got to see the sun."

My chin quivered, and I jutted my jaw forward, fighting back the tears stinging in my own eyes. "It's not too late," I said, my voice husky. I cleared my throat.

Ilyana was far too tough to let a little thing like death keep her down. Besides, I'd been dead once, too. More than once. And look at me now.

"Lay her flat," I told Caly. "I promise you; she'll see the sun."

Caly peered up at me, all tears and snot, but within her eyes, there was the faintest glimmer of hope. She trusted me. I wouldn't let her down.

Caly laid her mom out on the ground, and I created a stretcher out of pure psychic energy beneath Ilyana. With a thought, I raised her body until she floated a few feet off the ground. I extended my hand down to Caly, and when her palm slapped against my forearm, I gripped her arm tight and hauled her up to her feet.

"She'll see the sun," I repeated, my eyes locked with Caly's. I turned my head to look through the shimmering energy barrier toward the waiting psychics crowded onto the platform of the lift. "You all will."

[12]

I followed Caly's mental signature to the training room Meg had set up for the Zari psychics in anticipation of them joining us on the *Elysium*. They were here now, most settled in the Residential Sector getting some much needed R&R after the harrowing events of the last few weeks. Caly hadn't left the training room in hours. I had been keeping tabs on her mental status since leaving the Beta site. Since *the incident*.

It wasn't her fault, really. She was, in essence, a teenager, and like all teenagers, she still had an underdeveloped prefrontal cortex, rendering her impulse control *out of control* in times of heightened emotion. Times like watching her father execute her mother right in front of her. Caly's reaction to her mother's execution had been instinctive. Impulsive. And probably exactly what I would have done in her shoes. I wasn't sure what that said about me and *my* prefrontal cortex.

But it didn't change the fact that she had been mentally flogging herself since reality set in—since she fully comprehended what she had done to those warriors. To her own father. Her mental shields had crumbled under the weight of her emotions, and she was drowning in her inner turmoil. I wasn't sure she would survive this.

Worry for Caly wasn't the only thing weighing heavily on my mind. We had a meeting with the UN Security Council the following day, and unless Fiona came up with a viable way to integrate the Earth and Olympian simulations, we would have to be upfront with the Security Council about the reality of the situation —namely that the people who "boarded" the *Elysium* wouldn't be bringing their bodies with them. After the debacle with the Zari Council, I could only imagine how well that would go over.

But we wouldn't have a choice. If Fiona couldn't make the ship run dual simulations, we would have to upload the humans to the Olympian simulation, where it would be *very* obvious that their reality had gone from physical to virtual in the blink of an eye. We definitely wouldn't be able to trick them into thinking they were still on Earth. There was no saying how many people we would lose to consciousness suicide. A lot.

And then there was the chaos stone situation. We needed to destroy all evidence of the chaos stone—and the Atlantea Project —before the Tsakali arrived. If they discovered the blueprints for creating chaos energy, more than Earth was at stake. The entire universe would be in danger of succumbing to their hostile, consumptive nature. We needed the Security Council's help with destroying the evidence, but if they refused, we would have no choice but to initiate the planetary self-destruct. It was a matter of the greater good, and in the end, Earth would resemble the demolished colony we had visited not even a week ago, and any people we left behind would be obliterated.

My stomach twisted at the thought. I wasn't sure I could go through with it. And I wasn't sure I could live with myself if I did. *Or* if I didn't.

When I rounded the corner of the corridor leading to the training room and saw the figure standing in the open doorway, his shoulder resting against the frame and his back to me, I paused mid-step. Hades. My brow furrowed. What was he doing here?

I activated my regulator and continued forward. I cleared my throat when I reached him.

Hades glanced over his shoulder, worry lines creasing his brow. He pushed off the doorframe and turned to face me, relief smoothing out the lines on his face. His ice-blue gaze studied my features in that intense way that always triggered a slow, tingly burn low in my belly. "Oh good, you're here," he said, his voice hushed.

I narrowed my eyes at him, cocking my head to the side. "Yeah," I said, drawing out the word. "But what are *you* doing here?"

"The same as you, I imagine." He craned his neck to peer into the training room.

I followed his line of sight, my eyes finally landing on Caly. She was on the far side of the room, sitting on the floor mat nearest the viewscreen displaying a muted image of the sun, her back to us. Her head was bowed like she was staring down at something in her lap. Her hands, maybe? She had cleaned up and changed out of her bloodied hoplon suit and now wore the loose pants and tunic that served as the Olympian version of lounge wear, hers in dark gray, but I wondered if she still saw her hands covered in blood.

"I promised her I would deliver her mother's consciousness orb as soon as the extraction was complete," Hades explained.

So she wasn't staring down at her hands. She was staring down at the crystalline orb holding her mother's consciousness.

"The pain in her eyes . . ." Hades sighed and shook his head. He returned his attention to me. "It seemed reckless to leave her alone like that."

My shoulders slumped on my exhale, and I shuffled forward, crossing my arms over my chest as I leaned my shoulder against the opposite side of the doorframe and studied the broken girl within. I should have come sooner. I had been monitoring her mental state for this exact reason.

"Thank you," I said, glancing sidelong at Hades.

He reached for my hand, giving it a gentle squeeze. "I know her pain." His lips curved into a sad smile, sympathy filling his eyes. "I'll leave you two."

I held his stare for a long moment, then nodded.

Hades released my hand and started down the corridor. I watched him go, then pushed off the doorframe and hurried after him. "Hades, wait." When he stopped and turned around, I slowed to a walk, then stopped in front of him. "Did Fiona figure out the double simulation issue while we were gone?"

Hades pressed his lips together and shook his head. "But I have every confidence that she'll solve the puzzle," he said, his lips curving into a smile that was certainly meant to be reassuring, and maybe it would have been if his eyes hadn't shone with worry.

I chewed on the inside of my cheek and hugged myself.

Hades took a step closer, peering down at me with those worried eyes. "Something else is bothering you."

I inhaled and exhaled, feeling like I carried the weight of the world on my chest. "What if they don't agree?"

Hades tilted his head to the side. "Agree to what?"

"To destroy all evidence of the Atlantea Project."

"Ah." His focus moved past me, his stare distant, like he could see the planet through the walls of the ship. "We will find a way. I know how much this planet means to you, Cora, and I swear I will do everything I can to avoid that outcome."

I still wasn't used to him using my current name rather than the name he had known me by all those millennia ago, and his use of it now made his words resonate more deeply within me. I blew out a breath, exhaling some of the tension coiled in my chest. "I should—" I nodded to the doorway behind me. But before I turned away, I took a step closer to Hades and raised onto my toes to brush a kiss against his cheek. His faint stubble felt rough against my lips, and I lingered there, relishing the sensation.

"Thank you," I said, dropping my heels down and meeting his eyes. I found his hand, and his long fingers curled around mine. "Really. Thank you."

He didn't have to help the people of Earth. In fact, doing so ran counter to his primary objective—saving our people. He could have uploaded the contents of the Vault of Souls at the Omega site to the *Elysium* by now and cut ties with this doomed planet. He was risking our people by lingering here, helping me to save what we could of Earth and the humans. He was doing it for me, in part. But he was also doing it because he was a good person.

Spots of pink flared in Hades' pale cheeks, and his eyes searched mine, his longing palpable. "Cora…"

Heart lodged in my throat, I released his hand and took a step back. For literal lifetimes, we had been restrained by duty and regulation, and even something as innocent as a kiss on the cheek or simply holding hands had been forbidden. I wasn't sure there would ever be such a thing as a casual touch where we were concerned.

"I should go," I said and flashed him a smile—an apology.

I lingered there for a moment, my eyes locked with his, then turned away, retreating into the training room. I had asked him to give me the space I needed to figure out who I was and what I wanted, and he was giving it to me. Both he and Raiden were honoring my wishes, proving just how worthy they were to hold their respective pieces of my heart. It wasn't fair for me to blur the lines when I was far from ready to step across them, one way or the other.

I crossed the training room, heading straight for Caly. Meg had set up stations around the perimeter of the room for the Zari psychics to train with both practice dorus—simple steel staffs the same weight, balance, and length as a doru, but lacking the ability to channel psychic energy—and real dorus, as well as stations targeting the various attributes of a hoplon suit, like the invisibility cloak, the energy helmet, and the boots' built-in magnetic function. But the central area of the space was wide open, with twelve-by-twelve gray floor mats arranged in a checkered pattern over the metal grating for sparring.

My footsteps alternated from being muffled by the pads to echoing off the walls. When I reached Caly's mat, I paused at the edge. "Mind some company?"

She shook her head without raising it.

I stepped onto the mat, closing the final few steps between us, and sat down cross-legged beside her. I rested my hands on my knees and arched my back in a stretch, the faint popping of my spine the only sound breaking the heavy silence. I studied Caly out of the corner of my eye, assessing how she was doing *without* relying on my psychic senses for once.

The back of Caly's hand rested on her crossed ankles, cradling her mom's consciousness orb. Within, the glittering peridot ribbons of Ilyana's consciousness swirled in an endless dance. Caly's shoulders drooped, her posture hunched. Tears leaked in a steady stream from red, puffy eyes that stared down at all that remained of her mom. She looked broken. Her heart, her spirit, her innocence—all of it had shattered.

"Does she know I'm here?" Caly asked, her voice small and higher-pitched than normal.

"No," I told her. "Stasis in a consciousness orb is like being in a deep sleep. A blink between death and the next life, whether that life is in a simulated world or in the physical world."

Even if that blink lasted thousands of years, as mine had. Of course, psychics were the only ones with consciousnesses that could sustain themselves indefinitely in stasis without stimulation. Any other consciousness had a few years—a decade or two, at the most—before consciousness atrophy ate away at all that had made them the person they had been. Thus the need for a simulation to stimulate those stored in the Vault of Souls over long periods of time.

Caly sniffled. "What will it be like for her in the simulation?"

I raised my eyebrows, frowning as I thought through my response. I stared at the muted image of the sun blazing on the viewscreen in front of us. It was merely a projected image of the view of the sun from outside the *Elysium*. This room was far from the outer walls of the ship, after all. All a window would have shown was a view into the next room.

"I think it will be a lot like this reality," I started, "but without the current doom and gloom. Fiona is working hard to make it indistinguishable from the physical world, so the inhabitants won't be able to tell they're living in a simulated world." Assuming she could get the damn dual simulation situation to work *at all*.

More than ever, that perfect, hyper-realistic simulated reality seemed essential. The Zari Council's reaction to the idea of leaving their bodies behind when they boarded the *Elysium* had hammered the final nail in the coffin, quieting any qualms I had felt about lying to humanity, should Fiona solve the dual simulation problem. If the Zari, who had a better understanding of Olympian tech and history—and of the Tsakali threat—than any other people alive, couldn't accept temporary relocation into a virtual world, then I wasn't holding out any hope that the UN Security Council would be willing to go along with the plan with open eyes.

Yes, we needed their help, but that didn't mean they needed to know *everything*. Let them believe we had space for billions of humans on board the *Elysium*, however preposterous the idea seemed. Better yet, let them believe we had an entire fleet of ships. The human mind was remarkable when it came to believing in the reality it wished was true, however unlikely that reality might actually be.

Caly inhaled shakily and turned her tear-stained face toward me. "But my mom'll know, right? She'll know it's a simulation—that it's not real?"

I smiled gently. "If that's what you want. I'm sure Fiona could use an inside woman."

Caly sniffed and wiped her nose on the shoulder of her tunic. "And I'll really be able to visit her?"

I nodded. "Whenever you want. In fact..." I raised my eyebrows and leaned a little closer to Caly. "From what Hades tells me, the cryopods on this ship are rigged to hook into the simulation, so those in cryosleep can spend time with their loved ones in the virtual world. Once we start the journey toward our new home, you'll be able to spend every day together."

Caly sniffed again, her stare drifting to the image of the sun on the viewscreen. "We could visit a beach and—and just lay there under the sun."

A small, soft laugh bounced around in my chest. "You could *live* on a beach," I said. "Whatever you want, you'll be able to do it in there—together."

Caly flashed me a weak smile. "That'll be a nice change."

At the sound of muffled voices behind us, I peered over my shoulder. A pair of Zari psychics walked into the training room but stopped as soon as they spotted us sitting at the far side of the room. The shorter of the two offered an apologetic smile, and wordlessly, they turned to leave.

I watched them go, then refocused on Caly, who seemed oblivious to the near interruption. "How are the others settling in?" I asked her, dangling the distraction in front of her and hoping she would bite.

"Good, I think." She shrugged and laughed under her breath. "I don't know, really. Meg's been handling the transition."

I knew that, of course, but Meg's perception of the situation with her sisters didn't necessarily reflect reality. At the moment, she was riddled with a disorienting cocktail of anxiety, paranoia, and self-doubt, causing her to interpret every curious sideways glance as a glare, and every question as a challenge. My gut told me the situation wasn't nearly so dire.

"Well," I said, taking a deep breath, "let me know if you need anything. Fiona should have the simulation up and running in a few days." I shifted my right hand, hiding it under my knee as I crossed my fingers. We *really* needed her to figure this thing out. "Then, we'll get Ilyana situated in her new home."

Caly gazed down at the consciousness orb, rubbing her thumb over the smooth surface. "Thanks, Cora." She peeked at me out of the corner of her eye. "For everything."

Her words were like a knife stabbing into my heart. I had convinced Ilyana to lead the rebellion against her oppressors. Without me, Caly's mom would still be alive. But for how long? At least this way she had a future.

Before I could let my quickly souring mood drag Caly down further, I stood and said my goodbyes. I lingered in the corridor outside the doorway, deactivating my regulator long enough to take measure of Caly's emotional and mental states and to reassure myself that, for now at least, she would be all right.

I headed back to the Residential Sector, intending to return to my sleeping quarters to attempt to get some rest. But as I walked down the corridor leading to my quarters, I knew I would just end up rolling around restlessly in bed. I was too nervous about the meeting with the Security Council.

Making a last-minute decision, I bypassed the door panel to my quarters and headed to the next one over. I stood in front of the door panel and reached out to press the door chime, but I stopped short of actually pressing the button. If Raiden was asleep, I didn't want to wake him. I raised my fist and knocked lightly instead.

Standing at the door to Raiden's room, I had the most vivid sense of déjà vu. For a moment, I was back in Fiona's castle, standing at Raiden's door, waiting to declare my love for him. So much had changed in the two weeks since that stolen moment. *I* had changed. But some things remained the same. I still loved Raiden. When I needed grounding, he was still my go-to guy. Yes, I had changed, but in every way that mattered, I was still *me*. And I still needed *him*.

The door panel slid open, revealing Raiden's broad form standing there in gray sweats and a black T-shirt.

I met his warm brown eyes, and tension seeped out of me. "Hey," I breathed.

Raiden's lips curved into a gentle smile. "Hey."

I stared at him for long enough to start to feel awkward. "Were you sleeping? Because if you were sleeping, I could—" I turned partway, pointing over my shoulder with my thumb.

"I wasn't sleeping." Raiden ran a hand over his short hair and blew out a breathy laugh. "I tried to sleep," he added. "Couldn't."

"Yeah," I said, the word coming out as a sigh. "That's what I'm afraid of. So. . ." I flashed him a brilliant smile. "Want to help me kill the time?"

[13]

"We're getting close," I said, my eyes locked on the navigation chart hovering in front of the viewscreen as the *Cerberus* glided over a patchy field of cottony clouds at Raiden's direction.

The night sky stretched from horizon to horizon, an endless field of stars, their luster dimmed by the silver glow of the full moon. Raiden amused himself by dropping the ship down to touch the clouds intermittently, like a stone skipping along the water's surface. The top left corner of the navigation chart displayed the outlines of the islands I knew and loved.

I looked at Raiden. His eyes were bright, his mouth pursed in concentration. "You want to try your hand at landing?" I asked.

His eyes opened wide, and he looked at me, petrified by the thought. He jerked his hands away from the navigation sphere, and the ship stopped so abruptly that our bodies lurched forward, straining against our seat restraints.

"Ooof!" I grunted.

Raiden shot me a sheepish glance. "Sorry, but no. I definitely don't want to land this beast."

Chuckling, I reached for the bar running along the side of the shaft supporting the navigation sphere and pulled the controls closer to me. I placed my hands on the sphere, pressing ever so gently until my palms barely sank into the smooth, metallic surface, and the *Cerberus* glided forward once more. I rolled the sphere forward, guiding the ship downward through the spotty clouds. There was a moment of darkness as we flew through one of the larger, denser clouds, but then we emerged to see a midnight sea glittering below us. The dark outlines of the San Juan Islands hovered on the horizon, the golden glow of homes decorating the coasts of the southernmost islands like fairy lights.

My heart soared, but at the same time, I felt a deep, bruising ache in my chest. This would be the last time I ever saw my islands.

We soared over Lopez Island, then between Blakely and Shaw, heading straight for East Sound, the waterway that nearly divided Orcas Island in two. I lightened the press of my hands on the sphere and rolled it forward to guide the ship down to the water's surface. We glided over the water, breaking through the larger swells and sending sea spray splashing over the viewscreen.

As we closed in on Cascade Bay on the east side of the sound, I rolled the navigation sphere backward, lifting and slowing the ship to clear the bluff at the southern end of the Blackthorn estate. I guided the ship toward the sprawling expanse of lawn to the east of Blackthorn Manor and gently touched the ship down on the soft earth. The stately manor house was dark, lifeless. I had never seen its exterior like this at night, unlit by the dozens of lights on the porch. As I stared out the viewscreen at my home, the ache in my chest throbbed.

Maybe it would have been easier to have never returned, but this place had been my whole world for so long. Leaving it behind felt like abandoning my best friend. I needed to say goodbye.

I tucked the navigation sphere into the recess built for it in the control panel, then pressed a button off to the left of the sphere.

The sound of hydraulics filled the cabin as the loading ramp slowly lowered behind me. With trembling hands, I unfastened my seat restraints, and my chest ached in a way that let me know this goodbye wouldn't be tearless. Forcing a brave smile, I looked at Raiden, then stood and crossed to the ramp on the far side of the ship. I made my way down but hesitated before stepping onto the grass.

I stood at the edge of the ramp, staring out at the place that had been my home for the past twenty-six years of my life. Almost twenty-seven. Just a few more hours, and it would be my birthday. These few decades may have been a mere drop in the bucket of my long string of lifetimes, but they were the freshest. The rawest. The most directly defining of who I was today.

The lawn glistened in the moonlight from a recent rain. I closed my eyes and inhaled deeply. An intoxicating mixture of wet earth, grass, and pine scented the air, seasoned with the brine of the sea and the pungent odor of low tide. It was the perfume of this place, of my home, and to me, it smelled like heaven.

A million memories replayed in my mind of a life equal parts full and empty. Joyous and sad. For all the misery I had felt believing I suffered from some rare mental affliction, this lifetime had been my happiest. I wanted to bottle this scent and take it with me, to never forget this place or all I had experienced here. I inhaled again, attempting to cement the distinctive scent of home in my mind. I just hoped Fiona's simulation would do it justice when it recreated this place.

With one last deep inhale, I opened my eyes and stepped out onto the grass. For a long moment, I simply stood there, staring at the darkened manor house. It was as stately as ever, its white paint gray in the moonlight and the broad porch spanning the length of the house inviting me to sink into a teak rocker and stay for a while. I considered walking up the steps to the porch and going into the house. That wasn't why I had come here, but it would have been nice to walk between those familiar walls one last time. But I couldn't bring myself to lift my foot and move it forward.

I turned and started toward the tree line at the edge of the lawn instead.

"You don't want to go into the house?" Raiden asked, lagging behind. "Maybe grab a few things?"

I paused mid-step and glanced over my shoulder at him. Raiden stood where I had been a moment ago. I looked past him, peering through the darkened windows of Blackthorn Manor, seeing nothing but blackness.

I thought of all of my trinkets, the priceless antiques and treasures my mom had brought back for me during each of her adventures. Once, they had been my most prized possessions, but now they served as a reminder of the lie my life had been.

And then I thought of the damage that had been done to the house during the attack that had driven me away. I recalled the bodies—those I had seen, and those I hadn't—of the Custodes Veritatis soldiers Emi and Raiden had killed defending our home. Were those bodies still in there, tainting my home with the foul stink of decay?

I preferred my pristine memory of Blackthorn Manor, unmarred by the stain of my last moments there. *That* was the version of the home I wanted to lend to the simulation. Not what it had become. What it was now.

I shook my head and turned away from the house, resuming my walk toward the tree line. "You go ahead, though," I told Raiden. "You know where I'll be."

I found the head of the well-traveled trail easily and followed it as it wound through the woods. When the path split, I veered left, making my way toward the boulder at the edge of the bluff, overlooking the turbulent night sea. My thinking rock.

I rounded the base of the boulder until I arrived at the more gradual slope at the front. I reached up, gripping a ridge of stone I knew by memory, then climbed up the face of the massive rock, careful of the slick surface. When I made it to the top, I turned and sat, hugging my knees to my chest, and stared out at the sea and the darkness beyond.

If I could bring just one thing into the simulation from this place, it would be this rock. This view. This feeling. I would wrap it up and tuck into my pocket and carry it around with me everywhere.

The snap of a branch on the trail behind me told me Raiden had decided to join me. He climbed up onto the boulder and sat beside me, propping his forearms on his upraised knees.

If the sky had been clear of the patchy clouds and the stars and moon could have shone their fullest, the silhouette of Blakely Island would have been visible on the horizon. But a dark patch of clouds met the glittering, obsidian sea, making it feel as though Raiden and I were utterly alone in the world. Nothing existed beyond this bluff. This moment. Us.

I reached for Raiden blindly, and when my hand found his, I twined our fingers together. His stare burned into the side of my face, heating my neck and cheeks. Still, I didn't look at him. I continued to gaze out at the midnight sea. At that moment, we were the only two souls in existence. The only two hearts beating in all the universe.

"I—" I licked my lips and swallowed roughly. "I can't promise you all of me, forever," I started, my voice sounding faint against the crashing of the surf on the rocks below. "All I can give you is the part of me that's here with you right now."

I turned my face toward Raiden and rested my cheek against my knee. Our eyes locked, and my heart stumbled.

Raiden stared at me for a long moment, his eyes searching mine. He didn't say anything. He didn't need to. He reached out with his free hand and brushed his knuckles ever so gently over my cheek. My eyelids fluttered shut, and I lifted my head, leaning into his touch. My breath hitched when the pad of his thumb glided over my lips.

"Cora…" His breath mingled with mine, his fingers unfurling to cup the side of my face.

I peered at him through my lashes, wondering if he would follow through on the promise dripping from those two syllables.

He rested his forehead against mine, his hand gliding lower to curl around the back of my neck. And then his lips touched mine, the kiss hesitant and sweet and a little sad, just like this moment. Our moment. I reveled in everything about the kiss, about his touch, knowing that when this moment was over, it might never come again.

I relished the velvety feel of his lips pressed against mine and the way my heart galloped as he kissed me. I cherished the melody of our heavy breaths and the rasp of fabric rubbing together. I memorized the clean, masculine scent of Raiden mixed with the beloved smell of this place. I savored the taste of his kiss. His desire. His love.

Our lips parted as the kiss intensified. I raised my hand to the collar of Raiden's coat and dragged the zipper down. I pulled my other hand free from his and pushed his coat off his shoulders.

Raiden broke the kiss, pulling back a few inches, his eyes searching mine. My chest rose and fell with each too-fast breath. Whatever Raiden saw in my eyes prompted him to slide down the face of the boulder, putting some space between us.

I sat there, afraid to move. Afraid it was over. Afraid that what I was offering him was too brief. Too impermanent. Too casual.

And I wanted to scream at Raiden that even if this wasn't forever, it wasn't casual to me. This was as serious as it got. I wanted him to be my first. Not my first as Cora. My first *ever*. And not because he was the one who was with me right now, but because he was the right one for this. For giving me my first taste of the physical expression of love.

When Raiden's boots touched the ground, he turned back

toward the boulder, reaching up for me. His gaze was super-heated and hyper-focused on me. I nearly cried with relief. This wasn't over. It was only just beginning.

I scooted down the face of the boulder, placing my hands in his when I was close enough to reach him. I slid down the final, steeper section and dropped to the ground.

Raiden released my hands and raised his to cradle either side of my jaw. His thumbs caressed the column of my neck, the tantalizing touch sending shivers cascading down the front of my body. He angled my face upward toward his and leaned down to reclaim my lips. His hands slid down over my shoulders and grazed down my back, pulling my body closer to his. My fingers crept under the hem of his T-shirt, my nails skimming along the hard ridges of muscle on his abdomen, and his next inhale was noticeably shakier.

And then his whole body was shaking. For a moment, I thought he was crying, but a soft chuckle rumbled in his chest, suggesting otherwise.

I pulled back, my brow furrowing. "What's so funny?"

"You're scowling," he said, pressing a kiss to my brow.

"Because you're laughing at me."

His body stilled as his laughter died down. "I'm not laughing at *you*. I'm laughing at *me*." He stepped one foot backward and skimmed the length of my body, the mirth vanishing from his gaze as his desire flared. "I cannot, for the life of me, figure out how to get this damn thing off you," he said, his voice gruffer than before. "Is there a zipper, or . . .?" He shook his head, another chuckle rumbling in his chest, lower and more growl-like than before.

"Oh." My cheeks flamed. "Right."

I took a backward step, moving out of Raiden's hold. Of course, I had known we would need to take off our clothes. I just hadn't considered that Raiden wouldn't know how to take *mine* off.

I pressed my fingertip into the center point on the collar of my hoplon suit, releasing the magnetic fastener. The collar slackened around my neck as it opened. "It's kind of like a zipper," I said as I slowly drew my fingertip down the centerline of my body. The two sides of the suit parted like my fingertip was a knife cutting through the fabric. "Like a really high-tech zipper."

Raiden's eyes locked on my fingertip, following as it trailed between my breasts, down to my belly button, and lower, until just a hint of my underwear was visible in the opening. He blinked and dragged his stare up the pale strip of visible flesh. "I'm sorry, what did you just say?"

I smiled and moved one hand to the suit's collar, pushing it off over my shoulder. I did the same with the other, watching as Raiden's gaze was once again lured lower. I pushed the suit down over my hips, then unclasped my boots and kicked them off so I could remove the suit completely. I stood before Raiden in only the gray bandeau and boy-short style underwear I always wore under my hoplon suit.

"You . . ." Raiden took a step closer to me, placing his hands on my hips. His thumbs traced along the front band of my underwear, causing goose bumps to spread up my belly and sparking a slow, simmering tingle in the core of my being. "You are the most beautiful thing I have ever seen."

He leaned in and reclaimed my lips. Gone was all gentleness. All hesitance. Raiden was a creature of hunger now. Of desire. Of need—for me.

I responded in kind, tugging his T-shirt up and practically tearing it off his body. I tossed it away and turned my attention to the button on his cargo pants. I popped the button open, then dragged the zipper down. Raiden dipped his fingers under the band of my underwear, molding his hands over my hips. He kneeled in front of me, dragging the thin fabric down my thighs and past my knees before letting it drop to the ground.

He gazed up at me, his expression rapturous as he took me in.

I ran my fingers through his hair, drinking in his adoration. I had lived over a dozen lifetimes, but nothing I had experienced during all that time could compare to the way I felt when he gazed up at me like that. In that moment, I was his.

So I gave myself to him, wholly and completely.

[14]

"It's after midnight," Raiden said.

"Uh-huh," I murmured, not tearing my stare away from Black-thorn Manor, visible through the *Cerberus'* viewscreen. The navigation sphere was positioned directly in front of me, but my hands rested on my lap. The seat restraints were snug against my shoulders, chest, and hips.

I was filled with the purest forms of joy and sadness. I wasn't quite ready to go. To say goodbye to this place. I wasn't sure I ever would be. It now held the single happiest memory of all my lifetimes, along with one of my greatest heartbreaks—the moment I learned of my mom's betrayal. It didn't matter that I had forgiven her. Being here renewed the heartache.

"Happy Birthday, Cora."

I snapped my head to the right to look at Raiden. "What?"

He raised his eyebrows. "It's after midnight, which means it's April 3rd," he said. "Happy Birthday." He reached out and brushed the pad of his thumb over my cheek, wiping away a tear I hadn't realized had fallen. His brows bunched together, lines of concern etching into his forehead. "You all right?"

I blinked several times, and another tear escaped over the brim of my eyelid. I wiped it away, then sniffled. "I will be." I cleared my throat, my stare returning to Blackthorn Manor. "It's just—" I took a deep, shaky breath. "I spent so much time wishing I could leave this place. Now, all I want is to stay, but I can't."

"The grass is always greener."

I barked a laugh, the sardonic wisdom unexpected. And exactly what I needed. I glanced at Raiden sidelong. "Wow. Did you come up with that all by yourself?"

Raiden made a show of polishing his nails on the breast of his coat. "Maybe I did. Maybe I didn't." His eyes met mine, his lips twisting into a playful smirk.

Chuckling, I shook my head and returned my attention to the viewscreen. The sadness felt more distant now than it had a moment ago. Lifting my mood had always been one of Raiden's superpowers.

"I'll miss it," I said, the words little more than a whisper, like I was afraid speaking them too loudly would draw the grief back out of hiding.

"Yeah," Raiden said, his voice equally soft. "Me too."

We fell quiet for a long moment, both of us staring out through the viewscreen at the home we were forever leaving behind.

Out of the corner of my eye, I saw Raiden twist his wrist and peer down at his watch. "We should get back. At least try to get a few hours of sleep."

I nodded and raised my hands to the navigation sphere. The meeting with the UN Security Council was at two in the afternoon, Swiss time—just five hours away. Before I lifted the *Cerberus* off the ground, I looked at Raiden, my eyes lingering on the individual lines and angles of his face, and I imagined how much simpler our lives would be if I just chose him. If I let our connection in that moment stretch out into eternity.

But in the end, it wouldn't be fair to either of us because part of me would still love Hades. Would still yearn for him and wonder—*what if?* I would never be wholly Raiden's, even if I told him I was his and his alone. And something deep inside me told me that, over time, my lie would erode his love for me until it eventually tore us apart.

I broke eye contact and pressed my hands into the sphere. The *Cerberus* lifted off the ground. "I need to make a quick pit stop," I told Raiden. "Then we can head back to the *Elysium*."

I may have said my goodbyes to Blackthorn Manor, but there was one piece of my life on Earth I couldn't bear to leave behind.

The oversized door panel connecting the transport hangar to the rest of the ship slowly glided open, and Tila bounded forward to greet my mom, who waited in the corridor on the other side of the door. The pit bull jumped up when she reached my mom, and my mom stumbled backward under the force of the solid wall of dog muscle. Tila could usually keep her jumping impulses under control, but my mom had always been incorrigible about working the dog into an excited frenzy.

My mom braced her backside against the wall of the corridor while gripping Tila's paws and stretching out her neck to accept the bombardment of doggy kisses.

Tila finally tired of the strain of standing on her back legs and dropped her forepaws to the ground.

My mom crouched down to scratch the dog's enormous head and thick neck. "Who's a good girl?" she cooed. "Who's such a good girl?"

Tila's tail wagged so hard the entire back half of her body swayed from side to side.

My mom reached out to scratch Tila's back, right near the base of her tail, earning a series of grunt-like whines from the dog. "I missed you, you pretty, pretty girl."

Tila emerged from her euphoric haze just enough to drag her tongue over my mom's cheek.

My mom leaned away. "Oh boy, that was a wet one." She wiped her cheek on her sleeve, then patted Tila's back and stood.

Tila sat on her haunches and grinned up at my mom, her tongue lolling out of the side of her mouth.

My mom brushed off her hands, then planted them on her hips and looked at me. Her lips curved into a smile. "I didn't realize you were picking her up from the ranch tonight."

I shrugged one shoulder, averting my eyes to the dog. "I didn't really have anything better to do." But even as I spoke the blasé words, I could feel the heat of a blush climbing up my neck and warming my cheeks. I purposely didn't look at Raiden.

Thankfully, my mom had returned the bulk of her attention to Tila as she stroked the dog's velvety-soft ears, and she didn't seem to notice my body's telltale reaction to the attempted cover-up.

Raiden yawned audibly and stretched his arms out to either side as he arched his back. "Well, I think I'm going to go grab a few winks," he said. "Big afternoon ahead of us." After the briefest glance my way, Raiden skirted around my mom and Tila to retreat up the corridor.

My mom watched him go, then turned her attention to me. She raised her eyebrows suggestively, the corner of her mouth lifting into a sly grin. So it looked like she *had* noticed my blush after all and had put two and two together.

My cheeks flamed, the blush returning with a vengeance. "We went down to the house," I told her. "To say goodbye to it."

"Uh-huh." My mom continued to stare at me while stroking the contented dog's ears.

"We did!"

The grin widened on my mom's face. "Whatever you say, sweetie."

I huffed out a breath. "I'm going to bed." And before she

could snicker at any perceived implications to those words, I added, "Alone." I strode past my mom and dog. "Tila, come!"

The tags on Tila's collar clanged as she trotted after me.

"So," my mom said, laughter in her voice, "not alone?"

I clenched my jaw and kept walking. "Goodnight, Mother."

"Sweet dreams," she called after me.

Oh yeah, she definitely knew.

[15]

I lay on my side, teetering on the precipice of sleep. Tila snuggled close behind me, curled up in the curve of my legs, her heavy head resting on my hip. A snore rumbled in her barrel chest with each exhale. Snuggling with my dog in the narrow bed within my cramped quarters on the *Elysium* was the next best thing to being in my bed back at Blackthorn Manor. Tila's rhythmic snores lulled me closer to the land of dreams.

The door chime buzzed, and my eyes popped open, my heartbeat doubling in speed as my body shifted into high alert. At the second buzz, Tila raised her head, her floppy ears perking up.

Whoever was on the other side of the door pressed the chime again, holding it down to emphasize their urgency. I sat up and scooted to the edge of the bed, then stood and hurried to the door panel, grabbing my doru as I passed it. I deactivated my regulator, instinctively channeling psychic energy into the staff weapon's focus crystal.

Tila bounded ahead, nearly tripping me, and reached the door panel first. I slammed my hand against the controls on the wall beside the door, and the door panel slid open.

Fiona stood in the corridor, her thumb pressed against the door chime.

Tila pushed past my legs, the fur along her spine standing on end, and growled at Fiona. I barely snagged Tila's collar before she lunged at the perceived intruder.

Fiona retreated hastily to the far side of the corridor; her widened eyes locked on the menacing pit bull. Hands clutching her chest, she flattened herself against the opposite wall.

"Stand down, T," I commanded. When Tila didn't stop growling, I flicked her ear to get her attention. "Stand down. She's a friend."

Of course, I could understand why Tila was on high alert. She was in the strangest place possible, with strange smells and strange sounds and strange people. Hell, even the artificial gravity felt strange. On top of all that, she had been away from me for a couple of weeks, after having spent every day since she was a teeny tiny puppy at my side. She was a little on edge, which was making her a lot overprotective.

But just because I could understand her reason for overreacting didn't mean I was going to let her continue to scare the bejesus out of my best friend. I stepped through the doorway and out into the corridor, then used my knees to shove the dog back into my quarters. "Sit," I ordered, my voice stern. I still held her collar in my clenched fist.

Tila sat, grunting her displeasure.

"Stay," I told her. I waited a few seconds. When she didn't struggle against my hold on her collar, I let go. I tapped the exterior door controls, and the door panel slid shut, sealing Tila within my quarters.

I blew out a breath and turned to face Fiona, flashing her an apologetic smile. Her waning fear washed over me in waves. I touched my index finger to the stone in my regulator, activating it to dampen my psychic senses. We clearly weren't under attack—literally anyone else would have come in her place if we were—

and Fiona deserved her privacy in her own head as much as anyone.

"Sorry, Fio," I said, glancing back at the door panel.

I could hear the muffled sound of Tila whining on the other side. At least she wasn't scratching at the door. Yet.

I turned back to Fiona. "She's a little excitable right now, but I promise she won't hurt you."

Fiona let out a nervous, high-pitched laugh. "It's fine. I'm fine." Her eyes remained locked on the door panel, like she could see Tila through the metal. "I'm just more of a cat person, I think." Fiona let out another of those high-pitched laughs. "So, that's Tila? She's really—" Fiona lowered her hands from her chest and flexed her arms like a bodybuilder. "Sturdy. Like a solid piece of muscle. A really strong, really pissed-off muscle." Fiona blinked. "I mean, wow. Sturdy."

I raised my eyebrows, suppressing a laugh.

Fiona finally dragged her stare away from the door and looked at me. "Are you sure she's a girl dog?"

The laughter escaped as a snort. "Yeah, I'm sure."

A muffled thud suggested Tila had succumbed to her baser instincts and was now throwing her not insubstantial body at the door panel.

We both looked at the door in time to see it rattle from the force of another canine impact.

Fiona shook her head slowly. "She's just so . . ." Fiona made a growling, grunting sound and flexed her arms again.

"Yep, she's super strong." I stepped between Fiona and the door panel, recapturing her attention. "So what's up?"

Fiona's lips parted, and she blinked at me. "What?"

"You came here . . ." I glanced at the door panel. "Rang my chime . . ."

Fiona's eyes rounded. "Oh!" Her brow furrowed, and she shook her head more forcefully. "Right." Her face lit up with excitement, and she rubbed her hands together. "Right! I figured it out!" She bounced on the balls of her feet.

"You figured *what* out?"

"The simulation!" She started pacing in front of me, four steps up the corridor, four steps back. "I feel like such an idiot." She brought her hand up to her mouth to chew on her thumbnail. "I mean, it was right there all along. I don't know why I didn't think of it sooner." She rolled her eyes, scoffing a laugh. "Because I'm a dummy, obviously!"

I balled my hands into fists, fighting the urge to deactivate my regulator so I could pluck the information out of Fiona's mind. "You don't know why you didn't think of *what* sooner, Fio?"

Fiona stopped mid-step and faced me. Her excitement turned her eyes into bright green emeralds. "Allworld Online! We can create a simulation *within* a simulation," she explained, the words tumbling out of her in a rush. "I've been working on AO for years. I've got all the code on my external drive, which, of course, I brought with me because it's like my life's work, you know? I already uploaded it to the ship's system, and Gertie is converting the code to make it compatible with the current simulation."

She sucked in a breath, barely interrupting the outpouring of words. "You see, instead of operating two different simulations, all Gertie needs to do is expand the current simulation to incorporate another layer *around* the current simulation. So the Olympian simulation will become a smaller simulation contained within the new, greater simulation based on AO." She let out a compulsive, semi-hysterical laugh. "It's perfect!"

I eyed Fiona, wondering if the pressure had been too great and she had finally cracked. "I'm not sure I'm following," I said, narrowing my eyes. "How will this 'simulation within a simulation' thing work, exactly?"

She clapped her hands together giddily. "Allworld Online is the ultimate multiverse, right? All those separate worlds and universes, all linked up and ready to explore. So, all we need to do is to make the current Olympian simulation *one* of those universes within AO—a nice, tidy, self-contained universe—and build a 'real world' around it." She said that last part using air quotes. "We can release Allworld Online within the simulated 'real world' and give the humans access to all the goodies, but keep the Olympians in AO. By the time the humans meet the Olympians in AO, they'll already be in the mindset that the supposed 'virtual world' is a game and won't think twice about their presence."

I blinked several times, processing Fiona's explanation. "Wow, that was a lot of air quotes," I said, because what else was I going to say? Was I going to tell her I still didn't fully understand how this would work? Did I even *need* to understand? No. It just needed to work.

"I know," Fiona gushed. "I love air quotes. Totally under-used and undervalued. So, what do you think?"

"About air quotes?"

"No!" Fiona stepped closer and smacked my arm with the back of her hand. "About the 'simulation within a simulation' plan?" she clarified, pulling out the air quotes one more time. Her eyebrows were high, her eyes alight with hope.

"Oh, right." I frowned, then shrugged. "I guess I don't really know. You're the expert, and I trust you and Gertie, so I suppose it sounds like a good plan?" I pursed my lips, not wanting to get my hopes up for something that wasn't a sure thing. "Gertie thinks it'll work?"

Fiona nodded emphatically.

I chewed on the inside of my cheek. "And Gertie doesn't have an issue with restricting the Olympians to the 'virtual world'?" I asked, earning a grin from Fiona for my own use of air quotes.

"No," Fiona said. "Well, yes, at first she had a problem with it, but once I explained to her that the 'real world' would be so limited compared to the 'virtual world', she came to understand that really it was the humans who would be restricted. Plus, she didn't think the Olympians would be all that interested in spending time in the boring old 'real world', and they'll have access to the humans in AO, so their curiosity about the new inhabitants of the Vault of Souls should be sated fairly quickly. They'll be aware of the situation. It's not like we'll be trying to trick them, too, you know?"

I nodded slowly, finally letting myself believe Fiona's work-around might actually work. My lips spread into a broad grin, relief flooding my body, easing tension I hadn't even realized was there.

Now, thanks to Fiona, we could move forward with the orig-inal plan. We would hide the truth from the UN Security Council, letting them believe humans would board the *Elysium* in the tradi-tional, physical way. This would allow us to avoid the mass panic that would undoubtedly be unleashed by revealing the truth about the impending Tsakali attack, and the survival rate of those who uploaded to the Vault of Souls would be nearly one hundred percent, not the pittance it would have been if we were forced to reveal the truth of their virtual existence to the uploaded humans.

Grinning like a maniac, I reached out to grip Fiona's shoul-ders. I pulled her into a tight hug, earning a soft grunt. I released her and stepped back, gripping her upper arms. "Fio, I could kiss you right now."

Fiona leaned back, turning her head away from me. "I'm flat-tered, Cora, but you're a few bits and pieces shy of being my type."

I barked a laugh and released her. "Thanks, Fio."

I turned away from her and headed back toward the door panel to my quarters. I definitely wouldn't be able to get any sleep now, but there was barely an hour until our departure time. I figured I should probably start getting ready. We had a show to put on today. The literal fate of the planet depended on our performance.

"You just saved my bacon," I told Fiona.

"I don't know what that means," she admitted.

I stopped at the door panel, my hand hovering over the

controls on the wall. I peered at Fiona over my shoulder. "It means you're the best, and I owe you one."

"One what?" she asked. "One man? 'Cause you keep bringing women onto the ship, and despite a fun and fleeting experimental phase at uni, I really like penises. I mean, they're kind of weird to look at, but they're great for sex. And I miss sex." She raised her eyebrows. "I *want* sex."

"Noted." Chuckling, I pressed the button to open the door panel, catching Tila as she attempted to lunge through the opening. Gripping her collar with one hand, I pushed her back into the small room and hit the interior controls with my elbow, holding her tight as I waited for the door to close.

"With a penis!" Fiona reiterated.

The door panel slid shut.

[16]

A warm kiss of sunlight softened the crisp bite of the spring afternoon air as I ascended the grand stairway leading to the entrance of the Palace of Nations, the home of the United Nations in Geneva. I carried my doru extended to its full length, tapping the butt against each stone step as I walked. A pair of UN guards stood sentry on either side of the central pair of glass doors at the top of the stairs.

Hades and Niall, the Olympian walking around in Henry Magnusson's body, flanked me, followed by my mom and Raiden. Selene and Meg, dressed in hoplon suits and armed with dorus, drew up the rear of our procession. The channels running the length of their armor and weapons burned with a saturation of psychic energy—brilliant amethyst for Meg, and rich topaz for Selene to my electric blue. We were going into this meeting with our psychic senses fully awakened.

My mom's presence wasn't strictly necessary, but she helped to even out the human-to-Olympian ratio. Plus, we wanted to show the Security Council that she and "Henry" had set aside their feud for the good of humanity. Like my mom, Raiden was there for appearances only. In the eyes of the Security Council, a human soldier with an impeccable service record and a Purple Heart could only strengthen our position.

We weren't here to grovel or to make a deal. We were here to save a crap-ton of humans, and to do that, we needed to inspire trust in our ability to safeguard the human species during its journey across the universe to a new, safe home. The Security Council needed to see that we were strong. Confident. Capable.

I peeked over my shoulder at Niall, the new and improved Henry Magnusson. If we had to tell a few little lies to sway the council to support our save-the-world plan, so be it.

My focus shifted past Niall to my mom, our eyes meeting for the briefest moment before she looked away. She was on board with our use of subterfuge, but she wasn't happy about it.

Maybe this whole charade was a big fat lie, but we genuinely had humanity's best interests at heart. Maybe the road to hell was paved with good intentions, but you know what other roads were paved with good intentions? The road to not dying at the hands of the soulless Tsakali bastards, and the road to keeping as many humans alive as possible. Also, the road to not inadvertently destroying the universe by giving the Tsakali the means to create chaos stones on their own and spread like a cancer, unrestricted by energy constraints. Those were the roads we were taking.

When I reached the top step, one of the UN guards side-stepped to block the door. He was an inch or two over six feet and looked like he would be a match for Raiden, strength-wise, which was really saying something. He held his rifle across his body, and his stare locked with mine. He had intelligent eyes, shadowed by wariness.

I approached, stopping far enough away to show I wasn't a threat. Behind me, the others stopped as well.

I smiled at the guard, nodding once in greeting. "We have a meeting with the Security Council," I told him. "They should be expecting us."

The guard's gaze shifted past me, taking in all seven members of our group and lingering on Niall before returning to me. "We have orders to only admit Henry Magnusson," he said, his English accented with French.

I turned sideways, meeting Niall's eyes. We had been expecting this and had planned accordingly.

Niall stepped forward, taking the lead, and I retreated to his position alongside Hades. "These are my personal guards and guests," Niall said, his accent and intonation almost perfect for the self-righteous asshat he was impersonating. He had been studying videos of the real Henry Magnusson for the past week, since first taking over the body of the Primicerius of the Custodes Veritatis, preparing for the moment he would need to pass as the original.

"We cannot let them enter," the guard reiterated.

"Then we have reached an impasse," Niall said, nailing the snide haughtiness characterizing pretty much everything Henry Magnusson ever said. "Because I will not enter without them, and I know the Security Council is quite eager to hear what I have to say."

Focusing on the back of Niall's head, I forged a psychic connection with his mind. "Tell them to radio the Security Council," I told him, my voice audible only to him. "Tell them you're happy to wait."

Niall crossed his arms over his chest and made a show of standing up straighter. Looking down his nose at the guard, he delivered the message, his imperious show so spot-on that I wondered if any bits of the original Henry were still locked away in that head of his.

The guard looked unimpressed as he passed the message along through his earpiece. His focus strayed to me, suspicion wafting off him. The lightest skim of his mind told me he suspected I was the one really pulling the strings in our group.

The guard's focus snapped back to Niall as he received new orders through his earpiece. "We can admit the entire group," he said. He eyed my doru. "But no weapons are to enter the building." He shifted his assault rifle so it was slung across his back, then held his hand out to me, palm up and waiting for me to hand over my doru.

I exhaled through my nose, my stare locked with the guard's. Giving up my doru was annoying, but not really a big deal. Meg had trained her whole life to use her psychic abilities without a doru to focus her intent, and Selene and I had plenty of practice wielding psychic energy bare handed. Offensive blasts wouldn't be nearly as intense or precise, and shields wouldn't be as strong, but we were far from weaponless without our dorus.

After all, *we* were the weapons.

With a thought, I retracted the doru to its shortened length, then handed the two-foot golden rod to the guard. The electric-blue light faded from the grooves and focus crystal the moment it left my hand. Meg stepped forward, handing over both her and Selene's dorus, then fell back to her original position.

The guard cradled all three dorus against his body and stepped to the side to let us pass. His companion pulled the rightmost door open.

Niall entered the building first, followed by Hades and the others. I hung back, waiting until everyone was inside, then stepped forward. A stray thought from the lead guard stopped me short.

He was considering turning the Olympian weapons over to his CO in the hopes of receiving a commendation, something like a finder's fee.

I stood at the door's threshold and looked pointedly at the dorus cradled in the guard's arms. "We can sense those," I told him, lifting my stare to his. "Wherever they go, we'll find them. And I'm holding *you* personally responsible for their safekeeping." I tensed my cheeks, hinting at a smile. "Just so you know."

His eyes widened infinitesimally as he wondered if I had really known what he was planning, or if my warning was mere coincidence.

I let him keep on wondering and stepped through the doorway, entering the building. Strides long, I caught up to the others and fell in step beside Selene. In my absence, Meg had moved to the front of the procession to walk alongside Niall. The guards standing sentry at the double doors to the Security Council's meeting chamber stepped aside as we approached. The guard on the right reached out to pull his door open.

We entered the meeting chamber in single file, Meg first and me last. The fifteen Security Council delegates seated around the long horseshoe-shaped desk at the center of the cavernous space quieted as we filed in, as did the aides seated behind them. I counted a dozen guards stationed around the perimeter of the chamber. All eyes followed our group.

We headed for the seven chairs set up near the open end of the semicircular desk. Niall, Hades, Raiden, and my mom moved to stand in front of the chairs, while Meg, Selene, and I filed behind them, spreading out evenly to stand guard.

The woman seated at the apex of the curved desk pushed her chair back and stood. She was petite and middle-aged, with a keen, hawkish stare. I recognized her as Irina Petrov, the current President of the Security Council, whom we had locked horns with the last time we were here, requesting access to the Atlantea Project's chaos stone. Though, to be fair, much of that dispute had been Henry's fault, and he certainly wouldn't be causing any more problems.

"I am pleased to see you are well, Henry," Irina said, her Russian accent thin but noticeable. "I was worried when we didn't hear from you for so many days after your mission to Antarctica." She scanned the rest of our group. "Perhaps you will fill us in on the events that took place there, and how, exactly, you have come to be in this unlikely alliance."

Irina reclaimed her seat, and Hades, Raiden, and my mom sat as well. Niall remained on his feet, stepping forward to address the council. He bent his neck, bowing his head slightly. "I will gladly fill you in," he said, straightening. "But first I must request that all aides and guards leave the room. What I have to tell you is highly sensitive—for the delegate's ears alone."

Irina pressed her lips together, and I sensed a surge of annoyance and what felt a lot like disgust coming from her general vicinity. With so many other minds in such close proximity to her, it was impossible to say if the emotion was truly hers without skimming her mind directly, and I didn't want to risk her sensing my psychic touch. Most humans didn't notice, but some were more sensitive to a psychic's intrusion.

All around Irina, the delegates and aides exchanged looks ranging from curious to concerned. Irina's focus remained on us, her expression unreadable. She looked past Niall to Hades, and then to me. That sense of disgust—verging on hatred—amplified. Looked like Irina was a classic xenophobe; an unexpected trait for a senior member of a global peacekeeping organization.

After a long moment, Irina returned her attention to Niall. "We will excuse the aides, but the guards will remain."

The direct connection was still open between Niall's mind and mine, and I could feel his mounting uncertainty. He didn't know what to do.

"It's fine," I told him telepathically. "Agree to her conditions."

Niall relayed the message, then retreated to the line of chairs to sit between my mom and Hades while we waited for the aides to gather their belongings and leave the chamber. Reluctance and disappointment clouded the space. I couldn't blame the aides for not wanting to go.

"Now," Irina said as soon as the room was cleared of all nonessential people. "Please bring us up to speed on the events that have led you—" She raised her eyebrows. "*All* of you—together—to request this meeting with the United Nations Security Council."

Niall stood once more and stepped forward, launching into a made-up tale of his journey to the Alpha site in Antarctica and his interaction with us there, including an over-the-top battle with fictional Tsakali agents who invaded the Alpha site through the gephyra and were only defeated by us when we returned to Earth via the *Elysium*. He told the council we took a single, living prisoner and destroyed the bodies of the dead to prevent the coming force from reanimating their corpses. They were synthetic android beings, after all.

He concluded by explaining that only after seeing the enemy with his own two eyes—and nearly dying at their hands—had he come to accept that there was no bargaining with them, as he had previously intended to do. He now agreed that fighting the invading Tsakali force would be a hopeless endeavor.

"We would like to see one of these formidable Tsakali warriors," Irina said when Niall had finished.

I suppressed a smirk, having guessed the Security Council would want to see the enemy with their own eyes.

Niall shook his head. "Unfortunately, it is far too risky to release the prisoner from its holding cell on the ship, but we would be more than willing to transport a representative of the Security Council up to the *Elysium* to see the prisoner—and the ship."

A heavy silence settled over the room, and the delegates' frenetic thoughts charged the air.

"Based on what you have already shared," Irina said, breaking the silence, "am I to understand you believe there is no hope for us to survive the coming invasion?"

"Wait," I told Niall, speaking in his mind. "Let them stew in their worries a little while longer."

And wait, he did. Only when the sense of expectation had become palpable did he finally speak. "No." The single word rang throughout the chamber like a death knell for the entire human race. Niall paused, letting the ramifications of his answer sink in. "No, there is no hope for us . . . at least, not here on Earth."

The atmosphere of the room shifted toward disbelief and panic.

Irina remained outwardly calm, narrowing her eyes at Niall. "If we cannot remain here, is there some other place we can go to shelter from the coming storm?"

Hades stood and bowed his head. "I believe my people can help. If I may . . .?" He gestured toward the floor in front of him. When Irina nodded, he stepped forward, and Niall retreated to the line of chairs.

"The *Elysium* is not our only ship currently in orbit around Earth," Hades said, clasping his hands behind his back. "We have an entire fleet stationed here—cloaked, of course—large enough to transport as many humans as are interested in joining us on our journey to settle a new, safe home planet. The people of Earth are more than welcome to join us."

Irina pursed her lips as she studied Hades. "There are nearly eight billion people on this planet," she told him. "Are you suggesting this supposed invisible fleet of yours has the space and resources to house and feed that many people when our own planet is struggling to accomplish the task?"

"No, I am not," Hades said matter-of-factly. "I am *telling you* we have the space and resources to hold just under four billion humans in stasis for a potentially centuries-long journey across the cosmos."

Irina sucked in a breath to respond, but Hades continued speaking before she could start.

"All of our predictive models suggest that the number of humans who will be willing to join us falls far below what our infrastructure could support," Hades explained. "Let me be clear —we are not asking for your permission to do what must be done to save at least some of the people of this planet."

Irina bristled, sitting up straighter in her chair.

"We are fully capable of making our offer worldwide without your help," Hades continued. "However, we are all too aware of the chaos that will break out across this planet as soon as we reveal the impending Tsakali invasion to your people. Our goal here is salvation, not destruction. We will leave *that* to the Tsakali." He paused for dramatic effect. "You are peace keepers. We have come here today to ask for your assistance in keeping the peace while we save what we can of your people." He fell silent, letting his offer sink in.

"I see," Irina finally said. She inhaled deeply, releasing the breath in an exhausted sigh. "You have given us much to discuss. When do you need our answer?"

Hades straightened his shoulders. "By the end of the day."

[17]

One arm crossing my middle, I stood at the center of three windows in the conference room where we had been awaiting the Security Council's decision for hours, staring out at the manicured lawn and luscious trees of the Parc de l'Ariana. Through the foliage, I had a peekaboo view of Lake Geneva and the snowy peaks of the Alps beyond. It was a perfect day, with a smattering of white, puffy clouds dotting the clear blue sky. Countless people strolled along the park's paths and lounged on the grass, soaking up the golden rays of the late afternoon sun.

How different would this view be after the Tsakali arrived? Would the ground be reduced to scorched, wasted earth? Would the lake be dried up or turned toxic? Would the mountains be leveled? Would the sky burn red under a destroyed atmosphere? Would any people be left alive to attempt to survive, or would discarded bodies litter the grounds after spite drove the Tsakali to raze the surface of the planet?

I squeezed my side, my fingers digging into my waist. Or worse yet, would we have been forced to destroy the planet ourselves? At least we would know if we would need to initiate the planetary self-destruct soon enough.

The door to the hallway opened behind me, and I turned to see a pair of UN guards enter the conference room. One took up a post beside the door, while the other stood in the doorway, surveying us. Raiden, Meg, and Selene pushed away from the patches of wall they had each claimed, while my mom and Niall stood from their seats at the long table. Only Hades remained in his chair.

"The Security Council is ready for you to rejoin them in the meeting chamber," the guard standing in the doorway announced.

I exchanged a look with Hades, my stomach twisting into knots. What happened in the next hour would determine the fate of this planet. Only Hades and I were aware of the true significance of the coming negotiations.

We followed the guard out of the conference room, Niall heading up our group and the second guard trailing behind us. The eyes of the delegates followed us as we filed into the meeting chamber. A somber silence hung in the air.

"Please, sit," Irina said, her hand extended toward the line of chairs arranged at the opening of the semicircular desk.

Once again, Meg, Selene, and I took up posts behind the chairs while Hades, Niall, Raiden, and my mom sat.

"After much deliberation," Irina began, "we have decided that a coordinated evacuation effort will offer the human species the best chance of survival." She paused, letting the announcement settle over the room. "We would like to choose who boards the ships based on who can contribute the most to rebuilding human civilization on our new, shared home planet. This would also afford us the benefit of avoiding the inevitable chaos and death that would result from a global announcement."

I clenched my jaw. Ever the pessimist where humans in power were concerned, Raiden had predicted this outcome. I had hoped the delegates on the Security Council wouldn't be so cold and calculating, but there it was. I narrowed my eyes, already sensing how Hades would respond.

Hades stood and stepped forward, bowing his head in acknowledgment of the Security Council's proposal. "Agreed."

Of course, I knew for a fact that Hades' quick acquiescence was all bluff. We were going to save as many people as we could. Period.

"With one condition," Hades added.

The corners of Irina's mouth tensed and her eyebrows twitched higher.

Anxiety formed a tight knot around my heart. This was it. The moment of truth. They had taken the bait. It was time to set the hook.

"All records of the Atlantea Project must be eradicated," Hades said, "and no personnel with knowledge of the true nature of the source of chaos energy can be allowed to remain on this planet to fall into Tsakali hands. This is nonnegotiable."

I held my breath. They wouldn't back out now. They couldn't. Hades had them cornered.

"Is that everything?" Irina asked coolly.

Hades bent his neck in assent.

"Very well," Irina said. "All in favor of Hades' final amendment to the proposal?"

One by one, the delegates voiced their assent. I didn't release my held breath until the final delegate agreed. As I exhaled, relief rushed through my body, flowing into every cell, leaving me tingling and giddy. We wouldn't have to destroy the planet after all.

"Then it is done," Irina said, her voice resolute. She fell quiet, her eyes narrowing thoughtfully. "Tell me, Hades, why is it you are so keen to help us? Surely there must be an easier, safer path forward for your people."

Hades turned his head to the side and peered over his shoulder. His eyes met mine for the briefest moment before he faced forward once more. "Because what is easy and what is right are rarely one and the same. I have chosen the easy path before. Today, I choose to do what is right."

Irina studied Hades for a moment longer before her focus shifted past him once more, this time landing on me alone. She nodded infinitesimally, a silent thank you for whatever part I had played in convincing Hades to help humanity—to do what was "right".

The corner of my mouth lifted, and I returned her nod.

Irina refocused on Hades. "We will begin drawing up our plan for selecting the evacuees as soon as you depart. And we will begin destroying all evidence of the Atlantea Project tonight," she announced. "Do we need to discuss anything else?"

"Just one more thing . . ." Hades turned to the side, looking back at me.

Taking my cue, I made my way around the line of chairs and approached the delegates, coming to stand beside Hades.

Hades gestured to me with a sweep of his hand. "I would like to introduce Persephone, the leader of our psychic forces and the one who will coordinate the distribution of tracers to all humans who will be joining us for the journey to the new world."

"We have met," Irina said, pressing her lips into a thin line. The last time I was here, I struck the Security Council with a stunning psychic blast. Apparently, I had made something of an impression.

Amusement wafted off Hades. "Ah, yes. How could I forget?" Hades covered a laugh with a fake cough.

Eyeing him sidelong, I cleared my throat. "The tracers will allow us to lock onto each individual's location and remotely transport them onto our ships when the time comes," I explained, figuring it was best to just get on with it. I left out the part where we would only be transporting people's minds and genotype records onto the *Elysium*, not their bodies. "We have enough psychics to manage the distribution of the tracers to all chosen individuals in every major city on the planet, but we'll need your help distributing the tracers everywhere else. We can supply you with one billion tracers to be distributed via injection by the week's end. We'll need your list of chosen individuals by then, as well."

I glanced over my shoulder, locking eyes with Niall.

He stood and stepped forward, joining Hades and me. "Henry will remain here with you to act as our liaison and to assist in the coordination of these efforts. Once you have your list ready, give it to him. The sooner, the better." I scanned the faces of the delegates. "Henry is more than capable of answering all of your questions, but since I'm here now, is there anything you would like to ask me?"

Crickets.

Apparently, our last interaction had left an even stronger impression on the Security Council than I had thought. They were literally too afraid of me to speak.

For long seconds, the delegates sat silent and motionless, not even seeming to breathe. Finally, a petite Indian woman sitting two chairs to the left of Irina stood. She held her hands clasped before her, fidgeting with her fingers.

"The last time you were here, you were able to make yourself invisible," she said. "How is such a thing possible?"

I allowed the tiniest of smiles to curve my lips. "I'll be glad to share that secret with you," I told her. "Once you're on board the *Elysium*."

[18]

Today was turning out to be one hell of a birthday. Fiona had found a way to make the simulation work. The Security Council had voted to go ahead with the evacuation of Earth. And we didn't need to destroy the planet to protect the universe. Good things really did come in threes.

I lay on my back on my narrow bed, my regulator deactivated and all of my mental barriers down, basking in the psychic silence. The Residential Sector had been constructed with the psychically gifted in mind. A mild EM field charged between every wall, offering the maximum amount of privacy to psychics and norms alike.

Tila lay stretched out beside me, her nose tucked into my armpit. Each of her exhales carried with it a gentle snore. Idly, I stroked her velvety ears, ending the day exactly as it had begun. Only now, anxiety didn't twist my stomach into knots. I felt blissed-out on relief, eager to see what the future would hold for both of my peoples—Olympians and humans.

At the brief buzzing of my door chime, I begrudgingly scooted away from Tila without disturbing her and stood, tucking my feet into a pair of soft, cushy slippers. I activated my regulator as I shuffled toward the door, then pushed the button to open the door panel.

And blinked when it slid to the side, revealing Fiona bouncing on her toes in the corridor. "Fio," I said, my brow furrowing. I snuck a peek back at the slumbering dog, then stepped out into the corridor and tapped the button to close the door panel. "Déjà vu." I spoke through a yawn, making the words barely comprehensible.

"What?" Fiona waved away her one-word question. "Never mind." Her gaze dropped to my regulator, then returned to my eyes. She bunched up her nose, making a pained expression. "I hate to do this," she said. "You look like shit."

I guffawed lazily and leaned back against the door panel. "You hate to tell me I look like shit?"

She bit her bottom lip, her internal battle written all over her face. "I need your help with something," she finally said after a long moment of indecision. She pointed over her shoulder with her thumb. "In Gertie's room. It's for the simulation. It's quick, I promise."

It took my exhausted brain a few seconds to piece together what she meant by "Gertie's room." She must have been referring to the System Operator chamber down on the lower level, where I had found her cursing like a sailor a few days ago.

Had it really only been a few days? So much had happened since then. It felt like months had passed.

I closed my eyes and shook my head, forcing my tired mind to focus. Fiona needed me to help her with something. I yawned again as I rubbed the sleep from my eyes. All I wanted was to crawl into bed with my snoring dog and zonk out for a couple of days. "Can it wait?"

But when I opened my eyes and saw the apologetic smile curving Fiona's lips, I knew the answer. Heaving a sigh, I pushed off the door panel and held up one finger. "Give me a sec," I said before retreating into my private quarters.

I reemerged wearing a long, charcoal gray sweater over my

thin sleeping pants and top, and once again, I sealed Tila in the room. I let Fiona lead the way when we left the Residential Sector, and we were well on our way *away* from the nearest lift that would carry us down to the lower levels of the ship by the time I realized we were heading in the wrong direction.

"Wait," I said, stopping and turning to look back the way we had come. "The lift's back that way."

Fiona retraced her steps and tugged on my sleeve, pulling me along beside her. "I know," she said. "Quick pit stop." She flashed me another of those apologetic smiles. "It's been a long week. I need caffeine."

I fought a scowl. She couldn't have grabbed a cup of pseudo-coffee *before* dragging me out of bed? "No problem," I said, hiding my annoyance behind a half-assed smile.

The crew dining room was dark as we approached the open doorway. Hades rounded the corner at the far end of the corridor, and his features tensed with the hint of a smile when he spotted us.

This was my first semi-private encounter with him since I slept with Raiden. My human upbringing told me I should have felt guilty about what happened between Raiden and me. If anything, I felt guilt toward Raiden. Were Hades to find out I had slept with Raiden, he likely wouldn't care. In Olympian society, there was no concept of monogamy. We didn't even have a word for it.

From what I knew of our ancient traditions, even back on Olympus, when my people could still bear children naturally, there was no hard and fast "family unit." Humans often *say* "it takes a village" to raise a child, but Olympians fully embraced that idea.

But Raiden *was* from a society rooted in monogamy, and whatever agreement we had struck the previous night, I knew he was having a hard time accepting the strings-free nature of our relationship—more so now that we had actually been together.

"Good evening," Hades said as Fiona and I met him in front of the doorway.

"Hey," I murmured.

Hades gestured for us to enter the dining room first, that hint of a smile more prominent now. *Did* he know about what happened between Raiden and me?

Fiona linked her arm with mine and tugged gently, pulling me into the dining room. The motion-activated lights turned on when we stepped through the doorway. I barely had a chance to notice all the people huddled together in the center of the room. My mom, Raiden, Emi, Selene, Caly—everyone appeared to be there.

"What—"

"Surprise!" they shouted together, bright smiles on their faces.

I stumbled back a few steps until I ran into Hades. He gripped my arms, steadying me. I clutched my sweater closed over my chest, my heart hammering.

"I understand that felicitations are in order," he said, his lips close to my ear. "For the anniversary of your birth." He couldn't have sounded more uncertain. Olympians didn't celebrate birthdays. In fact, we didn't have any celebrations that focused on individuals, though we had communal holidays aplenty.

I choked on a laugh and craned my neck to peer at him. This was a surprise birthday party. For me. I grinned. "Thanks."

With a nod, Hades released me.

I turned to face my approaching loved ones.

My mom reached me first, wrapping her arms around me in a big hug. "Happy birthday, sweetheart." She pulled away, raising her hands to cradle my face, and smiled at me, her eyes gleaming with unshed tears. "My sweet baby." Her nostrils flared, and her chin trembled. "I am *so* proud of the woman you've become."

My eyes stung with a welling of tears.

My mom pulled me in for another quick hug, then released me and stepped aside, Raiden taking her place. Raiden curled his arms around me and pulled me in close, engulfing me in his strength and warmth. I returned the embrace, wrapping my arms around his waist and pressing my cheek against his shoulder. I inhaled deeply, breathing him in. With my body flush against his, it was impossible not to think about the last time we were this close. Closer.

I flushed with warmth and fisted my hands in the back of his shirt. Down on that bluff, I had told him I could give him only that moment. But that brief taste of the passion we could share wasn't enough. I wanted more. I *craved* more.

"Happy birthday, Cora," Raiden said, and I could feel the words rumbling in his chest.

I smiled against his shoulder. "You said that already," I reminded him.

Raiden chuckled, and the rough, familiar sound sent tingles cascading down my body. He gave me one last squeeze, then loosened his arms around me. His hand slid down my arm and captured my hand, his fingers slipping between mine, the caress slow, intimate. His eyes locked with mine, the honeyed depths filled with heat and promises.

"I have a gift for you," he said, his voice low, for my ears alone. "Can I bring it to your quarters after this?"

"I—" My cheeks burned, my words caught in my throat. I nodded.

Raiden released my hand, leaving me to mingle with the others who had gathered around me. The only person who was missing was Meg, but one of the Zari psychics arrived with her soon enough, and I figured they must have purposely kept her in the dark about the party—otherwise, it wouldn't have been a surprise.

For a while, my exhaustion was forgotten. I laughed with my loved ones, sipping on the boozy punch and nibbling on the cake my mom had concocted using the ship's food generator. But soon enough, even the excitement of my first ever surprise party—in fact, my first real birthday party that included more than four people—wore off, and I found myself casting longing glances at the doorway, wishing I could return to my bed.

My mom snuck in close, curling her arm around my waist and resting her head on my shoulder. "I know you're tired, sweetie. Thank you for humoring us. We needed this—a little happiness in these dark times."

I yawned and set my cup down on the nearest table. Much as I enjoyed the pleasant tingle humming through my blood from the alcohol in the punch, more than anything, it was making me even sleepier.

"It's all right, hun," my mom said, giving my waist a squeeze. "Go to bed." She leaned in, raising up onto her toes to press a kiss on my cheek.

I waited until nobody was paying me any attention and snuck away, retreating to my private quarters. I quickly brushed my teeth, then flopped onto the bed. Tila grunted and raised her head as I curled around her, but she was snoring again within a matter of seconds. I closed my eyes and felt the gentle lure of sleep pulling me under.

I was half-asleep when the door chime buzzed. I lay still, hoping I had imagined the sound. For seconds, there was nothing but the gentle rumble of Tila's snores.

The door chime buzzed again, and I groaned. It definitely wasn't my imagination. I dragged myself out of bed for the umpteenth time and smacked the button on the wall beside the door. The door panel slid open, revealing Raiden smiling tentatively in the corridor.

My lips parted, and I rubbed one hand over my eyes. "Raiden. Hey." I shook my head, laughing under my breath. "Sorry, I totally spaced." I flashed him an apologetic smile.

"No worries," he said, his lips spreading into a grin that crinkled the corners of his eyes. "Did I wake you?" His brows bunched together. "I was hoping to catch you before you fell asleep." He handed me a small jewelry box, the size that would hold a ring.

I raised my eyebrows, looking from the jewelry box to Raiden's eyes.

A flush crept up Raiden's neck. "Don't worry," he said, laughing softly and rubbing the back of his neck with one hand. "I'm not proposing." He reached for my wrist and pressed the jewelry box against my palm, curling my fingers around it. "Open it?"

I couldn't resist his hopeful tone. I uncurled my fingers and held my hand higher, then lifted the lid of the jewelry box. A ring-shaped band of bronze sat tucked into the depression in the tiny cushion within the box. My brow furrowed, my mind working sluggishly to process what I was seeing.

It was a ring, but not like anything I had ever seen before. It looked like a key that had been stretched and flattened, then curled around a rod to form a ring.

All the puzzle pieces suddenly snapped together in my mind. My lips parted, and my eyes locked with Raiden's once more. "Is this your key to Blackthorn Manor?"

Raiden ducked his head with a nod, hiding his bashful smile. He peered at me through his lashes, an adorable look on such a big guy. "I thought it would be nice for you to have something you could always have on you to remind you of home." He shrugged, raising his head. "Besides, it's not like I need it anymore."

Tears gathered in my eyes as I stared at the ring. My bottom lip quivered, and I looked up at Raiden, my lips spreading into a tremulous grin. "Thank you." I shook my head, at a loss for words. "This is—I—" I snapped the jewelry box shut and held it against my chest, directly over my heart. "It's perfect," I said, reaching for Raiden's hand. "Thank you."

"You're welcome." Raiden cleared his throat and shuffled his feet, glancing up the corridor toward the door to his private quarters. "I should, uh, go."

I tightened my grip on his hand. "Don't."

He looked at me.

"Don't go."

I walked onto the dock near the northern end of Gene Coulon Memorial Beach Park, the sound of my steps echoing under the thick, weathered boards. Water lapped at the piles under the dock, and a lone duck quacked intermittently as it floated along nearby. The surface of Lake Washington rippled with the faint breeze, the water appearing dark and murky under the overcast sky. Undeterred by the threat of rain, children played on the playground at the opposite end of the park, their squeals and laughter diluted by the time it reached my ears.

I wore loose-fitting jeans and a hooded sweatshirt over my hoplon suit, so as not to attract attention, and carried a small Olympian storage cube tucked under one arm. The box appeared to be a solid block of obsidian, just like those I had found below Vatican City.

Raiden followed me onto the dock, his clothes similarly casual. He walked with his hands tucked into the pockets of his jacket, his watchful gaze always moving, searching for any potential threats. His jacket hid the laser pistol tucked into the modified holster on the small of his back.

"Are you sure about this location?" Raiden asked. "It's not too distracting?"

I reached the end of the dock, where the platform widened to form a T, and glanced back at him.

Raiden was scanning the shoreline at the southern end of the park, where the children played in defiance of the gloomy weather.

I followed his line of sight, then closed my eyes and listened to the diffused laughter of the children. I inhaled deeply, letting the faintly musty lake air fill my lungs. Smiling to myself, I released the breath and opened my eyes to look at Raiden. "It's nice to have a reminder of why we're doing this," I told him.

And right now, I needed that reminder. This was my eleventh straight day of dispersing nanotracers to the general population, and I was exhausted—mentally, psychically, and emotionally. The Tsakali were due to reach Earth in a month, and we needed to be long gone by then.

We had divided the planet up by geographical regions, and each psychic had been assigned a region. I was responsible for spreading the nanotracers to as many people as possible along the west coast of North America. Mine was one of the largest and most populated regions, but besides Selene, I was the strongest of the psychics, so the assignment made sense. Selene was tackling Southeast Asia, moving along the coastline from the Bay of Bengal up to the East China Sea. Selene, Meg, and I had a jump start while Caly and the rest of the Zari psychics lost a couple of days recovering from the genetic treatment needed to reverse their solar urticaria.

The corners of Raiden's mouth tensed, hinting at a frown. He no longer scanned the surrounding area for potential threats. Instead, he focused on me, the concern in his eyes telling me he thought the most serious threat to our mission was, well, *me*.

"I'm *fine*," I told him, flashing him a reassuring smile. "Promise."

He grunted, and the slight narrowing of his eyes told me he wasn't all that reassured.

With a sigh, I turned away from Raiden and got to work. The dock offered two built-in benches, one on either end of the T. I strode over to the left-most bench and sat, setting the storage cube on the dock boards between my boots. I pulled my regulator out from the neck of my sweatshirt, quickly deactivated it, then tucked it away again. Channeling psychic energy toward the tip of my index finger, I traced the pattern on the top of the box to unlock it. The grooves in the shiny, black surface of the cube glowed with a silver light in the wake of my touch.

I watched Raiden out of the corner of my eye as I waited for the storage cube to open. He had turned his back to me and retraced his steps, moving closer to the place where the dock met dry land. He stood in the center of the narrow walkway, his stance wide and his arms crossed over his chest. I couldn't see his face, but it was easy enough to imagine the hard set of his features. Any passersby would take one look at him and decide to move on to the next dock.

The top of the storage cube split down the middle, then slid open, either side of the lid folding down to sit flush against the sides of the box. Within the cube, what appeared to be a thick, golden liquid gently swayed from side to side. It wasn't actually a liquid, but a mass of several hundred thousand nanotracers pooling together.

Taking a deep breath and sitting up straighter, I held my hands out over the open storage cube and closed my eyes. I sent threads of psychic energy pouring out of my hands to dive into the mass of nanotracers, activating them. At my direction, the thousands upon thousands of microscopic devices rose out of the storage cube, fanning out into the air around me like a swarm of glittering insects.

The nanotracers were beautiful little pieces of Olympian technology. Each one was laced with orichalcum, giving them their golden shimmer. The orichalcum not only allowed me and my fellow psychics to home in on and guide the minuscule devices, but since orichalcum was an element not native to Earth, once a nanotracer found its human host, the foreign element enabled the *Elysium's* tracking system to lock onto each individual host's location by detecting the trace amount of orichalcum in their body. The device itself acted like a virus, binding to a specific genetic sequence present in the mitochondrial DNA of all humans, passed down to them from Mitochondrial Eve. Once a nanotracer bonded to that genetic sequence, it would go dormant, awaiting activation from the *Elysium* while sending out a signal repelling all other nanotracers.

I raised my arms, guiding the swarm of nanotracers higher until they floated in an amorphous glimmering mass overhead. I inhaled deeply, securing my hold on them, and on my exhale, I sent them southward, guiding them to spread out in search of human hosts.

It took a little over an hour, but finally, the last nanotracer found its host and I released the constant flow of psychic energy. I slumped forward on the bench, bracing my elbows on my knees as a wave of dizziness crashed over me. I embraced the physical discomfort, knowing it stemmed from doing something that mattered, and stared down at the empty storage cube as I focused on taking deep, even breaths.

Once the worst of the dizziness had passed, I raised my head.

Raiden watched me, concern tightening the skin around his eyes. My tapped-out psychic senses could only pick up on the faintest hint of his disapproval floating along the breeze.

Ignoring him, I fished my regulator out from the neck of my sweatshirt and activated it with a sweep of my fingertip around the stone. His emotions faded away until I was, once again, alone in my head. I planted my hand down beside me on the surface of the bench and, groaning, pushed myself up to stand. I swayed, my legs unsteady, as a wave of nausea struck me.

Suddenly Raiden was there, one hand gripping my elbow, the other curled around the side of my waist. "You should take a breather, Cora," he said. "Let's call it a day."

I swallowed rising nausea and shook my head. "There's no time. We have to keep going."

Raiden stared at me for a long moment, his expression unreadable.

"Please, Raiden," I murmured.

His mouth flattened out into a thin line, his disapproval clear, but he didn't argue. Maintaining a firm grip on my elbow, Raiden bent over to retrieve the storage cube. He tucked it under his arm, then slowly guided me back to our waiting ship, a compact stealth shuttle similar to the *Argo*, but about a tenth the size. It was basically the Olympian version of a sedan.

When we reached the shuttle, I settled in the passenger seat and waited for Raiden to take his place at the helm.

I blinked, and he was in the pilot's seat, the engine on and the display illuminated. Raiden extended his arm across the space between our seats, a packaged protein bar in his hand. "Eat this," he said. "The sugar should keep you going a little longer."

"Thanks." I accepted the protein bar and offered Raiden a tight-lipped smile. I curled my fingers around the unopened bar, my stomach roiling at the thought of taking a single bite.

Raiden pressed his hands against the navigation sphere. "We'll stop and get some real food on the way to the next spot."

"Sounds good," I said and leaned my head back against the headrest and closed my eyes. I was asleep before we even lifted off the ground.

[20]

I stood on the observation deck at the top of Smith Tower, my eyes closed and my arms outstretched as I guided a swarm of nanotracers into the heart of downtown Seattle. My knees wobbled, and I lowered my hands to the railing, gripping it tightly to steady myself. There were just a few dozen more nanotracers in need of human hosts. I gritted my teeth, sweat dripping down my neck and temples, and pushed through the fatigue.

My brain throbbed from the oversaturation of psychic energy. Just three nanotracers left, now.

My heart fluttered in my chest, a trio of irregular beats. My eyes snapped open, panic worsening the heart palpitations.

"No, no, no . . . Not again," I breathed, a vivid flashback momentarily transporting me to another time and place. To the last time I died.

I dropped to my knees, head hanging. My heart continued to beat with that irregular rhythm, and my hopes weren't high that it would ever go back to normal. I had pushed myself too hard, too far, and something within me had broken. This body was nearing its end.

My breaths came in shallow, uncontrollable little bursts, and dark spots danced around the edges of my vision.

"Peri," Hades said, kneeling in front of me. He placed his hand on the side of my head and tilted my face up toward his. "Are you all right?"

My chin trembled, but I couldn't bring myself to tell him the truth. To tell him I was dying. "Yeah," I said faintly, feeling short of breath. It would only get worse. "I'm fine."

I took a shuddering breath. My heartbeat wasn't just irregular now. It was weakening too. The dark spots dancing around my vision closed in until Hades was all I could see. A tear broke free over the brim of my eyelid, streaking down my cheek.

My heart seized, and I collapsed forward.

Hades caught me, pulling me onto his lap. He brushed the hair out of my face, his touch gentle, and stroked my cheek. The sensation remained long after my awareness of who he was or why he was touching me had faded away.

Until even that, too, was gone.

Until there was nothing.

My awareness returned to the present. To the here and now. My heart gave another few irregular beats, and black spots danced around the edges of my vision. I couldn't catch my breath. I clutched at my chest, gasping for air.

My knees gave out, and I was vaguely aware of Raiden's arms closing around me before the darkness claimed me.

I woke lying on my back and feeling remarkably well-rested. It was lovely, except for the part where I hadn't felt well-rested in weeks and wasn't sure why I suddenly did now. I opened my eyes, expecting to see the familiar walls of my cramped room on board the *Elysium*. But that wasn't what I saw.

I was lying in a reclined recovery chair in a Med Sector pod, though the unfamiliar polished steel walls told me this was not the Med Sector on the *Elysium*. Propping myself up on my elbows, I glanced down at my body, taking in the loose-fitting pants and sleeveless tunic in a super soft, lightweight opalescent fabric, then scanned the three other empty recovery chairs but found no clues hinting at where I was. I narrowed my eyes, searching my memory for an explanation of how I had come to be here—wherever *here* was.

The last thing I could recall clearly was guiding nanotracers from the observation deck at the top of Smith Tower. I had been exhausted.

Had I passed out?

I touched behind my ear, intending to activate my comms

patch, but found only smooth skin and loose hair. My heart gave a nervous flutter as I realized my comms patch had been removed.

I sat up fully and draped my legs over the side of the recovery chair. "Hello?" I tried to call out, but the word was little more than a croak. I cleared my throat, only now realizing how dry it was, and tried again. "Hello? Raiden?" I cocked my head to the side, listening but hearing nothing. "Anyone?"

I licked my lips, my tongue tacky, and spotted a stainless steel tumbler on the small table beside my recovery chair. I reached for the cup and unscrewed the lid, then leaned over the clear liquid and gave it a sniff. It smelled like nothing—like water. I raised the tumbler to my lips and took a tentative sip. Yep, definitely water. I drained the cup, wiping my mouth with the back of my hand as I returned the empty tumbler to the table.

I touched a fingertip to my regulator, deactivating it without a second thought. My grasp of psychic energy felt thready and tenuous, and I had to concentrate harder than usual as I stretched out my psychic senses in search of other minds. I grew increasingly concerned until I finally touched Raiden's mind.

Relief washed over me, soothing my fraying nerves and pushing back the mounting unease. He was too far away for me to read much more from his mind than his location relative to mine and a general impression of his wellbeing. He was fine—bored, restless, and worried, but fine.

Closing my eyes, I extended my psychic reach, searching for more minds. I reached out for miles but found no other people, only the wild, unreadable mental signatures I recognized as belonging to animals. Where the hell *were* we?

I slid off the edge of the recovery chair and stood, the floor cool against my bare feet. I slowly approached the door panel. It slid open as I drew near, revealing a dark corridor. I poked my head through the doorway, looking first one way, then the other. The corridor stretched out in either direction, the smooth, stainless steel surfaces fading into darkness. The opposite wall appeared to be made of glass, suggesting it was a floor-to-ceiling window, but whatever lay beyond it was shrouded in darkness, and all I could see was my own backlit reflection.

When I stepped through the doorway, dim lights faded on overhead, illuminating a little more of the corridor but revealing nothing new. I spotted a tiny pinprick of light through the wall of glass and crossed the corridor. I stopped with my nose nearly touching the glass, my eyes narrowed on the light. It grew slowly, like it was drawing nearer.

Suddenly, a horrific monster with giant needle teeth swam into view.

I yelped and leaped backward, stumbling into the wall behind me as I stared at the *thing* on the other side of the glass. It took my frightened mind at least a dozen heartbeats to make sense of what I was seeing—not a monster but a huge, beastly angler fish. I watched the creature turn abruptly and swim on, disappearing into the darkness.

I let out a bark of nervous laughter and pushed away from the wall, hopping in place as I shook out my body to dissipate the bulk of the adrenaline surge.

So, it looked like Raiden and I were at an Olympian site deep under the ocean. The Gamma site, then. It was somewhere in the depths of the Pacific Ocean. That would explain why I hadn't sensed any other people, but I still had no idea *why* we were here.

Focusing on Raiden's mental signature, I looked up and down the corridor, then at the glass wall. Raiden was somewhere in that direction. Not that I had any clue of how to get to him. Only one way to find out.

I turned to the right and started up the corridor. Lights faded on overhead, following my progress. On my left, the solid wall of glass continued on, stretching out ahead as far as the light reached. I passed various door panels on my right, though they all remained shut. Curious, I paused at one door and pressed the button on the wall beside it. The door panel slid open, and lights faded on within the space beyond, revealing a sterile laboratory, all stainless steel and polished white. I frowned, my eyes scanning the space. The lab fit with my limited knowledge of the Gamma site. I knew it was primarily a research facility—and that was pretty much all I knew about this site.

I backed out of the lab and continued onward. I passed through a gentle bend in the corridor, angling me slightly more toward Raiden's location. After another long, straight stretch, I reached another bend, the slight angle the same as the previous bend. I paused and looked back the way I had come, then looked forward. A mental image of the layout of this place as a huge polygon was forming in my mind.

Holding onto that image, I continued on, my circuitous path gradually drawing me closer to Raiden's location. After seven more bends in the corridor, I sensed Raiden straight ahead. Eager to reach him, I picked up the pace.

The next bend in the corridor revealed a wide open space rather than a new extension of the hallway. I slowed, then stopped completely, taking a moment to admire the wonder of this new space.

The chamber was some sort of underwater ocean observatory, encased in a dome of glass, and the floor transitioned from shiny stainless steel to a polished alabaster stone. Lights spanning the perimeter of the dome's exterior illuminated the ocean depths beyond the glass, revealing the stunning alien landscape of the deep sea. Ridged spires rose out from the ocean floor, venting plumes of inky smoke. Beyond the field of spires, the ocean floor dropped away, diving even deeper underwater. Strange creatures swam around the spires lazily, some monstrous, some beautiful, some both.

Raiden lay on the floor in the center of the dome, his arms folded behind his head and his ankles crossed. Above him, huge bioluminescent eels performed graceful water aerobics.

I cleared my throat and started toward him.

Raiden craned his neck to look my way, his lips spreading into a broad grin as his relief and joy tickled my psychic senses. "Welcome back," he said, curling his body to sit up. He planted a hand on the floor and pushed himself up to his feet. "How do you feel?" he asked, starting toward me.

"I feel great," I said, frowning. I narrowed my eyes. "Why are we here?"

A crease formed between Raiden's brows as his expression turned quizzical. "You don't remember?"

I shook my head.

"You passed out," he said. One of his eyebrows quirked higher. "Pushed yourself too hard, just like I said you would."

Again, I frowned. I had no recollection of anything like that. At least, not from recent memory. I stopped just out of reach of Raiden and raised my hand part of the way. "Do you mind if I take a peek into your memory?"

Raiden shook his head. "Go for it."

A small smile of thanks touched my lips, and I stepped closer to Raiden. I raised my hand higher and touched my fingertips to his temple. The physical contact wasn't necessary or even all that helpful, but my limited experience using my psychic abilities around humans told me it set them at ease to believe physical contact allowed me deeper access to their minds. If their misperception that physical distance would shield their minds from me made them feel more comfortable around my alien powers, then I welcomed it.

"Think about what happened and why we're here," I said as I closed my eyes and delved into Raiden's mind.

I found the memory close to the surface, thanks to Raiden's focus. I saw myself through his eyes, a more perfect version of myself than existed in reality. In the memory, I stood on the observation deck at the top of Smith Tower, my arms outstretched as I directed the nanotracers throughout downtown Seattle. I watched as my body swayed and my hands lowered to grip the railing. A moment later, the memory version of me gasped and clutched her chest, and then her knees gave out. I got up close and personal with my past self as Raiden rushed forward in the memory, catching me before my body struck the floor of the deck.

I could hear Raiden calling my name, his voice garbled by his own ears. When the past version of me didn't respond, he hoisted me over his shoulder and carried me through the empty bar at the top of the tower to the elevator. When the elevator reached the ground floor, he rushed out through the lobby and across the street to the vacant construction zone of a demolished building where we had parked the ship.

I watched through Raiden's eyes as he spoke with Hades through his comms patch. Hades asked Raiden if I was alive, then reprimanded Raiden for letting me push myself too far. Raiden accepted the tongue lashing, his self-loathing seeping into me through the memory as he beat himself up worse than Hades' words ever could.

A navigation panel appeared on the holoscreen in front of Raiden, a beacon sent by Hades marking the location of the nearest asclypos. Hades informed Raiden he had uploaded a flight plan and warned him not to touch the controls. As the ship lifted off the ground, I slipped out of the memory and opened my eyes.

"This is not your fault," I said, pressing my palm to the side of Raiden's face and searching his eyes for the self-loathing I had felt in the memory. It was still there, simmering under the surface. "There's nothing you could have done to stop me." I offered him a gentle smile. "Hades knows that better than anyone."

I felt fairly certain that Hades' anger at Raiden was just as much directed at himself for the blame he still carried for my last death. I suppressed the urge to roll my eyes. Men.

I sensed Raiden wasn't ready to forgive himself yet, so I moved on to another topic. "How long was I out?" I asked, pulling my hand away from Raiden's face and quickly activating my regulator to give him some emotional privacy.

Raiden winced, telling me I wouldn't like the answer before he even gave it. "Two days," he said.

I planted my hands on my hips and pressed my lips together, inhaling and exhaling slowly, fighting the urge to scream. All that lost time equaled people who *wouldn't* be tagged by a nanotracer. Who *wouldn't* be saved.

It's done, I told myself. *Let it go.*

Clenching my jaw and not remotely close to letting it go, I made a show of looking around. "Where's the ship?" I refocused on Raiden. "We need to leave. I have to make up for—"

"Rest, Cora," Raiden said, placing his hand on my shoulder. He gave me a gentle shake. "What you have to do is *rest*. You were on the verge of cardiac arrest when I put you in the asclypos, and your treatment plan calls for one more session in the machine followed by another period of rest." The arch of his brows and set of his jaw told me he wouldn't budge on this. "*Then* we can leave."

I squared my shoulders and leveled a hard stare at Raiden. He threw it right back at me. I sighed, letting my hands slip from my hips.

Sure, I could have dug the location of the ship out of his mind, knocked him out with a stunning psychic blast, and dragged him unconscious away from the Gamma site, but deep down, I knew he was right. I would be more useful to the mission whole and healthy than dead, and as much as I wanted to believe I could push myself to the brink of psychic burnout without repercussions, my past experience of *dying* from that very thing convinced me otherwise.

My shoulders slumped, and I stared down at the shiny white floor.

Raiden flexed his arm and pulled me into a hug, holding me tight against him. "You scared the shit out of me," he said, his chest rumbling against my cheek as he spoke. "Please don't ever do that again."

I gripped the back of his shirt and squeezed my eyes shut, wishing I could tell him what he wanted to hear. But I couldn't.

We stood like that for a long time. I listened to his breaths and the beating of his heart. To the steadiness that was Raiden.

"Where's the control center?" I asked against his chest. I tilted my head back so I could see his face. "I should talk to Hades before that machine knocks me out again."

Raiden studied my face for a long moment, then exhaled heavily and nodded toward the corridor that had brought me into the domed observatory. "It's that way." He pulled back and turned to the side, keeping an arm draped over my shoulders as he started toward the corridor.

We followed the corridor around several bends, then Raiden guided me through a door panel into a large, boxy room of stainless steel floor, walls, and ceiling. An array of freestanding control pedestals surrounded a larger, crescent-shaped podium I recognized as a master control panel. Raiden's arm slipped from my shoulders as I strode ahead, making a beeline for the central podium.

I pushed a button, and a holoscreen appeared, hovering over the podium. I quickly navigated to the communications pane and swiped to select the external communications program. A list of symbols appeared—alpha, beta, delta, and epsilon—representing the four other official Olympian settlements on this planet. Since the Omega site had been kept secret from all Olympians except for Hades and his siblings, Poseidon and Demeter, it didn't appear on the list. The *Elysium* was listed below the settlements, as were all the other, smaller ships within the range of the ancient net of cloaked satellites surrounding Earth.

I tapped on the *alpha* symbol to open up a direct line of communication with all comms patches currently active at the Alpha site. Hades was supposed to be there, directing the move of equipment to Terra, the planet he had chosen for our new home. It was an idyllic planet my people had scouted as a potential colony eons ago, and thus had a gephyra, but it had never actually been settled due to the discovery of intelligent life on the planet. However, that species had long since self-extinguished, leaving the planet ripe for the taking.

It would take the rest of us sixty years to reach Terra via the *Elysium*—and that was with the ship's chaos-powered FTL drive cutting the trip in half compared to a ship relying on a standard FTL drive—but the transplanted Olympians would travel there through the gephyra to lay the groundwork for our new settlement.

I scanned the list of Olympians currently at the Alpha site. Hades' name wasn't there. I pursed my lips. He must have finished up there and moved on to the Omega site to start the transfer of Olympians from the terrestrial Vault of Souls to the one aboard the *Elysium*. I inhaled deeply, blowing out the breath through my nose. This complicated matters.

As the Omega site was a secret settlement, I couldn't forge a direct line of communication with Hades there. Although . . .

Squinting thoughtfully, I backed out of the Alpha site comms list and scrolled down through the ship names listed below the settlements. I found the *Argo* and selected it with a tap to forge a direct line of communication with the ship. I chewed on the inside of my cheek. There was no guarantee that this would work. Hades would only be able to hear me if he was in or near the *Argo*.

I waited a few seconds for the link to go live, then cleared my throat. "Hades? Can you hear me?"

No response.

"Hades?" I repeated a little louder. "Are you there?"

The responding silence stretched out for so long that I was preparing to abandon the effort to reach him.

"Cora?" Hades said, and my lips spread into a gentle smile at the sound of his voice. "Are you still there?"

"Yeah," I said, speaking through my smile. "I'm still here. Are you at the Omega site?"

"I am." He was quiet for a moment, and I pictured him standing in front of the *Argo*'s central control panel, grappling with his desire to berate me for being so reckless. "How are you feeling?" he finally asked. "When Raiden contacted me, I feared the worst."

"I'm all right," I told him, glancing at Raiden and flashing him a quick smile of thanks before returning my stare to the holo-screen. "*But*," I added, drawing out the word, "the asclypos prescribed me a second session, so I'm going to be out of commission for another day or two."

"I see," Hades said. "Well, if that's what the asclypos prescribed, then it's what must be done."

I nodded to myself, knowing he was right but not liking it. "Can you issue a warning to the other psychics? We only have a few weeks left to distribute the nanotracers, and we can't afford for any more of us to end up out of commission."

Hades took so long to respond that I knew he had bad news to deliver.

"How many have we lost?" I asked reluctantly.

"None have died," Hades said. "But three of the Zari psychics are recuperating from psychic overextension—one here, one at the Delta site, and one on board the *Elysium*."

The news was a punch to the gut, and I bowed my head. At least they weren't dead.

"Right after you collapsed, I warned the others not to push themselves too hard," Hades added. "But some didn't listen."

I nodded to myself again. I probably wouldn't have listened either.

"And there's something else, Cora," Hades said, his tone giving me chills.

I locked eyes with Raiden and could see that he had heard it too.

"The Tsakali have sped their approach," Hades told us.

I held my breath and shook my head, terrified of what he would say next. We should have had three more weeks until we needed to load up and ship out.

"We have one week until they arrive."

[22]

I stood on the Bridge in the *Elysium*, both hands gripping the curved edge of the navigation console's broad pedestal as I stared up at the large holographic projection of Earth hovering in front of me. The globe was depicted in gray scale and covered in a mass of glowing, golden lights, denser and brighter in the more populated areas—cities and along highways—forming a pattern that reminded me eerily of images I had seen of cancerous growths. The lights represented the nearly two billion nanotracers anchored in human hosts—all we had managed to distribute before it was time to pull back to the *Elysium* and prepare for upload.

Raiden stood on my left, Meg on my right, and my mom, Emi, Fiona, and Hades fanned out around the navigation console, bodies and expressions tense.

I dropped my focus to the smaller rectangular holoscreen floating below the globe. It displayed a real-time chart of part of the Milky Way Galaxy, Earth at the center. A blinking red beacon near the rightmost edge of the holoscreen marked the location of the Tsakali fleet. The beacon moved so slowly along its projected path—a dashed white line—as to appear to be stalled in place.

But I knew better. They were coasting along, using their slower-than-light engines while their FTL drive recharged.

Gertie estimated the Tsakali fleet would reach Earth in two more FTL jumps. That meant we had less than twelve hours, accounting for their FTL drive requiring one more recharge period. They would have been here much sooner, but their reduced speed suggested that at least some of their ships were running standard FTL drives rather than the faster, chaos-powered variety the *Elysium* employed.

A second line intersected with the Tsakali's projected path, this one in solid red, roughly halfway between their fleet's current location and Earth. It marked the point at which the Tsakali would be within range to detect the surge of chaos power emitted when the *Elysium* fired up its FTL drive.

That was our deadline, in the most literal sense of the word. If we were still here when the Tsakali crossed that line—if we jumped after they were within range to detect us—their scout ships, always equipped with chaos-powered FTL drives, would be able to track us, and we would be dead.

I focused on the bottom left corner of the holoscreen, where an eight-by-eight square of a real-time satellite image overlaid the navigation chart. It displayed the area immediately surrounding the hidden cliffside entrance to the Beta site. A team of Zari psychics had infiltrated the underground city with the mission to overthrow the Zari Council and give their people the eleventh-hour choice to either upload to the *Elysium's* Vault of Souls or to remain on Earth. The team had been radio silent for over two hours, and they had been scheduled to check in ten minutes ago.

I snuck a sidelong glance at Meg. She chewed on her bottom lip. A steady stream of anxiety and worry flowed through our bond.

"If we don't start soon," Hades said from the opposite side of the navigation console, "we won't have enough time to upload everyone who has been tagged."

I peered at him through the holographic projection of Earth, my grip on the edge of the pedestal tightening. "Just give them another minute," I said, my stare locking with his.

Hades nodded, the motion barely perceptible.

I dropped my focus back to the small square of rainforest on the holoscreen, willing the team of Zari psychics to emerge from the cliff wall. My heartbeat was a second hand ticking the time down until Hades initiated the upload, locking out all unlinked nanotracers. If the Zari weren't tagged by then, they would be left behind.

At least a minute passed, silent expectation slowly sucking all the oxygen from the room. Movement on the far side of the pedestal caught my eye, and I watched Hades raise his arm, positioning his holoband in front of his chest. His other hand hovered near the small holoscreen floating above the device on his forearm. I could see the big red button through the semiopaque holoscreen.

My whole body tensed.

"It is time," Hades said, raising his other hand to hover in front of the holographic button that would start the upload. "Initiating upload to the Vault in five, four, three—"

"Wait!" Meg croaked. Her hand was suddenly on my forearm, her grip painful even through the sleeve of my hoplon suit, and she pointed to the satellite image. A woman stood outside of the entrance to the Beta site, and another emerged from the cliff wall.

"We're out!" Caly proclaimed, her voice audible through both the ship's speaker system and the comms patch behind my ear. "All nanotracers have been distributed. We're not too late, are we?"

"No, you're not too late," I said as I looked at Hades through the holographic projection of Earth and nodded once, telling him to begin.

I watched him tap the button on his mini holoscreen, and then

I closed my eyes. My lips curved into a relieved grin as the tension seeped out of my body.

Meg released my arm, and I opened my eyes to look at her. Tears streamed down her cheeks, her sense of relief overwhelming. I reached for her hand, covering it with mine.

"Good job, Caly," I told the young psychic through my comms patch. "Now get back to the ship."

I exchanged a quick smile with Meg, then pulled my hand off hers and returned my attention to the large holographic projection of Earth, focusing on the brilliant glow of nanotracers lining the western coast of the United States. After each person's mind and genetic data were uploaded to the ship, their body would die and their nanotracer would go dormant, its glow fading from the projection. It was too early to see a difference yet, but that didn't stop me from looking for one.

"The first row is full," Selene announced, her voice only reaching my and Hades' ears through our comms patches. She was stationed in the ship's Vault of Souls, monitoring the progress of the upload there.

"That puts us at a rate of ten million minds uploaded every minute, so . . ." Hades fell quiet as he ran through the mental calculations.

"The upload should be complete in two and half hours," Fiona finished for him. "Assuming a constant upload rate, of course."

"Of course," Hades said dryly.

I shifted my attention back to the navigation chart on the smaller holoscreen and stared at the blinking red beacon marking the location of the Tsakali fleet. Our window to upload the tagged human minds depended on how long it took the Tsakali's FTL drives to recharge, when they made their next FTL jump, and where they landed when that jump was complete.

I looked up at the projection of Earth. Was it merely a figment of my imagination, or was the glow of nanotracers already perceptibly dimmer? I narrowed my eyes. The index finger on my right hand tapped steadily on the surface of the pedestal.

"Is there any way to speed up the upload process?" my mom asked.

Hades shook his head. "Not without diverting processing power from the simulation."

"If anything," Fiona added, "the upload process may slow as the simulation populates."

I looked from Hades to Fiona.

Fiona offered my mom an apologetic smile. "Gertie and I considered giving the simulation a delayed start, but neural variance suggested some people would notice the lapse in perception, and since we're prioritizing a seamless transition to minimize simulation rejection . . ."

We were all staring at Fiona now.

She looked around, her cheeks reddening under the sudden scrutiny. "Too much information? Right. Gertie's running the show here, and she's maxed out."

I pressed my lips into a thin line and returned to alternating between watching the equally imperceptible progressions of the upload and of the Tsakali fleet.

"Evacuation of the Alpha site is complete," a new voice announced through my comms patch. I recognized it as belonging to Tammyris, Hades' chosen second-in-command. She was slated to lead the transplanted Olympians while they awaited our arrival on Terra. "Permission to initiate the self-destruct sequence on all Olympian sites?"

I peered at Hades through the holographic projection of Earth. A deep sadness shadowed his eyes, and I could only imagine what he was feeling right now, on the cusp of giving the order to destroy all he had helped to build for our people here on this planet, a place that was supposed to be our sanctuary.

"Proceed with the self-destruct, but leave the Beta site off the list," Hades commanded.

"Yes, of course," Tammyris said. "I agree the data wipe should be sufficient there. Initiating the self-destruct." She fell silent, and the subsequent minute stretched out, feeling like hours.

"Gamma site is destroyed," she said.

My heart clenched as Hades' eyes met mine.

"Delta site is destroyed."

I held my breath.

"Epsilon site is destroyed," Tammyris continued. "Omega site is destroyed. Initiating the automated self-destruct sequence for the Alpha site."

A moment later, static filled the comms feed as Tammyris traveled through the gephyra to Terra.

"Safe travels," she said when the static cleared. "And good luck to you all." She was quiet for a moment. "Alpha site self-destruct in three, two—"

The comms feed died as the explosion at the Alpha site shut down the gephyra bridge.

Tears welled in my eyes, and I clenched my jaw, swallowing reflexively. All that effort. All that history. Gone, just like that.

Hades planted his hands on the navigation console and bowed his head, bending under the weight of what we had just done.

I closed my eyes, and a tear escaped from between my lashes, streaking down my cheek. I sniffed and wiped it away, then looked down at the navigation chart displaying the Tsakali fleet's location.

My heartbeat stumbled. The blinking red beacon was gone.

The Tsakali fleet had jumped.

[23]

My eyes felt dry and overtired from focusing for too long on the navigation chart without blinking. The Tsakali fleet was due to drop out of FTL any second now, and the only question was: how close would they be to the "go" line when they did.

I leaned forward, resting my elbows on the surface of the navigation console, and licked my lips. Any second now. Any second . . .

I blinked, and suddenly the beacon was there on the screen, and my heart lurched into my throat. I straightened, my eyes locked on the blinking red beacon. The Tsakali fleet was frighteningly close to the line demarcating the outer edge of our safe zone.

A moment later, a countdown timer appeared near the top of the holoscreen. It was Gertie's estimation of how long we had until the Tsakali fleet reached that fateful line. It was how long we had until we needed to jump.

I tore my stare away from the timer on the navigation chart to peer through the holographic projection of Earth at the only other person still posted around the navigation console. Hades stood on the far side of the pedestal, his brows pinched together as he swiped this way and that on the private holoscreen hovering in front of him.

I glanced over my shoulder to where Raiden and my mom huddled together with Emi and Fiona in front of the in-wall screen belonging to one of the multi-use control stations running along the side of the Bridge. The large screen was split into four, streaming multiple news feeds from Earth, showing shot after shot of crowded places filled with lifeless bodies. Malls, classrooms, stadiums—thousands of different settings, all filled with corpses. The most disturbing image was of an elementary school soccer field covered in the bodies of the children who had evacuated their school for a fire drill. The sight made my heart ache and my gut twist into knots.

A ticker scrolled along the bottom of the screen, displaying the growing number of casualties. Of the dead. At least, that's what the people who had yet to be uploaded thought. In reality, the former occupants of those discarded shells had a far more promising future than those who would remain on Earth, left behind to clean up our mess.

That part didn't sit well with me. But this was a far better outcome for humanity than leaving all of them behind in blissful ignorance of the danger hurtling toward their planet.

"How much longer until the upload is complete?" I asked Hades, facing him once more.

The corners of his mouth tensed, but he didn't stop swiping and tapping. "It's going to be close." He glanced up at me, just for a moment. "At the current upload rate, we should make it with about a minute to spare. But, if the rate continues to slow . . ." He left the implication hanging unspoken.

If the rate continued to slow, we wouldn't be able to upload every tagged person before we had to leave.

I pressed my lips together, tapping my index finger on the side of the pedestal as I thought through our options. Or rather, as I realized we didn't have any.

Again, I glanced over at the cluster of humans watching the news from Earth. "Hey, Fio," I called out.

Fiona turned her head to look at me, tears streaming down her cheeks. She knew as well as I did that those people weren't really dead, but that didn't make the visuals any less disturbing.

"Can you talk to Gertie?" I asked Fiona. "Maybe convince her to hold off on integrating the last batch of uploads until we have everyone on board?"

I understood the AI's reasoning for the immediate integration of the uploaded minds. The integrity of the simulation would be at risk if enough of the inhabitants resisted their new reality, which would endanger not only the new human uploads but the current Olympian denizens as well. Immediate integration was the best way to prevent an internal collapse of the simulation. To the new uploads, life *should* appear to be business as usual.

Gertie's primary objective during the active uploading process was to mold their new, virtual reality around their current perception of the world to create a seamless transition. The process required her to make constant tweaks to the virtual world, populating the simulation with digital doppelgängers of all those people missed by the nanotracers. We couldn't have little Sally wondering why Grandma suddenly vanished from the world. Essentially, Gertie had to adjust the simulation to accommodate each new upload, which meant each new upload sapped a little more of her processing power, diverting it from the upload process itself.

Fiona hastily wiped the tears from her cheeks and nodded. "I'll see what I can do," she said, hurrying over to another of the multi-use control stations, where she had set up shop by jacking her laptop into the ship's interface. She was already speaking to the AI through her comms patch by the time she perched on the edge of the built-in bench seat.

". . . hold steady at the current upload rate until the process is complete." Fiona fell quiet, listening to the AI's response. Then she started nodding and typing at the same time. "Yeah, I under-stand that, but if we want to upload everyone before we jump. . ." She paused typing, her fingers hovering over the keyboard and her focus distant as she listened to the AI. "Yeah, I can do that." She started typing again, faster than ever. "Uh-huh," she said, nodding. "Uh-huh."

Fiona glanced at me, flashing me a quick grin and raising her eyebrows, her fingers never ceasing their endless tapping on the keyboard keys.

I swallowed roughly, nearly choking on my anxiety, and checked the countdown timer. Seven minutes.

The voice of a female news anchor drew my attention back to the screen displaying the news feeds from Earth.

". . . sorry to report we still don't know how or why this is happening," the news anchor said. "And we have no way to know who will fall victim to this terrifying affliction next. Current esti-mates suggest nearly one-tenth of the world's population has perished in the last two hours, but some experts are estimating the impact is actually much higher. If you're still here, hold your loved ones close and—"

The news anchor's expression went blank, and she hunched forward in her chair, face-planting on her desk. She had just been uploaded. Saved. But to the people who remained down on Earth, she was dead. It was all a matter of perspective.

Their estimate of the number of people who had "fallen victim" was far too low, and at the same time, not nearly high enough. We had distributed nearly two billion nanotracers, tagging one-quarter of the world's population for upload. Six billion souls would remain on Earth, awaiting an alien attack they didn't know was coming, and there was nothing we could do about it.

I had been so focused on those we *could* save that I had given little thought to those we would leave behind. What would their next few hours look like? Their next few days? Would they have much more time than that? What would the Tsakali do to this planet and these people in their desperate search for the secret to creating chaos energy? Would they torture the ignorant masses of humans in a futile attempt to dig out the truth? When they were finished, empty-handed and enraged, would they destroy Earth out of spite? Or would they leave what was left of humanity to their ravaged planet, scrambling to survive?

I wasn't sure which outcome was worse.

My hands balled into fists. Silently, I vowed to return. One day, centuries in the future, when the settlement on Terra was safe and stable, I would return to Earth and do whatever I could to help the shreds of humanity that remained. If any remained.

An alarm blared, and I started. The harsh beeping echoed off the walls of the Bridge. The countdown timer was flashing red. Less than a minute until we *had* to jump. On the far side of the navigation console, Hades tapped the holoscreen in front of him, silencing the alarm.

I stared at the blinking red beacon representing the Tsakali fleet, watching it inch closer to the line each time it winked out of and back into view. Every few seconds, I glanced down at the countdown timer. Tension wrapped a tight fist around my heart. The timer reached the final twenty seconds, and I couldn't look away.

Nineteen. Eighteen. Seventeen. Sixteen.

"The upload is complete," Hades announced. He raised his arm and tapped the screen hovering above his holoband. "Initiating FTL jump. Brace yourselves."

Ten. Nine. Eight.

A new alarm blared, warning an FTL jump was imminent.

I leaned forward against the navigation console, my arms spread wide to either side of me, my hands clutching the edge of the pedestal. And still, I stared at the countdown timer.

Five. Four. Three. Two.

The blinking beacon touched the line, and the ship shuddered. A heartbeat later, the news feed from Earth went dead.

[24]

I deflected a sunshine-yellow doru blast with an energy shield that flickered into and out of existence in the blink of an eye. Then I spun around, using my own golden staff weapon to sweep Selene's legs out from under her. She jumped at the last second, and while she was in the air, I finally broke through her mental barriers—just for a moment—and could sense her next moves. I rolled to the side, narrowly avoiding the stunning web of energy she shot out of her palm, and blindly sent out an energy blast from the charged focus crystal of my doru.

The ball of shimmering electric-blue energy struck Selene squarely in her belly, sending her flying backward. She knocked over the Zari psychics unfortunate enough to be standing in her path. A chorus of shouts and yelps followed her as she skidded across the floor on her backside, coming to a stop two floor mats over. Her doru rolled away from her limp hand, clattering on the metal grating beyond the floor mat. A hush fell over the training room as Selene lay on her back, unconscious and limbs akimbo.

Breathing hard, I rolled onto my knees, then climbed to my feet, retracting my doru to its shorter length and stashing it in the sheath on my back as I stood. The crowd of Zari psychics who had gathered to watch us spar stared at Selene, all held motionless by hushed expectation. The channels running the length of every single hoplon suit glowed with a subtle amber light, indicating that their regulators were active, suppressing their psychic gifts. Selene's had reverted to amber the moment she lost consciousness.

I touched my own regulator, activating it with a swipe of my fingertip, joining the others in their duller view of the world.

Selene sucked in a harsh breath, and her body shuddered. The room filled with a collective exhale. I strode over to her, the sound of my steps changing as I moved from floor mat to metal grating and back.

Selene groaned, curling in on herself and rolling onto her side.

I extended my hand down to her, and a moment later, her palm slapped against the inside of my forearm. I gripped her forearm in turn and hoisted her up to her feet.

Selene stretched her neck, first one way, then the other, wincing slightly. Her eyes met mine, and she grinned. "Point to you, Cora."

I chuckled and shook my head.

Movements still a little stiff, Selene retrieved her doru, retracting the staff weapon to its shorter length before sliding it into the sheath on her back.

I turned away from her, facing the gathered warriors, and scanned their faces. I lingered for the briefest moment on Meg, whose eyes shone with pride as she relished my victory over Selene nearly as much as I did. "Tell me," I said, my voice raised to reach all the gathered women. "How did I defeat Selene?"

The Zari psychics exchanged hushed whispers and uncertain glances. A few looked at Meg, knowing she would have the exact answer I was looking for, but Meg's secretive smile told them she wasn't going to spill.

"Did I overpower her?" I asked, raising my eyebrows. Again, I scanned the line of watchful faces. "Battling another psychic is less about strength or skill, and more about feeling. To beat another psychic, you must rely on your deepest instincts—on your gut instead of your head—because while your head is busy trying to figure out her next move, she already knows yours."

Selene came to stand beside me, her hands planted on her hips.

"When fighting another psychic," I continued, "your conscious mind is your greatest weakness."

Selene nodded along as I spoke. "You must stop *thinking*," she added, "and simply *react*. The battle will be won by whichever psychic can sink into her instincts faster, for only then will she be able to slip past her opponent's mental barriers and not only *anticipate* her next moves, but *know* them."

I waited a few seconds after Selene fell silent, studying the gathered psychics' faces and letting her words sink in. "As the newest members of the Order of Amazons, it is up to each of you to keep our precious cargo safe." I hardened my expression, letting them see the gravity of their responsibility. "Two billion souls are in your care. *You* are all that stands between them and the greatest foe you will ever face."

The gathered women stood a little taller, held their heads a little higher.

"A Tsakali Titan may have psychic gifts," Selene said, "but it is still a machine, like all other Tsakali. It has no gut. It is pure consciousness. Pure thought. At any other time, this is their greatest strength, but when fighting an Amazon, it is their greatest weakness—their *only* weakness." She paused, her gaze traveling up and down the line of psychic warriors. "You have a single advantage over the enemy—your baser instincts, that part of you that is more animal than conscious, thinking being. You must learn to trust that part of yourself. To sink into it and embrace it."

I exchanged a look with Selene, nodding my thanks for her help with this lesson, then returned my attention to the gathered psychics. "All right," I said, clapping my hands together. "I want you to break up into pairs and deactivate your regulators. We'll spar with hand-to-hand this afternoon, and tomorrow morning we'll hold a tournament using dorus."

The buzz of excitement filled the training room as the women dispersed, pairing off and grouping around the floor mats spread throughout the space. I caught Meg's eye before she could find a partner, and she strode over to join Selene and me.

"For the tournament," I started, "do you think we should—"

The overhead lights flickered, and my question hung unfinished. All three of us looked up in time to see another flicker.

"Is that normal?" Meg asked, lowering her gaze to my face.

I exchanged a look with Selene. Worry lined her brow, and I had no doubt mine looked the same. "No," I told Meg and tensed the corners of my mouth as I again angled my gaze upward. "No, it's not." But for now, the glow from the light bars appeared as steady as ever.

I touched Meg's arm, just above her elbow. "Practice with Selene." I turned away and strode toward the doorway. "I'll be back in a bit," I tossed over my shoulder.

Walking quickly, I made my way to the wide central corridor running the length of the ship and hurried to the Bridge. The broad door panel remained stubbornly shut as I approached, and I stopped in front of it, momentarily at a loss for what to do. It should have sensed my approach and opened for me.

I narrowed my eyes at the motion sensor above the doorway. Had Hades deactivated it? There were only two reasons for such lockdown action—a hull breech or an enemy on board the ship. And if we were in the midst of either situation, Hades would have alerted me immediately through my comms patch. So, what was up with the door panel?

Something similar had happened earlier that morning. I had been forced to open the door panel leading out of the Residential Sector manually, as well. At the time, I dismissed it as a minor technical malfunction. But now, I wasn't so sure.

Feeling slightly unsettled, I sidestepped to the right of the door panel and punched the heel of my hand against the door controls. The door panel slid open, and I spotted the back of Hades' silver-blond head peeking over the headrest of the captain's chair, high on its platform.

I hurried into the command center, heading straight for the captain's station. The massive viewscreen at the front of the Bridge displayed the stars streaming past the ship like multi-hued laser beams, a telltale sign we were in the middle of an FTL jump.

As I neared the captain's station, I could see that Hades was leaning forward, his elbows on his knees. He stared at a long progress bar stretching across the holoscreen in front of him.

The floor suddenly shuddered, shaking violently enough to unbalance me. I stumbled sideways, catching myself on the curved podium of a weapon's station. The shuddering stopped as suddenly as it started, and when I looked up at the viewscreen again, the stars appeared as the usual pinpricks of light, confirming we were no longer traveling at faster-than-light speeds.

And the *Elysium* had dropped out of an FTL jump *without* an alarm.

Icy dread poured over me. Something was very wrong with the ship.

I straightened and rushed to the captain's station, taking the steps up the platform two at a time.

Hades glanced at me, only moving his eyes. The rest of him was locked in the same tense position as before.

"Door panels are malfunctioning and lights are flickering, and now this," I said, stepping onto the platform. I planted one hand on my hip, cocking it to the side, and stared down at Hades. "Please tell me you know what's going on."

"I'm already running a full systems diagnostic," Hades said, flicking the fingers of one hand toward the progress bar on the holoscreen.

I glanced at the progress bar, then returned my attention to him. "So we should know what the problem is soon?"

Hades didn't respond. He didn't even move.

"Right?" I prompted.

Hades exhaled a long, heavy sigh, and life seemed to bleed back into him. He scrubbed his hands over his face, then lowered them to his thighs and sat back in his seat, finally settling a bleary-eyed stare on me. "I've been attempting to run a full systems diagnostic all morning."

The progress bar flashed red, drawing my attention, then vanished from the screen.

"Five times," Hades said, his voice laced with defeat. "I've attempted to run a systems diagnostic five times, and it has failed every time."

I tore my stare from the holoscreen to look at Hades. He looked straight ahead, weariness draining the luster from his otherworldly features. "Why would that happen?" I asked him.

Hades shook his head, the motion barely perceptible. "I don't know." I saw it in his eyes the moment the idea struck. He leaned forward and swiped a finger over the holoscreen, navigating to another part of the system. When he spoke again, steel had entered his voice. "But I'm going to find out."

He tapped the holoscreen, and the overhead lights went out, plunging the Bridge—and likely the rest of the ship—into darkness.

[25]

Perched beside Hades on the wide armrest of the captain's chair, I watched him open a window displaying a list of ship-wide systems on the holoscreen in front of us. He started moving his hand down the list, tapping the name of each system. Each system name he tapped grayed out.

I chewed on the inside of my cheek, my brow furrowing. "What are you doing?"

"Shutting down all nonessential systems," Hades said, continuing to tap his way down the list. He only skipped a few essential systems: life support, artificial gravity, the cryogenerator, the Vault of Souls, the System Operator—a.k.a. Gertie—and both the visibility cloak and defensive shields protecting the ship.

Hades raised his free hand and touched his fingers to the comms patch behind his ear. "Shutting down artificial gravity in ten seconds," Hades announced, his voice echoing in through my comms patch. "If you're not wearing mag boots, find a secure location and sit tight. This shouldn't take long."

"Don't worry about Tila," my mom said to me through a private comms feed. "I've got her with me."

"Thanks, Mom." I scooted closer to the edge of the armrest,

planting both of my feet on the metal grating of the floor. My boots' magnetic feature would automatically kick in as they sensed the pull of the artificial gravity dying out. The process would be gradual, as centripetal force created the *Elysium's* artificial gravity, and it would take some time for the ship's spinning rings to slow and for the sense of gravity to fade.

Hades flicked his fingers to scroll back up to the top of the list of systems, then pulled his hand away from the holoscreen to secure the seat restraints over his lap. He reached for the holoscreen once more, his finger hovering over ARTIFICIAL GRAVITY as he waited a few more seconds, giving everyone a chance to prepare for the coming plunge into zero gravity.

He tapped the holoscreen, then slid the window containing the systems list to the side of the screen, revealing the diagnostic window. He tapped the holoscreen one more time, and the progress bar reappeared, seeming to fill much faster than it had before.

I stood slowly as the progress bar filled, not because I wanted to stand, but because the force holding me down was weakening by the second. A sense of glorious weightlessness overcame my body, and my hands floated upward, my braid lifting off my shoulder.

"This is the farthest it's made it all day," Hades said, his stare locked on the progress bar, now three-quarters of the way full.

I held my breath.

Finally, the progress bar filled completely.

Hades exhaled a laugh, and I reached out to give his shoulder a squeeze. He glanced up at me, the fine silver-blond hairs that had escaped from the leather tie holding back his hair floating around his head, making him look electrified. He hitched his eyebrows higher, his expression hopeful, then refocused on the holoscreen.

The progress bar vanished, replaced by a lengthy report.

I followed along as Hades scrolled through the report,

frowning to myself. It looked to me like all the ship's systems were running just fine. So far, the diagnostic report hadn't flagged any issues—software, hardware, or mechanical.

Until we reached the end of the report, where glowing red lettering emphasized the words: *SYSTEM OPERATOR*. Gertie. Something was wrong with the AI system.

I narrowed my eyes, then peered down at Hades.

His stare shifted from side to side rapidly as he scanned over the details of the error report. He brought one hand to his face, rubbing his fingers over his mouth as he processed what he had just read.

I stood beside his chair quietly, waiting until he was ready.

After nearly a minute had passed, Hades lowered his hand. "It's the simulation," he said, looking up at me. He shook his head. "I should have known. It's sapping up so much of the AI processing power that Gertie can't devote enough attention to the ship's other systems to run them properly."

My brows bunched together, and I touched my comms patch. "Fio, we need you on the Bridge." I returned my attention to Hades. "So what does this mean for us?"

Hades returned his attention to the holoscreen, where he dragged the window containing the systems list back into view. "Manual doors and lights," he said and tapped the screen, turning the artificial gravity back on but altering the setting to low. "Low gravity."

He scrolled to the top of the list and moved down it system by system, reactivating most but altering the individual system settings as he went. He switched to manual operation whenever possible and set many of the systems to dormant status. By the time he reached the end of the list and had adjusted the settings of the final system, the artificial gravity was strong enough to keep him from floating away.

Hades unfastened his seat restraints and sat back in his chair, raising his weary gaze to me, and named one more change to our status quo. "And manual navigation."

The words hung in the air between us, absorbing all the oxygen.

I stared at Hades, my eyes bulging. "Manual navigation? But —" I shook my head, words escaping me as my mind reeled from the implications. "But is it even possible to make an FTL jump using *manual navigation*?" So far as I knew, attempting such a thing was certain death.

"It is possible to execute such a jump, but the chances of us surviving such a jump are extremely low, nigh impossible," Hades said, confirming my fears. "No FTL."

My lips parted, and I covered my mouth with my hand as I dropped back down to the armrest. I searched Hades' eyes for answers to questions I had yet to ask. "Cryopods?"

It was the only way I could see for us to complete the journey alive. We would be cryogenically frozen for thousands of years, waiting for the ship to reach Terra traveling at slower-than-light speeds. Someone would need to wake from cryosleep every decade or so to adjust the ship's programmed course to account for celestial drift. So many things could go wrong. The ship could be attacked. We could fly into a hostile environment. A wayward gravitational field could pull us off course. A million unseen dangers lurked in the shadows along that path, waiting to destroy us. Failure was almost as assured as if we had made a blind FTL jump.

"We don't have the resources for the cryogenerator to support more than one, maybe two of us on such a lengthy journey in cryosleep," Hades informed me, sounding the death knell on that option.

Numbly, I shook my head. "But if we can't make FTL jumps, and we can't rely on the cryopods . . ."

"Then we will die long before we ever reach Terra," Hades

said, his voice monotone. He raised one hand to massage his temples with his thumb and forefingers.

"If the simulation is the problem," I said, thinking out loud, "can't we—I don't know—pause it or something like that? Just when we need to make an FTL jump?"

Hades was shaking his head before I even finished. "Not without shutting down the AI completely."

Right, because maintaining the Olympian simulation was part of Gertie's prime directive. To shut *it* down, we would have to shut *her* down. I inhaled and exhaled through my nose.

"Which obviously wouldn't help our situation," Hades added.

I nodded to myself. "Because we need Gertie online to navigate the FTL, of course." I pursed my lips and stared through the holoscreen at the stars dotting the way ahead, squinting like I could see Terra far off in the distance. "Exactly how long would it take the *Elysium* to reach Terra using only the STL engines?"

Hades chuckled morosely. "Our bodies will be dust before we have even made it halfway."

I swallowed, my mouth suddenly dry. Much as I hated the idea of dying—again—we would still have the chance of rebirth alongside all the humans and Olympians stored within the Vault of Souls. The prospect was far from ideal. We would reach Terra millennia after those who had traveled through the gephyra from Earth. There was no way to predict what state the settlement would be in by then, or if there would even still be a settlement.

But even if we had to start over with a completely blank slate, we could set the regeneration system to cycle our core group out first, raising us as the prime generation so we could oversee the regeneration process and ensure the settlement's infrastructure was in place to support the first full resurrection wave. The scenario was incredibly inconvenient, but it wasn't impossible.

"That's not the worst of it, though," Hades informed me.

Tension knotted in my belly, coiling out through my muscles.

"We couldn't have dropped out of FTL in a more dangerous location." Hades reached for the holoscreen and tapped an icon along the side that opened a window displaying a navigation chart.

A blinking white beacon representing the *Elysium* sat at the center of the chart, and stars spread out around the ship. A string of coordinates marked each star, some in white, some in blue, some in yellow, and some in red. The white coordinates marked neutral stars and planetary systems, usually those that had yet to be explored by our people. The blue coordinates marked safe places. The yellow coordinates marked mixed or suspected danger zones. And the red coordinates marked hostile locations, the kinds of places we generally avoided landing near when we completed an FTL jump.

Hades tapped three stars surrounding the ship's beacon in a rough triangle, each marked by red coordinates. Names appeared below the coordinates. "The last time we charted these planetary systems, they were under Tsakali control," Hades explained. "We have to assume their status remains the same."

Hades spread his thumb and index finger wide, zooming in on the navigation chart. "I am fairly certain we're not close enough for them to detect the latent energy signatures from our chaos stone through our energy screen—yet. We should be safe enough if we remain in this location. But if we move much closer to any of these hostile systems, the odds that they will detect our presence increase drastically."

I stared at the navigation chart, studying each of the glowing red points representing a hostile planetary system in relation to our location. There was no path out of the deadly triangle that didn't first bring us dangerously closer to the Tsakali. And if we did attempt to eek our way out of this precarious trap, we would have two options: make a series of blind FTL jumps and hope we lost them, or hold our ground and self-destruct. No matter what, we *could not* let the Tsakali get their hands on this ship. It would be akin to handing them the formula to create chaos stones on a silver platter.

"Tell me there's a way out of this, Hades," I said, my voice low and laced with threads of desperation. I turned to him, pleading with my eyes. "Please. After everything we've been through—after everything we've done—it can't end like this."

As I stared into Hades' ice-blue eyes, I could almost see the gears spinning in his mind. "Our only guaranteed way out of this," he said, "is to get the FTL drive running safely. Until we can do that, we are stuck here."

I pursed my lips and nodded slowly, returning my attention to the navigation chart on the holoscreen. "We're sitting ducks," I said, and I could feel Hades looking at me, no doubt confused by the saying. "It's just an expression," I said with a dismissive wave of my hand. "So, what can we do to make that happen? Shut down all nonessential systems to free up more processing power?"

Was there a way to defragment a spaceship? Or was that a hard drive thing, not a processor thing? I glanced over my shoulder toward the open doorway leading out to the main drag. I wished Fiona would get here already. Once she and Hades put their heads together, they were bound to figure out a solution to the problem.

"Shutting down all nonessential systems won't be enough," Hades said. He steepled his fingers and leaned closer to the holoscreen, studying the navigation chart closely. "But I wonder if . . ."

Hades inhaled and exhaled slowly, thoughtfully, and reached out with one hand to double tap the topmost red point in the deadly triangle trapping us. The chart re-centered on the selected point and zoomed in to display a detailed model of the planetary system, complete with dashed lines showing the orbital trajectories of the major celestial bodies contained within the system.

Hades tapped one of the outermost planets, highlighting it. It was a relatively small, rust-colored planet, surrounded by a thick ring of debris. A name appeared below the planet in glowing red letters: NYKTA.

"You may recall that Nykta was the site of one of the largest Olympian offensives against the Tsakali during the war," Hades said. "The ring is a graveyard of destroyed ships. If we could find an intact Olympian processor amongst the debris, we should be able to splice it into the *Elysium*'s existing array. And that *should* allow us to bring all systems back online and running at full power."

Hope had returned some of the spirit to Hades' voice, and I was loath to point out that the Battle of Nykta had happened over twelve millennia ago. What were the odds that any useful parts orbiting the planet hadn't already been scavenged? Or that any of what remained was even still usable?

I cast a sidelong look at Hades. "I don't suppose the *Elysium*'s manufacturing compartment could *make* a new processor?" I asked, assuming Hades already would have considered our ability to produce the part ourselves but tossing it out there anyway. Because why the hell not? The highly advanced 3D printer could make just about everything else, so it wasn't outside the realm of possibility that it could make a highly advanced AI processor.

"We don't have the raw materials," Hades said, killing that idea.

I swallowed compulsively. "So we go to Nykta. But what if we can't find an intact processor there? What then?"

Hades glanced up at me, then returned his attention to the navigation chart. "*Then* we make a blind FTL jump."

"That's suicide," I breathed.

"Most likely, yes," he agreed. "But our odds of survival would still be better than if we triggered the self-destruct." He peered up at me. "At least with a blind FTL jump, we would have a chance. Not a good chance, but a chance nonetheless."

"I'll gather a team," I said. "How long will the trip take?"

"In STL?" Hades frowned, studying the navigation chart. "About three years."

I nodded to myself, expecting something along those lines. "And the *Elysium* will be fine sitting here for that long?"

Hades was quiet for a long moment. "I can't guarantee it," he finally said.

I snorted a soft laugh. Because if I didn't laugh, I would cry. "Nothing new there."

[26]

I woke to the hiss of air releasing, a chill lingering in my bones, and a deep ache pulsing throughout my body. I felt weightless, like I was underwater, except I could breathe. My eyelids snapped open, and I watched a thick, frosted pane of glass slide out of view above me through a white, misty fog.

Where was I? I couldn't move. I could only blink and breathe. My heart hammered in my chest and panic electrified my muscles, waking my lethargic limbs.

My mind reeled, thoughts spinning, reaching, searching. *Where* was I?

The misty fog thinned, slowly revealing my surroundings. Stainless steel walls rose on either side of me, mere inches from my body, and white lights winked in and out of existence high above.

I blinked, then blinked again. The array of flashing lights oriented into something familiar to my brain. I was gazing up at the ceiling panel on a ship.

With that realization, my fractured memories snapped back together. I was on the *Argo*, waking from cryosleep. I was leading a team of Amazons to search the debris field surrounding Nykta for an Olympian processor. The journey had been slated to take three years, but I wouldn't know exactly how long I had been in cryosleep until I checked the ship's log. To my brain, it felt like I had barely been out for three minutes. Only the lingering discomfort of cryosleep told me it had been much longer than that.

I reached up, my clumsy fingers fumbling to release the restraining strap stretched tight across my forehead. Once my head was free, I moved on to the straps crossing my chest and hips. Groaning, I sat up, my braid lifting off my shoulder to float beside my head. Only the straps across my thighs and shins held me down in the zero gravity environment.

Now that I was sitting up, I was just able to peek over the lip of the sub-floor cryopod. Selene's head poked out of the floor, three cryopods to my right. Nobody else was sitting up yet, though all six cryopods had opened. It didn't surprise me that Meg and the three other Zari psychics were taking longer to wake. Emerging from cryosleep was disorienting, even when one was familiar with the experience, and this was their first time.

I nodded to Selene, who returned the gesture, and then I unfastened the straps stretched across my thighs and shins. I reached up to grip the lip of the floor on either side of me and pulled myself out of the recessed cryopod. With a gentle push, I propelled myself toward the front of the ship with a singular focus. I needed to check on the *Elysium*.

The planet Nykta filled the viewscreen ahead, the debris field looking like a glittering silver stream ringing around the bloated red planet. I caught the headrest of the pilot's seat and hooked my arm through one of the looped seat restraints to anchor myself in place. I activated the holoscreen and checked the ship's logs, pleased to discover that the journey to Nykta from the *Elysium* had taken just under three years. Right on target. I was even more pleased to find the *Elysium's* encoded signature in the expected location on the ship's interstellar radar.

I recorded a brief audio message letting the *Elysium* know we had arrived safely and sent it off via the photon transponder. The message would take several months to reach the *Elysium*, and if all worked out according to plan, nobody on the ark ship would ever hear it. Everyone who had remained behind would still be blissfully unaware in cryosleep, including my dog, and they wouldn't wake again until we had returned. Unless we never did.

I set the *Argo*'s radar to maximum sensitivity, then propelled myself back toward my cryopod, catching the lip of the recess to stop myself. I opened the storage cubby beside my cryopod and tucked my toes under the foot straps hidden in the floor along the edge. Once my feet were secure, I shucked my silken cryosuit and stuffed it into the pouch in the storage cubby, then pulled out my rolled-up hoplon suit. I shook it out and slipped it on over my leaden limbs. Only the lingering effects of cryosleep could make someone feel sluggish and heavy in a zero gravity environment.

Meg sat up as I was pulling on my boots, and by the time I planted both feet on the floor, held fast by the boots' magnetic feature, all four Zari psychics were emerging from their cryopods.

Boots clanging against the metal floor, I made my way to the aft of the ship, where Selene stood, staring out at the debris field through a small porthole on the side of the hull. My shoulder brushed against hers as I peered out at the remnants of a battle that had happened thousands of years ago. If I hadn't already been familiar with the Battle of Nykta, I might have guessed it had happened yesterday based on the pristine state of the remains.

Soon enough, the others joined us at the rear of the ship. Only Meg remained behind, strapping herself into the pilot's seat to man the *Argo* while the rest of us were out scavenging.

Psychic abilities unleashed, we activated our energy helmets to prepare for our spacewalking scavenging trip, then shuffled into the rear airlock. It was a tight fit, not intended for more than a couple of bodies at a time. Once we were all crammed in and the interior door was sealed shut, Selene opened the exterior door.

I moved closer to the edge, consciously reining in the panic that surged as I stared out into the yawning void of space beyond the debris field. The transparent barrier of my energy helmet colored the debris, crimson planet, and expanse of stars beyond with a shimmering electric-blue veil.

I took a deep breath, glanced over my shoulder at the small team of psychic warriors gathered behind me, then tapped my heels together to deactivate the magnetic function on my boots and launched myself out of the ship. I used tiny bursts of psychic energy from my palms to adjust my trajectory as I glided toward the debris field. I could sense Selene and the other three psychics trailing behind me as I plunged into the wreckage.

With a few more bursts of psychic energy, I slowed until I was floating along with the flow of the debris. I took in the disturbing setting, a shiver creeping down my spine.

This wasn't just a graveyard of ships. It was a graveyard of bodies, too, all pristinely preserved by the sterile vacuum of space. It was impossible to differentiate organic Olympian bodies from synthetic Tsakali remains without looking closely at the corpses, especially considering that most of the remains were mere bits and pieces of what had once been a person. An arm here. A leg there. The worst I saw was a torso, complete with arms and head, trailing ribbons of intestines as it flowed along with the current.

We spread out from the *Argo*, the cloaked ship's shields set to maximum strength, rendering it invisible to all means of detection. Meg's mental signature was the only indicator that the ship was still there at all.

I moved through my designated zone slowly, searching for any ship fragments that looked even remotely similar to the images of Olympian processors Hades had shown us. Over and over again, I spotted some piece of wreckage that resembled the images, but each time I scanned a promising item with my holoband to see if it matched the specs Hades' had uploaded, my holoscreen flashed red. No match.

I was staring at my holoscreen, waiting on the results of my umpteenth scan, when the faintest tickle of an unfamiliar awareness tripped my psychic radar. The hairs stood up on the back of my neck, and goose bumps rose on my skin in a wave that moved down the length of my body. For a fraction of a second, I felt certain I was being watched by some unseen stranger.

The sensation dissipated almost as soon as it started, a mere blip on my psychic radar. I wasn't even sure I had really felt anything at all, or if it had been a mere figment of my imagination created by the creep-out factor of this eerie setting.

I whipped my head around, searching the detritus surrounding me. A nearly complete body floated out from behind the shredded hull of a fighter ship, and my heart stumbled for a few beats. I stared at the body—hard—making sure it really was a corpse and wasn't the source of whatever I thought I had sensed.

A flash of blue drew my attention back to the holoscreen. My heart skipped a beat for an entirely different reason, and I grinned. We had a positive match.

I reached for the bulky, boxy piece of tech, gripping it with both hands, and let out a whoop of victory. "I've got something!" I proclaimed gleefully. "Meg, do you have a lock on my position?" She was sticking closer to the Zari psychics, who were having a harder time spacewalking.

"I do," Meg said through my comms patch, my own excitement rebounding off her and doubling back through our bond, making me tremble with giddiness. "I'm on my way to you now," she informed me.

I focused on Meg's mental signature, following it with my mind as it closed in on my location. When it felt like she was practically on top of me, what looked like a tear in the fabric of reality appeared mere yards away. It widened, revealing the airlock of the *Argo*. I could see Meg's grinning face through the small window on the inner door.

Ever so carefully, I guided the processor through the exterior door and into the airlock, tapping the heels of my boots together to activate the magnetic function. I hugged the processor as the soles of my boots stuck to the metal floor, but inside I still floated on a sea of relief. We had done it. We had found a compatible processor, and as soon as we got it back to the *Elysium* and Fiona hooked it up to Gertie's processor array, we were finally getting the hell out of the Tsakali triangle of death.

Meg waited until the outer door was sealed shut and the airlock was pressurized to open the inner door. I walked the weightless processor into the main cabin of the ship, and with Meg's help, strapped it down securely in the cargo area near the rear loading ramp.

While Meg piloted the *Argo* through the debris field to pick up the others, I recorded and sent a message to the *Elysium*, then ran a full systems check on the *Argo* before programming in our return flight plan. The *Argo* had its own AI operator—nowhere near as sophisticated as Gertie, but plenty able to tackle a job like auto-piloting such a small ship for a relatively short trip at slower-than-light speeds.

Meg, Selene, and the others were already settling into their cryopods by the time I floated back toward mine. I quickly shucked my hoplon suit and stowed it in the storage compartment beside my cryopod, then slipped on my cryosuit. I strapped myself into my cryopod, starting with my legs, barely able to keep my hopeful excitement in check.

Grinning, I glanced over at Meg, the only other member of the team who was still sitting up. She flashed me a closed-mouth smile and nodded once, letting me know she felt exactly the same way.

I opened the control pad hidden under a metal panel on the

floor and typed in the code to activate the cryosleep sequence, then laid down within my cryopod and finished strapping myself in. I watched the lid of the cryopod slide shut above me and smiled to myself as the sedative mist filled the enclosed space, dragging me into a deep, dreamless sleep.

[27]

The next time I woke from cryosleep was just as disorienting as the last. Once I remembered where I was and why I had been in cryosleep, the excitement returned, mellowed from giddiness to eager anticipation. It was time to bulk up Gertie's processing power with the scavenged tech and get the hell out of Dodge.

Once again, Selene and I were the first to shake off the pervasive discomfort of cryosleep and emerge from our cryopods. My first glance out of the front viewscreen brought a rush of relief. The endless string of landing bays in the *Elysium's* cavernous transport hangar stretched out of sight. A private smile touched my lips, and a thrill of excitement hastened my movements as I changed out of the silken cryosuit and into my hoplon suit.

I propelled myself toward the back of the *Argo* and pressed the button on the wall to open the loading ramp. While I waited for the ramp to lower, I looked back at Selene, who was helping the others orient themselves as they emerged from their own cryopods.

"I'll let you know when Fiona is awake," I told Selene.

She nodded at me. "We'll have the processor waiting for her in Gertie's room."

The loading ramp clanged against the floor of the landing bay. I flashed Selene a quick smile and deactivated my regulator, then turned toward the opening to launch myself out of the *Argo*.

Anything could have happened on the *Elysium* during our six-year absence while all the remaining occupants slumbered in cryopods, especially with so many systems off-line. Hades had assured me as much as he could that the Tsakali wouldn't sense our presence—or the chaos stone powering the ship—so long as we didn't stray from our current location. And thankfully, I didn't sense any minds on the *Elysium* that weren't supposed to be there. I could feel Meg, Selene, and the rest of the Nykta team still within the *Argo*, and that was it. Hades and the others' minds would be dormant while they remained in cryosleep, not perceptible to my psychic senses.

I propelled myself through the ship, grateful for the speedy travel that was only possible in a zero gravity environment. I was almost to the Bridge when an alarm blared, the sound harsh and discordant to my tender ears. Cryosleep had a tendency to leave the physical senses hypersensitive for a time.

Wincing, I smacked my palm against the controls for the door to the Bridge and waited as the door panel slid open. I propelled myself toward the captain's station, and when I reached the top of the platform, I knocked the heels of my boots together to activate their magnetic function. Feet firmly planted on the floor in front of the holoscreen, I tapped the flashing red box warning us of danger.

The box vanished, and a new window appeared, displaying a navigation chart. The blinking white beacon representing the *Elysium* stood at the center of the chart, as expected. The cluster of flashing red beacons closing in on our ship, however, was very much *not* expected.

There were at least a dozen ships, all approaching the *Elysium* from the direction we had traveled in the *Argo*. It couldn't have been a coincidence. Whoever was flying the incoming ships must have somehow tracked the *Argo* during our return trip from Nykta, something I hadn't thought possible while the *Argo* was cloaked and shielded. For a stunned moment, all I could do was stare at the approaching ships on the navigation chart.

"Damn it!" I hissed, slamming the heels of my boots together to turn off the magnetism. I launched myself off the platform, aiming for the staircase down to the cryovault tucked away in the back corner of the Bridge. I caught myself on the semicircular railing surrounding the opening in the floor, then used the descending railing to pull myself down the spiral staircase.

When I reached the cryovault, I propelled myself off the face of the second to the last stair toward the third cryopod on the right side. Through the fogged glass, I could see Hades slumbering within. I tapped my heels together as I neared the cryopod and angled my boots down toward the floor. The magnetic pull stopped my forward momentum, and the soles of my boots clanged against the metal floor. I clomped the final few feet to Hades' cryopod and entered a code into the small control panel set into the wall to the immediate right of the cryopod to start the wake sequence.

While I waited for Hades to emerge from cryosleep, I pulled a pair of mag boots from the narrow storage closet on the left side of the cryopod and tapped their heels together to activate them before setting them on the floor in front of the curved glass door. An opaque cocktail of restorative gasses had filled Hades' cryopod, almost completely obscuring my view of him. It would still be a few minutes before he was fully awake.

I sidestepped to the right to stand in front of Fiona's cryopod. I started her wake sequence, set out her mag boots, then moved on to Raiden's. I had just set out the boots in front of the nineteenth cryopod on the right side of the cryovault when Hades stepped into his mag boots.

I hurried back up the line toward him. "We've got a problem,"

I told him as I pulled his coat from the narrow storage closet beside his cryopod and handed it to him to wear over his cryosuit.

Hades looked at the proffered coat, then at the rest of his clothing, still tucked away in the storage closet.

"There's no time for that," I said, shaking my head. "We've got incoming." I glanced at Fiona, who was dazedly slipping her feet into her mag boots. "Selene and the others are waiting for you with the new processor."

Fiona blinked at me, the lingering disorientation of waking from cryosleep fogging her brain.

"We got the processor," I said. "It's waiting for you in Gertie's room. We need you to get it hooked up as quickly as possible."

Recognition lit Fiona's eyes, and her mouth formed a tiny O.

Hades glided toward the staircase behind me as I marched past Fiona and stopped in front of Raiden's cryopod. Raiden was still working on unfastening the straps holding him in place. I pressed my hand against his thick biceps, drawing his attention to me.

It took him a few seconds, but his eyes finally focused on mine.

"Finish waking the others, but leave Tila, then meet us upstairs," I told him. I waited until my instructions registered in his muddled mind, then tapped my heels together to kill my boots' magnetic charge and pushed off the floor to fly up the staircase.

By the time I reached the Bridge, Hades was already standing on the platform of the captain's station, studying the damning navigation chart. I pushed off the railing and glided over to join him, watching as he double-tapped the holoscreen to pull up more information on the incoming ships. I left my regulator deactivated; this was no time to prioritize mental privacy.

"How is this possible?" I asked, catching the rail curving around the back half of the platform to stop my forward trajectory. I swung my lower body down toward the floor and tapped my heels together. My magnetized boots stuck to the floor, and I took a step closer to Hades and the holoscreen. "The *Argo* was cloaked the whole time we were out there."

Hades narrowed his eyes. "It shouldn't *be* possible," he said as he continued to read through the information listed in a small box hovering beside each of the flashing red beacons. A faint frown turned down the corners of his mouth. "This is strange. The ships' energy signatures are muddled, some reading as Tsakali and some reading as Olympian." His frown deepened. "And some reading as neither."

My brows drew together, and I shook my head. "What does *that* mean?" I asked, looking at him.

"I've only seen such a confusing array of tech once before," he began, glancing at me sidelong. "It was during the final days of the war. I had stayed behind on Olympus to activate our last defenses after the ark ships left the planet. I evacuated through the gephyra and was picked up by a team of Amazons and escorted to the *Tartarus*, but we had some issues while we were en route. Their ship's cloaking mechanism had been damaged, and we were stalked by a small fleet with similarly confused readings."

At the telltale clang of mag boots, I twisted to peer back toward the staircase that led down to the cryovault. Fiona emerged a moment later, offering me a quick salute before deactivating her mag boots and launching herself through the doorway and up the main corridor.

I turned back to Hades. "So, who were they?"

Hades clasped his hands together behind his back and inhaled deeply through his nose. "It's less of a *who* and more of a *what*." He looked at me, his expression grim. "Pirates."

I choked on a guffaw as I battled a rising tide of hysteria.

Pirates. God damned space pirates.

Once again, I was struck by the dizzying notion that I had been sucked into one of the video games I had spent so many hours playing during my years at Blackthorn Manor. I mean, *space pirates*.

I stood shoulder to shoulder beside Hades, weightless despite the tug of my magnetized boots holding me to the floor, and watched the discordant fleet of ships slowly surround the blinking white beacon of the *Elysium* on the navigation chart. Hades tapped an icon on the side of the holoscreen, opening another window displaying the list of *Elysium's* systems beside the navigation chart. Hand swiping and tapping faster than I could track, he brought some of the dormant systems back online and adjusted others to redirect resources to our defensive shields.

The *Elysium* wasn't a warship and was by no means equipped for battle. It was an ark ship, meant to be the nexus of a fleet carrying our people across the universe to colonize new worlds, escorted by a variety of support ships, including a swarm of fighters. It had never been intended to journey alone.

There was no fight-or-flight option where an ark ship was concerned. There was only flight. The *Elysium* had two means of defense against an attack: the ship's assortment of shields, including a defense shield that protected from physical attacks, and the chaos-powered FTL drive. And until Fiona hooked the scavenged processor into the ship's existing array, any FTL jumps would be made blind—and would be about as deadly as taking fire unshielded. For the time being, we were relying on shields alone to protect us.

Hades pulled his hand back from the holoscreen to touch his comms patch behind his ear. "Reactivating artificial gravity in five, four, three, two, one." He reached out and tapped the screen.

"Won't that divert power from the shields?" I asked, shooting Hades some serious side-eye.

"Quite the opposite," Hades said as he continued to scroll through the systems list, tweaking settings at a more relaxed pace. "The centripetal force actually reinforces the shields by condensing the defensive barrier at an atomic level. It seems counterintuitive, but the loss in energy directed into the shields themselves to power the artificial gravity is more than made up for by the effects of the condensing force."

I frowned, pondering his explanation.

An alert box appeared at the center of the screen, the border flashing yellow. At the same moment, one of the red beacons surrounding our ship on the navigation chart flashed yellow in time with the alert box. The details and specs listed underneath the ship noted it comprised parts from several Olympian warships pieced together.

"They're hailing us," Hades said, his fingers hovering in front of the flashing window for a heartbeat before he tapped the screen.

Three sharp beeps sounded through the overhead speakers, announcing a live audio feed had been established between the

Elysium and an outside ship. On the navigation chart, a solid yellow ring surrounded the red beacon of the hailing ship.

Hades cleared his throat and clasped his hands behind his back. "*Elysium* receiving," he said, projecting strength and calm when I knew for a fact he felt little of either. But thus was the cunning and deceptive nature of an Olympian prince.

"We have you surrounded," a woman announced through the audio feed. Her voice was rich, resonant, and eloquent—not remotely close to what I had imagined for the voice of the leader of a band of space pirates, assuming this was the leader speaking. "Send over your chaos stone and FTL drive on an unmanned cargo ship, and we will let you go."

I snorted derisively, not believing for one second they intended to follow through on such a "generous" offer.

Hades looked at me, visually assessing my reaction.

"Refuse," the space pirate continued, "and we will take your ship and kill everyone on board. You have five minutes to respond."

Hades tapped the alert box on the holoscreen, closing the audio feed. "Obviously we cannot comply with their request," he said, his body humming with tension.

"Obviously," I said dryly. "What are the *Elysium's* battle capabilities?" I was really hoping the old girl had some tricks I didn't know about hiding up her sleeve.

"Non-existent," Hades said absently. He was deep in thought, the workings of his mind open to me, but so far beyond my technical understanding that his potential solutions for how to reinforce the shields might as well have been gibberish.

I blocked out his thoughts and refocused on the holoscreen, studying the ring of hostile ships surrounding us on the navigation chart. Maybe I wouldn't be much help with the technical aspects of our defense, but I *could* strategize.

Once Fiona hooked the scavenged processor into the existing array, we would be out of the pirates' reach in the blink of an eye, but that would take longer than the five minutes the pirates allotted us to respond. I needed to figure out a way to buy Fiona some more time.

"How long will the defense shield hold?" I mused aloud.

"It depends on how much fire we take," Hades said, his words quiet and clipped. "I'll have a better idea once we're under fire and can assess their weapons' capabilities. Regardless, the defense shield will not hold indefinitely, and once it is depleted, the other shields will lose efficacy as well."

Icy dread washed over me. If the defense shield fell, so would the visibility cloak and, more importantly, the energy screen, which dampened the chaos signature emitted by our ship. Without the energy screen, the *Elysium* would be detectable to Tsakali radar throughout this galaxy. Then, not even a blind FTL jump had a chance at saving us. We would have no choice but to self-destruct.

I raised my hand behind my ear and touched my comms patch. "Fio," I said, opening a direct audio feed to her. "How much longer do you need to get the new processor patched in? We need to get the FTL drive back online ASAP. I'd say no pressure, but we're *kind of* about to be under attack . . .so, sorry, but yes, pressure. Lots of pressure. *All* the pressure."

I expected a snarky response, possibly even a colorful cursing out. I did not, however, expect radio silence. A spark of worry quickened my heartbeat.

"Fiona?" I said, momentarily catching Hades' eye. He could easily hear the concern in my voice. "Can you hear me?"

"She's not responding?" Hades asked, his focus now completely on me.

Pursing my lips, I shook my head and touched my comms patch again, opening a new audio feed. "Selene, are you still with Fiona?" I said, then inhaled and held the breath.

The answering silence fanned that spark of worry into a full-blown inferno.

"Selene?" I repeated, already bracing myself for the lack of response. I waited a few seconds before touching my comms patch again, this time to open up a ship-wide feed. "Does anyone have eyes on Fiona or Selene? They should both be in the System Operator chamber, and neither is responding to my calls."

Within seconds, I received a handful of negatives.

"Do you want me to check on them?" Meg asked. Through our bond, I could see that she was still in the *Argo*, taking care of the post-trip maintenance.

"No," I said, leaping over the railing curving around the back of the captain's platform. I floated down to the floor, pulled by a combination of partial gravity and my magnetized boots. "I'm just as close," I told her. And I wasn't nearly as busy. As soon as my soles hit the floor, I started running toward the doorway at the back of the Bridge.

I was barely three steps into the ship's main corridor when Hades' voice sounded over the *Elysium's* speakers. "We are under fire," he announced. "Brace for impact in five, four, three, two, one."

The floor bucked under my feet, and I stumbled to the side, my shoulder slamming against the wall of the corridor. I pushed away from the wall, but before I could even take a step, I was thrown back against it as our defense shield deflected another strike. I braced myself against the wall, waiting as a series of impacts shook the ship. Each was less intense than the previous until the shield had adapted to the pirates' attack enough that each strike caused the floor to merely shudder rather than quake.

Again, I pushed away from the wall and ran up the corridor. I kept my psychic radar on high alert as I rode the lift down to the bowels of the ship, and I grew increasingly concerned at the lack of mental signatures detected on the lower levels. At the very least, I should have sensed Fiona and Selene down there. The rest of the Nykta team should have remained in Gertie's room with them to provide protection and assistance as well. The future of two species depended on the success of this operation. We weren't taking any chances.

The lift stopped its descent, I deactivated my mag boots and bounced on the balls of my feet as I waited for the doors to slide open. I leaped through the opening as soon as it was wide enough to fit through and sprinted down the hallway. We were still taking fire, though the impacts were barely perceptible now.

I touched my comms patch as I rounded a corner, working my way through the maze of hallways. "Hades, how long will the old girl hold out?"

"The defense shield can hold for ten, maybe fifteen minutes at this rate of fire."

"Understood," I said as I rounded another corner. "I'll pass that along."

I ran down one more straight section of hallway, then rounded the last corner, and entered the corridor leading to Gertie's room. I slowed to a jog as I approached the shut door panel, then stood in front of the door, closing my eyes and reaching into the room beyond with my psychic senses.

And I felt . . . nothing. So far as my psychic radar was concerned, nobody was on the other side of the door. In fact, nobody was down on this level at all.

Deeply unsettled, I opened my eyes and reached over my shoulder to draw my doru. I extended my hand toward the small control panel set into the wall beside the doorway and pressed my thumb against the button to open the door. The door panel slid open, and for several heartbeats, all I could do was stare in horror at the scene that greeted me.

Bodies. Nearly a dozen women, unmoving. Not dead. Now that I was in the room, I could sense the faintest threads of their minds. I *should* have been able to sense them from outside, but I hadn't, which only compounded the disturbing scene.

Selene lay in a crumpled heap in the far corner, the bodies of the other psychics scattered around her, half on top of one another, limbs splayed this way and that like discarded dolls. Fiona lay on her side, her back against the far wall, her hands and forearms still encased in the mech gloves that remotely controlled two of the three large robotic arms hanging down from the ceiling. The scavenged processor hung in midair, held steady by the clawed hands of the robotic arms.

I ducked into the room and slammed my fist against the button to shut the door, keeping it depressed for a three count to lock the door from within. Nobody would get in here without my permission. Whoever had done this might still be down here, and I didn't want them sneaking up on me while my back was turned.

I rushed around the processor and robotic arms and dropped to my knees beside Fiona's limp form, setting my doru on the floor nearby. I pressed my index and middle fingers against the side of Fiona's neck and expelled a breath of relief when I felt the faint thrum of her pulse against my fingertips. Peering at the jumble of bodies fanning out from the corner, I touched my comms patch and sucked in a breath to issue a ship-wide warning about the apparent incursion.

"I don't think so," a woman said from behind me.

Pain burst out from the base of my skull, and stars filled my vision. My hand dropped from my comms patch as my body went boneless, and I collapsed on top of Fiona.

I blinked, my eyelids impossibly heavy. My thoughts were a slippery, incoherent jumble.

A second burst of pain erupted from my temple, and the world went dark.

I tried to lift my eyelids, but they weighed about a thousand pounds, and the effort intensified the pounding in my head. My brain throbbed in time with my heartbeat, feeling like it was too big for my skull.

I finally cracked one eyelid open enough to let in a sliver of blinding light. I winced, squeezing my eyes shut.

Hands gripped me by the armpits, and I groaned as I was hoisted up and off Fiona's unconscious form. I was dragged to a clear patch of floor beside Fiona, and I flopped onto my back.

With a massive amount of focus and effort, I dragged my eyelids open, squinting as my eyes adjusted to the myriad of lights blinking and flashing all over the walls and ceiling. A dark silhouette hunched over me, straightening my arms and legs. The silhouette slowly coalesced into a hooded woman wearing a hoplon suit. The thin channels running the length of her hoplon suit glowed faintly with blood-red energy, telling me she was a psychic. The diminished intensity of the glow suggested she was dredging the bottom of her psychic reserves.

A horrifying thought crossed my mind. Had one of the Zari psychics turned against us?

The dark hood draped over the woman's head obscured my view of her face as she bound my ankles together tightly. The fabric of the hood shimmered with a subtle golden hue every time she moved.

My sluggish mind slowly processed what I was seeing, and it took me a painfully long time to conclude that the hood's material must have been laced with threads of orichalcum, shielding the woman's mental signature completely from psychic detection. Such a hood would be a double-edged sword for a psychic, both shielding her from detection and blocking her ability to detect others' minds. She would still be able to use psychic energy as a weapon, however, and access most of her hoplon suit's features, like the ability to cloak herself to invisibility.

The psychic finished binding my ankles and glanced up at my face, finally giving me a good view of hers.

She definitely wasn't one of the Zari psychics. So, she must have been some sort of rogue Amazon, then. But how had she snuck onto the ship? Or was it possible she had been on the *Elysium* since we found the ship in the frozen colony? Even dazed as I was, I thought it much more likely that she was linked to the pirates who currently had us surrounded.

Her eyes widened upon seeing me awake and watching her. "You're a stubborn one, aren't you?"

Before I could even think about flinching away, she swung her elbow around, cracking me against the side of the head. And once again, the world went dark.

The next time I woke, I was lying on my side. The pain in my skull was a not-so-gentle reminder that I hadn't simply fallen asleep. That I had been attacked. Knocked out. Twice.

My brain had been rattled around enough, and I absolutely did not want the rogue Amazon to hit me again. On the off chance she had lowered her hood and could now sense my return to consciousness, I shielded myself as heavily as possible.

Keeping my eyes shut and my face relaxed, I took a mental inventory of my aches and pains. A concussion was pretty much a given at this point. The rogue had bound my wrists behind my back, the faint tingle encircling them suggesting she had used ribbons of psychic energy for the bindings. I figured she must have used the same to bind my ankles together, though I couldn't feel any tingle through my boots. My shoulder and hip didn't ache yet, telling me I hadn't been lying on my side for very long.

I cracked my eyelids open to peer through my lashes, careful not to flinch or tense any other parts of my face. My current position gave me a view diagonally across the room to the door, and I assumed the wall was just a few inches behind me. Most of the Zari psychics who had been incapacitated when I arrived were piled in a heap in one corner, the glazed-over look of their eyes telling me they weren't merely unconscious. My heart ached for them, but I suppressed the sorrow. There would be time for mourning later.

Three women lay in a line in front of me, rolled onto their sides, their wrists and ankles bound, just like mine. Selene counted among them, much to my immense relief. I couldn't see Fiona, but I hoped she was all right.

The rogue Amazon kneeled near the center of the room, facing me, her hood still draped over her head. She hunched over the body of one of the Zari psychics, a stream of sizzling green psychic energy arcing from the unconscious woman's chest to the rogue's concealed face. The channels in the rogue's hoplon suit glowed brighter than before, the red energy more of a vibrant ruby now, almost like she was stealing the unconscious woman's psychic energy.

Not *almost*. She *was* stealing the other psychic's energy.

Shock at what I was seeing made my heart beat faster. This woman was no rogue *Amazon*. She was a *Titan*, the Tsakali version of a psychic warrior. I had never met one of her kind, but I had heard plenty about them. Unlike Amazons, Titans couldn't self-generate their own psychic energy, probably because their bodies were synthetic, as I now knew. When a Titan depleted her stores of psychic energy, she had to refuel from an external source.

I shifted my focus past the Titan to the pile of discarded psychics in the corner behind her, figuring she must have killed them by draining them of their psychic energy. Apparently, another psychic was a perfectly viable refueling source.

I felt a nagging tickle at the edge of my mind, like a mosquito buzzing around inside my aching head.

Meg. She was reaching out to me through our bond, trying to capture my attention.

I closed my eyes and focused on our connection. Meg was in

the lift, alone, on her way down to me. Fear at the thought of the energy-drunk Titan capturing Meg nearly wrested a sob from my chest.

"No, Meg!" I practically screamed through our connection. "Don't come here. It's too dangerous!" My silent protestations slammed into a solid wall of obstinance.

"I won't abandon you to that—that *thing*!"

We didn't have time to argue. In a few minutes, Meg would be here. Yet another psychic snack for the ravenous Titan. "At least wait for backup—lots of backup. She's taken down too many of us already."

Through Meg's eyes, I watched as the lift doors opened and she ran out into the hallway.

"Please, Meg," I begged. "Wait. Please."

She slowed to a walk, then paused in the intersection of two hallways. "Fine," she agreed sullenly and crossed her arms over her chest. She touched her comms patch, updating the reinforcements that were already on their way to meet her.

Some of the tension left my body, and I relaxed as much as I could while hogtied and awaiting my death at the hands of a psychic vampire. Regardless of what happened to me, at least Meg wouldn't be facing this monster alone.

"Tell Hades to put the ship into lockdown," I told Meg, watching the stream of emerald energy flowing from the unconscious psychic to the Titan thing. "Our only advantage right now is that the Titan is contained." She currently held the psychic energy of several Zari psychics, and there was no saying how much more she could absorb. As superpowered as she already was, if she vanished from sight again—especially with her hood up, preventing us from detecting her—we would have little chance of defeating her.

An alarm blared out in the hallway, barely audible through the sealed door panel, and a grim smile curved my lips. The ship was going into lockdown.

The stream of psychic energy fizzled out, and the Titan raised her head, staring at the door for a few seconds before snapping her head around to spear me with a hard stare. Her eyes narrowed to vicious slits. Was it just my imagination, or did her irises glow with a fiery red light?

"What do you want?" I asked, thinking our best chance to defeat her was to get the jump on her, which meant I needed to keep her distracted while I waited for Meg at the team of Zari psychics to arrive.

The Titan's lips spread into a wicked grin. "Your ship, of course." She tilted her head to the side, the hostility bleeding from her expression. "You can't stop us. You must know that."

I gulped. "Why do you want our ship?"

She stared at me for a moment longer, then stood and stalked toward me.

"How many of you are there?" I asked, adrenaline surging in my blood, making my whole body thrum with the need to act. I figured she was the pirates' only psychic since she seemed to have infiltrated our ship alone. I really hoped I was right.

The Titan crouched beside me, balancing on the balls of her feet and resting her forearms on her thighs. Again, she cocked her head to the side and studied me through narrowed eyes. "I gleaned the purpose of your mission from your friends' minds over there," she said with a sideways nod toward the pile of discarded bodies in the corner. "You're attempting to save not one, but two species from destruction at the hands of my brethren." She raised her eyebrows. "Very noble."

I ground my teeth together as I glared up at her.

She sighed and shook her head. "I almost feel bad about interfering." She fell quiet, her stare contemplative. "Almost," she said and leaned forward, planting her knees on the floor.

I wriggled backward as quickly as I could but stopped when I hit the wall behind me. My whole body tensed. I was trapped.

"This will not be pleasant," the Titan said, planting one hand on my forehead, the other on my hip. The contact gave her access to my mind, and she shredded my mental shields like they were made of tissue paper. The corner of her mouth rose, forming the ghost of a smile. "I would offer to knock you out again, but we both know you would refuse."

She leaned forward and closed her eyes. Her lips parted, and she drew in a deep, almost laborious breath.

A groan slipped through my lips at the horrible tugging sensation in my chest, like she was trying to pull my heart out through my sternum. The Titan inhaled again, and electric-blue energy exploded out from the center of my chest and arced toward her mouth.

Pain whited out my mind, and I screamed.

[31]

For a time, the excruciating pain of having my psychic energy ripped from my body was all I knew. But ever so slowly, I became aware of something new. Something foreign. Something that wasn't pain. That wasn't *me*.

A connection to the Titan.

It was thin and tenuous, but it seemed to grow stronger with each agonizing draw she made from my personal well of psychic energy. I pushed through the fog of pain, following that fragile thread stretching between us. And once I was in her head, I mined her thoughts for anything that might prove useful to defeating her.

The first thing I learned was that the pirates really were after our chaos-powered FTL drive. They were tired of living under the constant threat of being hunted down by the Tsakali for any number of perceived transgressions. With our FTL drive and chaos stone, they could flee to uncharted areas of the universe. For the first time in any of their lives, they would be truly free.

The second—and far more important—thing I learned from the Titan's mind was that she was indeed the only psychic among the pirates. I latched on to that thought, following it through a string of related thoughts and memories.

She had been lying when she told me she *almost* felt bad for interfering with our mission to save both the humans and the Olympians. She genuinely felt terrible about what she was doing. Even now, as she slurped down my psychic energy, her commitment wavered.

I followed that sense of discord within her, searching for the source. And when I found it, I would have gasped had I not already been choking on a scream.

The Titan had fled from her people. The Tsakali had been planning to destroy her for being defective. For asking why. For questioning their endless need to consume and destroy. They had wanted to destroy her for having a conscience. What some might call a soul.

I squeezed my eyes shut, and a tear slipped between my lashes to trail across my temple. I gritted my teeth, struggling to inhale enough air to speak. "You don't . . . have to do . . . this." I sucked in another shuddering breath. "You could . . . join us." I whimpered, my chest convulsing. "Help us . . . fight them."

The Titan's eyes widened. She had finally noticed my psychic touch in her mind. She slammed a wall down between us and drew deeper from my well of psychic energy, compounding the agony.

A scream clawed up my throat.

Guilt and grief swelled within me, gradually overtaking the physical pain until I was drowning in the emotions.

This was it. The end. After everything. After fighting so hard for so long, this was it. The end of the Olympians. And of the humans. The end of me.

I gazed up at the Titan, who now glowed with an electric-blue aura of psychic energy. She gazed down at me, letting the stream of energy arcing between us fizzle out. Her eyes softened, filling with pity. She looked so beautiful, like an angel. An angel of death, but an angel, nonetheless.

She brushed a strand of hair out of my face with gentle

fingers. "I know it is difficult to surrender," she said, her voice surprisingly tender. "Surrendering can be more difficult than continuing to fight. But there comes a time for each of us when we must ask ourselves—what are we fighting for?" Her eyebrows rose, and a sad smile touched her lips. "The chance to keep fighting, on and on, forever?" She shook her head. "Aren't you tired? Don't you want to rest? To just take a break and stop fighting for once in your many, *many* lifetimes?"

A silent sob quaked in my chest, and a fresh tear slid across my temple. I *was* tired. So damn tired. And part of me really did want it all to be over. To just be done. Even as Cora, ignorant of all the lifetimes that had come before this one, every day was a struggle. I had never known a day of peace, and I feared I never would—at least, not so long as I continued fighting. What if there was no way to win? If there was only the endless struggle to survive?

The Titan brushed her knuckles over my cheek. "I can end your struggle," she promised. And then she leaned over me again and began to suck the last dregs of psychic energy from me.

An odd sense of relief spread out from my chest, tingling along my arms and legs, out to my fingertips and toes. There was nothing more for me to do. The burden of protecting my two peoples slipped from my shoulders. Each pull of psychic energy was less painful than the last. I closed my eyes, relaxing my limbs. Accepting my fate.

At the whoosh of hydraulics, my eyelids snapped open just in time to watch a clawed robotic hand clamp around the back of the Titan's neck. It lifted her up, stretching the sizzling strand of electric-blue energy connecting us until it stuttered, then fizzled out. The Titan's feet dangled above the floor, kicking fruitlessly as she attempted to pry the metal claws from around her neck.

I scrambled to the side along the wall, shrinking away from the Titan's violently kicking legs, and dragged myself up to a slouched sitting position out of range of her feet. With the shift in perspective, I could see Fiona slumped in the corner nearby, her arm outstretched in front of her as she used one of the mech gloves to control it.

Fiona gritted her teeth, the tendons in her neck tensing from the strain. She squeezed her hand within the glove, and the Titan howled as the robotic claw tightened around her neck.

Three balls of crimson psychic energy shot out from the Titan's hand, blasting burning holes into the floor and wall. The last barely missed Fiona's head.

Fiona grimaced as she squeezed her hand harder.

There was a sickening crunch, and the Titan went limp, hanging from the robotic arm like a rag doll. Her feet and fingers twitched spasmodically. Apparently, not even a synthetic Tsakali body could survive a crushed neck.

As the life faded from the Titan's eyes, the energy restraints vanished from around my wrists and ankles. I rubbed my left wrist and sat up the rest of the way. I tore my focus away from the dead Titan to look at Fiona.

Fiona stared straight ahead, not at the Titan, but at the boxy processor hanging precariously from the clawed end of one robotic arm in the center of the room. A blackened hole cut cleanly through the processor.

"No," I breathed, staring at the destroyed processor. We were so screwed.

[32]

Head pounding with each step, I jogged up the main corridor of the *Elysium* with Fiona on one side of me and Meg on the other. A swarm of Zari psychics trailed behind us as we hurried to the Bridge. The floor trembled every few seconds with each attack on our shield.

We poured through the doorway to the Bridge, and I ran ahead to join Hades at the captain's station.

Raiden waylaid me, stopping me short and pulling me into a tight embrace. He tucked my head under his chin, and I could feel the tremble coursing through his body. "I was so scared, Cora. I thought—"

Hands on his chest, I pushed my upper body away from his enough that I could see his face. "I'm okay," I affirmed, my eyes locked with his. "Really." I pressed a quick, gentle kiss to his lips, then slipped out of his hold and hurried to the captain's station. I rushed up the stairs to join Hades on the platform.

Hades' hands flew over the holoscreen, swiping this way and that.

When I reached the top of the platform, Hades paused to glance my way and flash me a relieved smile. "You survived," he said, his eyes conveying so much more emotion than his simple words. He had never doubted me.

I returned his smile. "I survived," I agreed, burying the memory of the craven thoughts that marked what had nearly been my last moments. "And thanks to Fiona," I said, "the Titan is dead." I shifted my jaw to the side, hesitating before delivering the devastating blow. "Unfortunately, so is the new processor. One of the Titan's death blasts burned a hole through its core. Fiona says it's unsalvageable."

Hades stared at me for another few heartbeats, blinked twice, and shook his head. He returned his attention to the holoscreen, his fingers frantically swiping and tapping, opening and closing windows faster than I could track. I may not have had much left in my inner well of psychic energy, but there was enough for me to skim his mind. He was shutting down entire systems, freeing up resources to redirect to the defense shield while he charged up the FTL drive.

My eyes opened wide at that, and I delved a little deeper into his mind.

The energy screen was losing efficacy quickly. Once it went out, all deep space radar systems surrounding us in the Tsakali triangle of death would be able to sense the energy signature emanating from our chaos stone. The Tsakali would come after us like slavering dogs, hungry for their bone. Our only hope of escape was to make a blind FTL jump. It was almost certain death. But that *almost* still gave us a better chance of survival than the *absolute* certain death we would face if we fell back on our only other means of evading the Tsakali—activating the ship's self-destruct.

"Wait!" I all but shouted. My hand shot out, and I caught Hades' wrist, his fingertips mere inches from the holoscreen. One tap, and the FTL drive would start charging.

Hades looked at me, panic brightening his ice-blue eyes, making him appear slightly unhinged. He tugged against my grip, trying to free his wrist. Rationality had fled from him. He was a mortally wounded animal, operating on pure instinct, grasping at what he perceived to be his last remaining means of survival.

The adrenaline coursing through my blood cleared the haze of pain from my head, and an idea coalesced. I recalled how the Titan had snuck onto the *Argo* when our guard was down. "I have an idea," I said, my voice low but resonant.

Hades shook his head vehemently, his arm shaking as he strained against my hold. He glanced longingly at the small window open in the center of the holoscreen. "This is the only way!" he proclaimed, his words tinged with hysteria.

"No, it's not," I said, keeping my voice level and speaking quickly. Hades needed something else to focus on. He was lost in the dark, flailing in search of a way out. So I would turn on the light and show him the way. "Announce our surrender. Let them board the ship."

Hades looked at me like I was mad. I flashed him a grim smile, all calm confidence. We had a veritable horde of Zari psychics on board. Their *one* psychic was dead. There was no way they could stand against us on this ship and win.

"They're waiting for a signal from the Titan," I said. "Let's give them that signal, and when they board our ship and all of their attention is here . . ."

I pulled Hades' hand away from the holoscreen with minimal resistance, then released his wrist and reached out to swipe the jumble of open windows off to the side of the screen. I opened the navigation chart and maximized it to take up nearly the entire holoscreen. At least a dozen ships formed a nearly perfect circle around the *Elysium*. I tapped on the beacon of the ship that had hailed us—the Frankenstein craft built from the corpses of Olympian warships.

"We'll be there," I said, sensing Hades' panic fade into the background as he followed along with interest. "Stealing what we need to get the hell out of here." I glanced at Hades. "Unless you think another ship would be more likely to carry a compatible processor . . ."

Hades' eyes locked with mine, and he shook his head. "No. That's the one," he said, pointing to the screen with his chin. "I can almost guarantee that ship has a processor we can use."

"Perfect," I said, my lips spreading into a sly grin. "Then we surrender."

Hades' attention returned to the navigation chart. "We surrender."

[33]

I crouched behind a tied-down stack of storage crates in the transport hangar, the contents of which were surely little more than
dust after however many thousands of years the *Elysium* had sat
unused. Selene's shoulder brushed against mine, and I glanced at
her sidelong. Her stare was distant as she focused on the input
from her psychic senses rather than from her eyes.

I, however, was relying on my eyes alone as I watched the
inner airlock door through a crack between two crates. As soon as
Hades and I settled on a plan, I had activated my regulator to
reserve what remained of my psychic energy for the coming
mission. We had considered sending Selene alone or sending
another psychic with her in my place, but both alternatives to my
participation presented higher risks for failure. A solo mission was
out of the question—eggs and baskets and such—and the Zari
psychics hadn't had nearly enough practice spacewalking to
survive the mission.

With a hiss of compressed air, the enormous inner airlock
doors split down the middle and slid open. A small, bullet-shaped
shuttle hovered forward out of the airlock and into the cavernous
hangar, its engines nearly silent as it inched forward using

magnetic propulsion. There was nothing Olympian in its design, but I wasn't familiar enough with alien technology to tell whether the ship was of Tsakali origin or had been crafted by one of the hundreds of other advanced civilizations that had developed extra-planetary travel. The inner airlock doors slid shut behind them, and I took a slow, silent deep breath.

We had left Hades on the Bridge, where he was pretending to be held hostage by the Titan as he directed the pirates on how to board the *Elysium*. Emi, Raiden, my mom, and roughly a third of the Zari psychics were with Hades, waiting to ambush the pirates. Meg and another chunk of Zari psychics hid with Fiona in and around Gertie's room, guarding Fiona as they awaited our return with yet another scavenged processor. The rest of our psychics had hunkered down in the ship's core, ready to defend the chaos stone and FTL drive with their lives. If everything went according to plan, the pirates currently disembarking their ship to take ours would be dead by the time Selene and I returned.

The clang of mag boots on the metal floor marked the pirates' path as they filed down their ship's loading ramp. They were dressed in a hodgepodge of body armor covering the full spectrum of grays and black, and so far as I could tell, the only unifying element on them were the black hoods draped over their heads, the thin fabric shimmering with the faintest hint of gold. I did a head count while Selene attempted to graze their minds. Twenty-three pirates marched off the shuttle, and Selene's hard expression told me she hadn't been able to touch even a single enemy mind.

I clenched my jaw and pursed my lips, biting back a curse. Our psychics would easily wipe out such a paltry force—without the orichalcum-laced hoods shielding their minds from us. Twenty-three shielded foes posed a much greater threat. Not enough to make me worry. Much.

Selene and I waited until the door panel slid shut behind the pirates and we were *most likely* alone in the transport hangar to let Hades know the headcount as well as the inconvenient use of the orichalcum-laced hoods. Then, staying low, Selene and I crept closer to the shuttle. I hid behind a rolling tool chest while Selene vanished from sight to sweep the interior of the enemy ship.

Within a few minutes, she reappeared at my side. "The ship is indeed empty."

I nodded and straightened from my crouched position. Once again, I touched my comms patch to update Hades. "Maybe we should wait," I added after a brief pause. The situation wasn't sitting well in my gut. "Make sure the ambush goes as planned."

"No," Hades said with no hesitation. "We don't have time for such precaution. The integrity of the energy screen is tenuous at best. It could shut down at any moment. Go. Get the processor and get back. We're ready for them."

"If you're sure," I said, understanding his reasoning but not liking it.

"I am," Hades said. "Opening the inner airlock door now. Good luck."

Selene and I were already running toward the oversized doors by the time they split down the middle and slid open. As soon as we were inside the airlock, I slapped the button on the wall panel displaying the manual controls while Selene ran ahead for the controls to the exterior door. The inner airlock doors started to slide together, and I turned to follow Selene. I deactivated my regulator while I walked, and with a thought, a thin barrier of psychic energy formed a helmet around my head, giving the steel walls a sizzling, electric-blue sheen.

Her own energy helmet in place, Selene raised the guard over the exterior door's manual controls and flipped a switch to begin decompression. The border of light surrounding the small control panel flashed red, and the hiss of escaping air filled the airlock. When the border stopped flashing, instead, settling on a steady red glow, Selene pressed the big red button to open the exterior door.

The floor vibrated beneath my boots, and I tapped my heels together to magnetize my soles. The large door slowly rose, revealing a vast, glittering darkness, and the vacuum of open space tugged me forward toward that yawning void.

I joined Selene at the edge of the airlock and raised my arm in front of me, bending at the elbow. I tapped my holoband, and the screen appeared, floating above my forearm, augmenting my view of space with information from the *Elysium's* radar.

It was impossible to see any of the ships surrounding us with the naked eye. They were all too far away, any light they emitted camouflaged by the glimmering stars. But through the transparent screen of my holoband, the enemy ships appeared as glowing red beacons accompanied by a tiny info box containing any detectable specs. I scanned the ships to the right of center while Selene scanned the ships to the left.

"I've got a lock on our target," Selene said, her body angled sharply to the left.

I turned in the same direction and found the target ship on my holoscreen. I tapped the beacon, locking in the target, then shut down the screen and lowered my arm. I looked at Selene, locking eyes with her and nodding once.

Moving in unison, we tapped our heels together to demagnetize our boots and let the vacuum pull us out of the airlock. We sent out tiny bursts of psychic energy from our palms to alter our trajectory and speed up to a velocity that would have been terrifying with any kind of air resistance or reference points to mark our progress. The target ship finally came into view, a monstrous and bloated pieced-together behemoth with dozens of laser cannons poking out from the hull like the spines on a blowfish, all aimed at the *Elysium*.

Selene held her holoband out in front of her and scanned the ship. "Three on board," she said, her voice reaching me through the open link between our comms patches as we slowed our approach with more tiny bursts of psychic energy. "All on the Bridge."

As we closed in on the ship, we activated our hoplon suits'

stealth capabilities and disappeared from sight. I didn't exactly have psychic energy to spare, but we couldn't risk the ship's external motion detector sensing our approach. Only my psychic senses told me Selene was still there, floating along beside me toward the enemy ship.

I continued to use tiny bursts of psychic energy to slow and adjust my approach until, finally, I reached the ship. I grabbed the rung of a ladder that formed a ring around the hull and clung to the ship's exterior, and while I waited for Selene to get a secure foothold, I dragged myself from rung to rung along the ladder in search of a way in. My efforts were rewarded by finding a circular maintenance hatch some ten feet from my landing spot.

"I've found our way in," I told Selene, who had latched onto the hull further up the ship and was carefully crawling her way back to me.

"Sit tight for a minute," she said when I sensed she was settling in beside me.

I felt a pulse of supercharged psychic energy, and a moment later, I sensed the energy fade from the ship as the power core overloaded and died.

"All right," Selene said. "The ship is dark."

No power core meant no lights, no radar, no motion detectors, and no artificial gravity, which would help our mission immensely. But most importantly, it meant local comms only—no external comms. We had cut this ship off from the rest of the fleet. They couldn't send out an alarm.

I stopped the flow of psychic energy feeding into my hoplon suit to make me invisible, and a moment later, Selene winked back into sight beside me.

I waited as she placed her hands flat against the maintenance hatch and closed her eyes. The door lock released, and the hatch cracked open. Selene pulled the circular door open the rest of the way, then dove in feet first. I followed, pulling the hatch shut behind me.

I floated in the absolute darkness of the cramped airlock, waiting for Selene to override the interior hatch, as well. The hiss of pressurized air marked the seal on the hatch releasing, and the red glow of emergency lighting seeped into the airlock. With a thought, I dispensed of my energy helmet.

Selene pulled herself into the ship through the interior door, making the airlock less cramped, and I glided through the hole feet first behind her. The hatch dropped us into a narrow hallway lit only by the red emergency lighting. We followed the hallway toward the center of the ship, where it intersected with the broad central corridor, which we then followed to the Bridge. We needed to immobilize the remaining three crew members.

When we reached the Bridge, we could see the three pirates working frantically to figure out the problem through the open doorway. Selene activated her suit's stealth mode, vanishing from sight, while I hung back in the corridor, remaining hidden the old-fashioned way to conserve psychic energy.

I sensed a burst of psychic energy within the Bridge, and a moment later, Selene reappeared. I peeked around the edge of the doorway to see the three unconscious pirates floating in the zero gravity environment, then touched my comms patch. "Hades, the ship is cleared," I said. "What's your status?"

It couldn't have been more than ten minutes since we left the *Elysium*. Assuming the artificial gravity was still on and the invading pirates weren't sprinting straight to the Bridge, it would likely take them at least another ten minutes to reach Hades' position.

"No change," Hades said, confirming my assumption. In my mind's eye, I could easily visualize him standing before the holo-screen on the platform of the captain's station, his hands clasped behind his back and his expression unreadable. "Where are you?"

"The Bridge," I told him. "Where do we go from here?"

"On a warship, the System Operator chamber is usually

directly beneath the Bridge, where our cryovault is located," he explained. "Do you see the door to a lift anywhere?"

I pulled my weightless body through the doorway to the command center and scanned the walls.

"It should be near the back of the Bridge," he added, just as I spotted the narrow, dinged door panel on the left wall, near the back corner.

"I think I see it." I launched myself toward the door and sensed Selene floating along close behind me. When I reached the wall, I waited for Selene to provide a small burst of power to the lift, psychically opening the door panel.

"Good," Hades said. "Take the lift down to the lower level. You should be able to psychically interface with the ship's AI. It will direct you on how to remove the processor. But remember that once you begin the extraction process, the AI will go off-line."

I nodded, despite knowing he couldn't see me.

"Let me know if you have any issues," he said.

My eyes locked with Selene's, and she channeled a continuous stream of energy into the lift to power it. "You got it," I said as I stepped onto the lift.

[34]

The processor extraction was quick and easy, and Selene and I flew down the central corridor toward the cargo bay at the aft of the pirate ship, the bulky, boxy processor hovering in front of us. Selene held it encased in a protective bubble of benign psychic energy and guided it with her outstretched hand.

I touched my comms patch to update Hades on our progress. "We've got the processor and should have it back on the *Elysium* within ten minutes," I told him. "What's your status?"

"A small team broke off from the group and is heading down to the ship's core," Hades said, a hard edge to his voice. "The primary group approaches the Bridge as we speak. Entering radio silence. I'll check in after we neutralize the threat."

"Understood." A soft chime let me know Hades had dropped out of our comms loop.

Selene emitted a tiny burst of psychic energy from her palm as we hurtled toward the door to the cargo bay, gradually slowing. My reserves of psychic energy were extremely limited, however, so I opted for the old-fashioned, tried-and-true zero gravity deceleration method of waiting until the last minute, finding a handhold on the nearest wall-ceiling-floor-whatever, and holding tight as the jerk of stopping suddenly reverberated up my arm and through my shoulder.

Wincing, I rubbed my shoulder while Selene floated serenely onward with the processor to join me at the door to the cargo bay. I waited as she closed her eyes and shifted the oversized door panel open with a surge of psychic energy. We made our way through the cargo bay to the airlock—one of the few on the ship that would be large enough for the processor to fit through—and quickly sealed ourselves within.

I tapped my heels together to magnetize my boots, then clomped over to the exterior door. Selene stood behind me, her energy helmet shimmering a sunny yellow as I strained to activate my own energy helmet.

"I'm fine," I said, purposely ignoring Selene's concerned gaze.

"I think I should tow you back," she said, not a hint of a question in her voice.

We had planned on sharing the burden of guiding the processor back to our ship, preferring the added stability of a joint effort. But I wasn't too stubborn to admit I probably didn't have the psychic juice to make such a trip. I would only get in the way. Which meant Selene would need to balance two burdens during the trip rather than sharing one.

Shame heated my cheeks, and hindsight's perfect vision made me doubt the soundness of me joining Selene on this mission. But with the knowledge we had at the time—and all the unknowns about what we might face on the pirate ship—a two-person team had been the smartest and safest option. Maybe my presence hadn't been necessary, but it was better to have some dead weight on such an important mission than to be undermanned.

I squashed the shame and buried the self-doubt, then turned to face Selene. "Where do you want me?"

She pursed her lips and shifted her focus from me to the processor, her eyes narrowing in thought. Finally, she looked at me, her lips spreading into a sly grin. "You know, this whole a-Titan-sucked-out-all-my-psychic-energy ploy is a really strange way of asking for a hug." She held out her arms, waving me closer with a bend of her fingers. "Come on, give us a squeeze."

Chuckling, I shook my head and stepped closer. I wrapped my arms around her torso and tucked my head into the crook of her neck.

"Hold on tight," she said, all seriousness now. "And don't move a muscle until we get back to the *Elysium*."

I tapped my heels together to demagnetize my boots, then hooked my ankles around Selene's calves, completing my transformation into a barnacle. I felt a surge of psychic energy followed by the hiss of pressurized air releasing as Selene forced the exterior airlock door open. Her muscles tensed, and she bent her legs, then tapped her heels together to release her boots' hold on the metal floor and launched us out into space.

I closed my eyes and focused on taking slow, deep breaths. I was scraping the bottom of my psychic energy reservoir, like a car engine running on fumes, and it took a conscious effort to maintain my energy helmet. I focused on my heartbeat and sank deeper into my body, pulling on those last remaining strands of psychic energy.

The barrier of my helmet thinned, and then it flickered. Suddenly, it was a lot harder to breathe. Burnout was imminent. I had to deactivate the helmet and risk exposure to open space, or I was most definitely going to die.

I opened my eyes, my heart hammering in my chest. If I was going to do this, I needed to do it now.

I blew out a breath, expelling all the air in my lungs as quickly as I could. If I held any air in my lungs, the loss of external pressure would make my lungs explode. I was still exhaling when the shimmering electric-blue barrier sizzled out, exposing me to the vacuum of space, and I reflexively squeezed my eyes shut.

The cold was shocking—so far beyond the parameters of what

my nerves could sense that my brain wasn't able to process it fully. The sensation of freezing quickly faded under the overwhelming pressure within my skin. I felt like a sausage casing shoved full of too much meat. My hoplon suit was suddenly too small, the constriction on various parts of my body agonizing.

Selene's hand cupped the back of my head and her arm curled around my back a moment before my shoulder and hip slammed into something hard. I would have screamed from the excruciating sensation that I was about to explode had there been any breath left in my lungs.

Selene released me, leaving me lying on my back on a hard, flat surface. The physical pain was too much, and I teetered on the brink of unconsciousness.

Suddenly, the internal pressure making me feel like an overblown balloon released. My lungs spasmed, sucking in air in fits and starts. I coughed, then groaned, the sharp motion sending shock waves of pain outward through my chest. It felt like my cells themselves were bruised.

"Cora?" Selene said, her voice urgent. She gripped my shoulders. "Cora? Can you hear me?"

I opened my eyes and found Selene gazing at me, her face lined with concern. I nodded, pleased to note that movement didn't hurt quite as much as coughing had. The pain caused by the abrupt shift in external pressure was fading, enabling me to feel the less urgent joys of surviving an unprotected space walk, namely that my lips were cracked and flakey, and that my face felt like I'd basked unprotected in full sun from the top of Mount Everest for a solid twelve hours.

Selene wedged her arm under my shoulders and raised me up so I was sitting. "We need to get you to the asclypos," she said, her voice urgent. She slid her arm lower, curving it around the back of my rib cage, and gripped my elbow with her other hand to support me as she hauled me up to my feet. "The radiation you were just exposed to will kill you if you're not treated soon."

I stumbled forward, dragging Selene with me, and leaned against the stolen processor. It hovered about a foot above the floor, still encased in its protective bubble of topaz energy from the space walk.

"After we get this to Fiona," I said, my voice raspy. And by *we*, I meant I would tag along as *Selene* transported the bulky piece of tech to Gertie's room.

The radiation might kill me—eventually—but if Fiona didn't get this processor hooked up ASAP, I would already be dead. The asclypos could wait.

I touched my comms patch as I trailed behind Selene and the floating processor, following both across the sprawling floor space of the transport hangar. Every inch of my body felt bruised, and mild nausea was setting in, courtesy of radiation sickness. It would only get worse. Lucky me.

"Hades," I said, sounding like I had been a pack-a-day girl for the last decade. "We're back. Delivering the processor to Gertie's room now."

When he didn't respond after a few seconds, I frowned. There was no need to maintain radio silence after dispatching the pirates. And hadn't he said he would check in once the Bridge was secured?

"Hades?" I repeated, meeting Selene's eyes as she glanced over her shoulder, her brow furrowed. "He's not responding," I shared unnecessarily.

I reached out to Meg through our bond and found her exactly where she was supposed to be, holed up with Fiona and a team of Zari psychics in Gertie's room, awaiting delivery of the processor. From Meg's mind, I gleaned that they hadn't heard a word from

Hades or the team on the Bridge since he initiated radio silence nearly ten minutes ago.

"We sent a scout to the Bridge," Meg explained, sensing the direction of my probing. "But she hasn't reported back yet."

I jogged ahead—painfully—to catch up with Selene, and I fell in step beside her as I relayed the new information.

"The pirates could be jamming the comms signal somehow," she mused. She didn't say she thought the pirates had somehow overwhelmed our forces and taken the Bridge. She didn't have to. I had already made that terrifying leap.

"But a jammer doesn't explain why the scout lost contact," I pointed out. She should have been able to communicate with Meg's team using her psychic abilities.

Selene pressed her lips together, the corners of her mouth turning down in a faint frown.

"I'm going to head to the Bridge and check it out," I said and reached over my shoulder and started to draw my doru, then paused and tucked it back into its sheath. I didn't even have the fumes of psychic energy to extend the staff to its full length. Better to have my hands free.

Selene shook her head, her eyes bulging in disbelief. "You're in no shape to—"

"You don't need me," I said, raising my eyebrows. "But they might." I let that sink in, then added, "I'm going."

Selene's lips parted, and again she shook her head, clearly at a loss for words.

"I'll be careful," I said before she could find her voice. We both knew it was a lie. I sent a pointed look at the processor floating along ahead of us. "Get that thing to Fiona and make sure she has everything she needs to get it hooked up, then meet me at the Bridge. I'll update Meg when I have a better idea of the situation. If I can help, I will. But if I can't, I'll wait for you."

A dark scowl settled over Selene's face, but she didn't argue.

I jogged ahead and took a sharp left down an intersecting corridor before she could change her mind and *make* me stay with her. I managed not to stumble until I had rounded another corner and allowed myself a five-count to lean against the wall and close my eyes, taking steadying breaths. After one last deep breath, I pushed off the wall and set out at a horribly pathetic stumble-jog. If nothing else, I could lure the pirates into complacency by looking about as dangerous as a wounded kitten.

I wound my way through the warren of corridors on the service level, slowly making my way toward the front of the ship. Once I was directly below the Bridge, I squeezed into a service chute and climbed up the ladder to the front of the cryovault five levels up. My limbs ached from the strain, and strands of hair stuck to the sweat on my neck and face. It was with the sheer force of will that I climbed the final few rungs.

I flopped out of the service chute like a calf being born and lay on my back with my limbs sprawled for a solid thirty seconds, catching my breath and reminding myself that the pain was a good thing. It meant I was still alive.

Once I had quieted my breaths enough that I was sure I wouldn't alert any interloping pirates to my presence by merely breathing nearby, I sat up. I shucked my boots and tottered to my feet. Carrying my boots, I crept toward the spiral staircase in the back corner of the elongated room.

I tiptoed up the metal steps until I could peek over the lip of the top stair and visually assess the situation on the Bridge. I looked to the raised captain's station first, hoping to find Hades standing in front of the holoscreen, signaling that everything was all right. But Hades wasn't on the platform, and nothing was right about the situation on the Bridge.

A hooded figure occupied the captain's chair like it was a throne, the dark fabric draped over their head shimmering with the hint of gold. This had to be the pirates' leader. Only someone used to being in charge could sit so imperiously. Over and over, the leader tossed and caught a small, gleaming silver device about the size of a tennis ball. A psychic dampener.

Biting back a curse, I ducked down, hiding in the staircase as I processed this new information and mentally regrouped. Psychic dampeners were crazy rare, in no small part due to the resources required to create each one—namely, a chaos stone. The process didn't simply *use* a chaos stone; it *destroyed* a chaos stone.

Not that the presence of a psychic dampener really mattered to me in my current state. My tanks were dry. If I tried to do anything powered by psychic energy before my energy stores had replenished themselves, I would end up burned out and uncon- scious—or worse, dead—and then I wouldn't be of any use to anyone.

At least the dampener was relatively small, covering an area not much larger than the Bridge itself. And it explained why Meg's team had lost contact with their scout.

With the utmost caution, I peeked over the lip of the floor. Maybe a dozen pirates migrated around the Bridge, hoods pushed back as they scoped out the various control panels like they were assessing their spoils. I gritted my teeth and visualized cutting off their greedy, grubby hands.

I spotted the bodies of three women dressed in hoplon suits sprawled on the floor throughout the space, the severity of their injuries and the amount of blood splattered in their immediate vicinities making it highly unlikely that they were still alive. How many more were there that I couldn't see from my vantage point?

Fear cinched around my heart, and dread was a leaden weight in my belly. What about my Mom and Raiden and Emi? What about Hades? Without him, our odds of completing the interstellar trek to Terra dropped to, oh say, a snowball's chance in hell.

I crept up one more step and slowly straightened to increase my field of view. There, at the front of the Bridge, below the enormous viewscreen. The broad pedestal of the navigation console had been blocking my view before, but now I could see them.

Raiden, Hades, my mom, and Emi—they were all there, along with four more psychics. And based on the existence of the opalescent energy barrier surrounding them within an electric cage, they were all alive. There would be no need to contain them if they were dead, like the discarded bodies of the other three psychics.

I focused on the haggard group, absorbing as much information about their situation as I could within the span of a dozen heartbeats.

Only Raiden and two of the psychics were conscious. None of them appeared to be restrained, but then they wouldn't need to be within their prison, especially not with the psychic dampener in play. One of Raiden's arms hung uselessly at his side, and he cradled his mom's body on his lap with his other arm. Enough blood soaked Emi's shirt to make me question my earlier assessment about the wellbeing of those contained within the cage. Hades and my mom lay side by side on their backs near Raiden and Emi, their legs straight and arms tucked against their sides in a way that suggested they had been dragged to their current positions, already unconscious.

I watched my mom's chest for a few seconds, then Hades', but I was too far away to tell if either of them still drew breath. My only solace was in them having been moved into the cage at all. They hadn't been dead when they had been captured, which meant there was a chance they were still alive now.

Clenching my jaw, I retreated into the stairwell. Rage-fueled tears stung my eyes, and I balled my hands into fists, digging my nails into my palms. I could wait for Selene, but then what? We would likely just end up captured along with the others.

I stared into the glazed eyes of the nearest of the dead psychics.

Or worse.

And Emi might not have the five or ten minutes left in her to wait for backup. It was now or never.

Which meant it was *now*.

[36]

I retreated further down the spiral staircase and sat to carefully stuff my feet back into my boots. Standing, I rolled my neck and shook out my arms, psyching myself up for the performance I was about to put on. My head still pounded from the encounter with the Titan, and my entire body ached from the impromptu space walk. The skin of my face felt hot and swollen, and nausea roiled in my gut. I was basically a walking corpse and absolutely was not in shape to take on a veritable swarm of space pirates.

But I would not let a little thing like that stop me from saving the people I loved.

I climbed one stair, then paused as the world did a not-so-fun tilt-a-whirl impersonation. I gripped the curved railing and squeezed my eyes shut, waiting for the wave of vertigo to ebb. The radiation sickness was advancing faster than I had expected. I breathed through the unsteadiness, willing it to pass.

After one more deep breath, I raised my head and opened my eyes. Just a few more minutes. I needed to hold it together for just a few more minutes. Take out the pirates, save my people, get my butt into the asclypos.

I started up the stairs, shoving as much of my physical

discomfort into the back of my mind as I could. I fell into an easy saunter as I ascended the final few stairs and stepped out onto the floor of the Bridge. I leaned my shoulder against the steel post at the top of the staircase and crossed my arms over my chest. The pirates were so preoccupied playing with all the bells and whistles on their new toy that they hadn't noticed my arrival.

I cleared my throat loudly and forced my face into something within the smirk family. It was hard to say how well I pulled it off, but at least I tried.

"Looks like you're going to need a new psychic," I said, projecting my voice as much as I could. I still sounded like a chronic smoker, but at least my voice was a little stronger.

Pirates froze all around the Bridge, then drew their weapons and aimed in my direction. Up in the captain's chair, the leader caught the psychic dampener and gripped it tight, turning their head toward me so their profile was just barely visible beyond the brim of their hood.

"You're Titan tried to space me," I said, gesturing to my cracked and burned face. I flashed the pirate leader a grim smile. "So I killed her." I pushed off the post and strolled toward the captain's station. "She was weak. Very *conflicted*." I coated the word in a thick layer of condescension. "You're better off without her."

I stopped near the body of one of the Zari psychics and nudged her shoulder with the toe of my boot. Yep, definitely dead. I made a show of sniffing in disgust. "You would be much better off with *me*."

"*You* wish to join us?" the leader asked, the familiar feminine timbre of her voice confirming that the woman Hades spoke to earlier had indeed been their leader.

"Why not?" I said, planting a hand on my hip and shrugging one shoulder. "I'm an opportunist. And here you are—an opportunity." I scanned the Bridge, casually assessing the situation from my new vantage point.

Raiden caught my eye, then glanced at the pirate leader and shook his head, the movement barely perceptible.

I returned my focus to the pirate leader, offering her a sly grin. "So, what do you say?"

A mental presence suddenly invaded my mind, leaving me momentarily disoriented. Meg. She was behind me, standing on the other side of the broad door panel. She must have left Gertie's room as soon as she sensed I was heading for the Bridge, and I had been too focused on getting here to notice she was on her way, too.

Her presence buoyed me, and I fought the urge to glance over my shoulder. To grin. If I could only take the psychic dampener out of play, we would squash these asshats like the opportunistic cockroaches they were. "Wait for my signal," I silently told Meg.

"We could never trust you," the pirate leader said, dragging my attention back to her.

"Can you ever really trust anyone?" I asked, raising my eyebrows.

The pirate leader resumed her steady tossing and catching of the psychic dampener. She was relaxing, settling into her false sense of security. Good. People always underestimated a psychic's other skills and abilities, like once we no longer had access to our psychic gifts, we were rendered powerless. Fine with me.

I resumed my slow stroll across the Bridge. "You can trust me to survive," I said, passing by the stairs leading up to the platform of the captain's station and heading for the navigation console. Or rather, for the armed pirate—a male—watching me from the far side of the console pedestal. "Which is more than I can say for your Titan," I added.

I attempted a come hither gaze as I neared the pirate at the navigation console. His narrowed eyes and general show of confusion reminded me I currently looked like hell from my brief walkabout in open space—not exactly vixen material. Oh well. Confusion was almost as distracting as flirtation. I rolled with it.

I glanced up at the navigation chart on the holoscreen hovering over the pedestal, feigning disinterest in the handful of blinking red dots moving toward the *Elysium* from the larger beacons of the ships surrounding us. The pirates were waiting for reinforcements. They must have called them in when they lost contact with the people they sent down to the ship's core to secure the chaos stone and FTL drive. I doubted these pirates had *two* psychic dampeners, and the team of Zari psychics stationed in the ship's core would have made quick work of the pirates, regardless of how well armed they were.

I returned my attention to the pirate watching me warily from the far side of the navigation console, his laser pistol trained on me. I inched around the broad pedestal, my eyes locked with his. "Have you ever *been* with a psychic?" I winked at him, enjoying his increasing discomfort as I drew closer. I blew him an air kiss, and his discomfort ramped up to outright revulsion. Maybe I looked worse than I had thought.

"Want to be *friends*?" I asked, pressing my sternum against the nozzle of his laser pistol.

His brow furrowed. He may even have suppressed a gag.

I capitalized on his moment of preoccupation to grip his wrist, breaking it with a sharp jerk. I twisted the laser pistol out of his grip and shot him in the gut, then whipped my arm out behind me and sniped the psychic dampener while it was in midair. The small orb shattered, spraying the pirate leader with razor-sharp shards of shrapnel. Awareness of my psychic powers returned, though, without a reserve of psychic energy, they were all but useless to me.

"NOW!" I mentally shouted to Meg. Her psychic powers were another matter entirely.

The door panel slid open, and I ducked down, hiding behind the navigation console as a trio of laser blasts intersected above my head. Shouts filled the space, and the pirates scrambled around, reacting to the abrupt change in circumstances.

I peeked around the side of the pedestal in time to see Meg stalk through the doorway like a Goddamn terminator, and it might have been the most glorious thing I had ever seen. Meg deflected a barrage of laser blasts like they were butterflies and slammed the butt of her doru onto the floor. A shock wave of supercharged air blasted out of the blindingly bright focus crystal.

The force of the blast knocked me onto my back, and it took my lungs a painfully long time to remember how to draw breath.

Ears ringing, I rolled onto my side, then onto my hands and knees. Laser pistol still in hand, I crawled toward the electric cage, leaving Meg to dispatch the remaining pirates. At this point, I would only get in the way.

My eyes locked with Raiden's through the shimmering wall of electricity separating us, and the sound of laser blasts and the screams and cries of dying enemies faded into the background. Pain and worry etched new lines into Raiden's face, and tears cut tracks through the blood smudge on his cheeks. Whether it was his blood, Emi's, or another's, I couldn't tell. I peered down at Emi, bloody in Raiden's arms, then at my mom and Hades lying on the floor nearby.

"Are they—" I choked on fear, unable to complete the question. I licked my lips, and my eyes returned to Raiden's. "Are they okay?"

"They're alive," Raiden said, his voice gruff. *For now* hung between us unsaid, trapped in the energy barrier like a mosquito caught in a bug zapper.

Chin quivering, I nodded once. I pressed my lips firmly together and clenched my jaw, pulling myself together. I could fall apart later. Right now, I had work to do.

Bracing a hand on my knee, I stood and turned to face the pirate leader. She cowered on the captain's chair, her hood torn and her bloodied hands raised to cover her wounded face. She shrank away from Meg as the pissed-off psychic terminator walked up the steps to the top of the platform. Meg grabbed the injured woman's arm and yanked her up to her feet, then dragged her down the steps to the main level. Meg shoved her prisoner down the final few steps.

The pirate leader stumbled forward, catching herself on the edge of the navigation console.

Meg leveled the charged focus crystal of her doru on her prisoner.

"Please, mercy," the pirate begged.

Grip tight on the laser pistol, I stalked around the navigation console, hard glare spearing the groveling pirate. "You think you deserve mercy?" I barked a laugh. "You?" I glanced at the navigation chart displayed on the holoscreen, watching the blinking red dots close in on the *Elysium*.

I slid my jaw to the side and narrowed my eyes, then shifted my focus back to the pirate. "Call them off," I said, nodding toward the navigation chart. "There's been enough bloodshed today. Send your reinforcements back to their ships, and you'll get your mercy."

The pirate leader stared at me for a long moment. Even without my gifts, I could almost feel her gauging my sense of honor and weighing her odds of survival. She touched a small device attached to her belt, no larger than a deck of playing cards. A burst of static from my comms patch told me she had turned off the jammer that had been killing all radio signals to and from the Bridge.

"Retreat," she said, unwavering strength in her voice despite her weakened appearance. "Turn back now. Your lives depend on it."

Breath held, I stared at the navigation chart. The blinking red dots stopped moving, clustered close together near the aft of the *Elysium*. Finally, they started to move again, fanning out as they retreated. I exhaled, closing my eyes and bowing my head under the weight of my relief. I granted myself three heartbeats to bask in the victory.

Then I opened my eyes, straightened my neck, and raised the laser pistol to point it at the pirate's forehead.

Her eyes opened wide, and she raised her hands defensively. "But I did what you asked," she pleaded, shaking her head. "Mercy, please!"

"After what you've done, this is me showing you mercy," I said. And then I pulled the trigger.

[37]

I ran back to the energy barrier imprisoning Raiden and the others. The two conscious Zari psychics stalked along the perimeter like caged animals. I searched the floor along the outside of the barrier for the shield generator and found the unobtrusive device set flush against the wall at the left-most edge of the cage, looking from a distance like an oversized beetle.

I hurried closer to the wall and raised my boot, then stomped down hard, crushing the shield generator beneath my heel. The energy barrier fizzled out, and I rushed forward to crouch beside Raiden, trading places with the two psychics, who hurried out to assist Meg in checking for signs of life among their fallen comrades.

I placed a hand on his uninjured shoulder. "How bad is your arm?"

"Just dislocated, I think," he said, his eyes never leaving his mom's face.

"Any other injuries?"

He shook his head.

I peered down at Emi, visually assessing her wounds. She had been struck in the gut by a laser pistol. She looked worse close up, which was saying a lot because she didn't look great from farther away. If it had been a gunshot wound, she would likely already be dead, but the partial cauterization caused by the laser blast prevented her from bleeding out.

"She was protecting me," Raiden said hollowly. "She stepped right in front—" A stifled sob choked off his words.

"Is she—" I inhaled shakily, then attempted a slow, even exhale. "How is she?"

"She's holding on," Raiden said. He raised his eyes to meet mine, the pain and fear in his gaze transforming him into the little boy I had grown up with. "But I'm afraid to move her."

"We'll take care of her," I said, mentally calling Meg over. I rubbed Raiden's shoulder, then pulled my hand away and crawled closer to my mom. I pressed my fingers to her neck, and relief flooded me when I felt the strong, steady thrum of her pulse.

Sensing Meg approaching, I sat back on my heels and twisted to meet her eyes. I offered her a grateful nod, then turned my attention to Raiden. "Meg will cauterize your mom's wound," I told him. "That should keep her stable while you carry her to the Med Sector."

Raiden's nostrils flared and his jaw tensed. He nodded to me, then looked to Meg as she kneeled in front of him, leaving a space of several feet between them.

Meg swept her hand over the floor between them. "Lay her down on her back."

While Meg worked with Raiden and Emi, I reached over my mom to press my fingers against Hades' neck. I didn't even have a chance to feel his pulse before he groaned, his eyelids fluttering.

I sat back, resting my hands on my thighs.

Hades opened his eyes, then winced. He lifted one hand and gently touched his fingertips to his temple.

"Hold on," I said, scrambling around my mom to reach Hades as he attempted to sit up. He propped himself on his elbows, and I extended my arm behind his shoulders to help him up the rest of the way.

Raiden stood, scooping up Emi and hurrying away.

I looked at Meg as she climbed to her feet. "Will you take my mom to the Med Sector?" I asked. Her prolonged stretch of unconsciousness concerned me. "I'd like to have her assessed by an asclypos."

"Of course," Meg said, spreading her hands in front of her in a smooth gesture. A flat, shimmering energy stretcher formed in front of her, and she guided it down to rest on the floor beside my mom.

I moved to kneel by my mom's head, and Meg crouched by her knees. With a twist of her fingers, Meg formed a brace of psychic energy around my mom's neck and shoulders. Working in unison, we rolled my mom onto her side, and once the stretcher was in place, settled her on her back again.

"You should come with us," Meg said, her concern for me bleeding through our bond.

"I will. As soon as I'm finished here." I leaned over to kiss my mom's forehead, then straightened and watched as Meg smoothly raised the stretcher and guided my mom away.

"What did I miss?" Hades asked, drawing my attention back to him. He appeared much more clear-headed than he had been a moment ago. He scanned the Bridge, taking in the bodies and the damage dealt to the controls during the struggle, his focus landing on the pirate leader's corpse.

"The pirates won't be a problem any longer," I said.

Hades turned his attention to me, his gaze tracing a complicated path around my no-doubt horrifying visage. His brow creased, his concern palpable.

"It's nothing the asclypos can't fix," I told him.

Movement drew my focus to the doorway from the main corridor. Caly rushed in with team of Zari psychics. The women spread out to help their sisters with the bodies scattered around the command center.

Hades' stare lingered on my face, but he nodded to himself. "And the processor?"

I touched my comms patch to open a private feed. "Selene, stay with Fiona," I ordered. "The Bridge is clear, and I have Hades with me."

"Understood," Selene said through the comms feed.

"What's the status on the processor?" I asked.

"Fiona is still working," Selene said. She fell quiet for a moment but started up again before I could ask for more. "She says she should have it hooked up and ready to go in about an hour."

I relayed the status update to Hades.

"I need to check on the energy screen," he said and shifted to his knees to stand. His extreme unsteadiness made me doubt his ability to stand on his own.

I gripped his elbow to stabilize him and curled my arm behind his back, at the same time dragging his arm over my shoulders. With a grunt, I hoisted him up to his feet. I helped him make his way to the captain's station and climb the stairs to the top of the platform, only releasing him once he was easing down into the captain's seat.

Hades skimmed through the windows the pirate leader had opened on the holoscreen, then cleared the screen with a flick of his wrist. He opened a new window and tapped the holoscreen a few more times.

His expression darkened. "The energy screen has failed."

Numbing dread washed over me.

Hades tapped one of the icons running vertically along the side of the holoscreen, and a navigation chart appeared in a new window. It displayed the bright white beacon of the *Elysium* surrounded by the pirate fleet. Hades pinched his thumb and forefinger together in front of the screen, then spread them wide, and the view on the navigation chart shifted, zooming out to include Nykta's planetary system. A cluster of seven blinking red dots hovered near the outer edge of the system. A Tsakali fleet.

I blinked, and one of the dots vanished.

"That was a Tsakali scout ship entering FTL," Hades said, his voice monotone. "And now that we no longer have an energy screen, I think it's safe to assume it's heading our way."

One by one, the remaining ships winked out of sight.

Brow furrowing, I chewed on the inside of my cheek. It had taken us three years to reach Nykta while traveling at top slower-than-light speed. The time it would take the Tsakali fleet to reach us using FTL jumps depended on whether their ships used chaos-powered FTL drives or not—an hour per year of standard travel for non-chaos FTL, with that time cut in half for a chaos-powered FTL drive. The Tsakali tended to reserve their chaos energy for self-propagation and scout ships.

"It should take them several hours to get here, right?" I said, thinking aloud. "Even if the entire fleet is equipped with chaos-powered FTL drives—"

"Highly unlikely," Hades said, shaking his head.

"Even if they are," I reiterated, "it should take them at least an hour to reach us. If Fiona's estimate is accurate, we should be long gone by the time they drop out of FTL."

Again Hades shook his head, his gaze haunted. "The navigation system recorded those ships leaving Nykta's system nearly an hour ago."

My lips parted, my eyes widening in horror. I sank down to sit on the arm of the captain's chair.

"If that scout ship drops out of FTL before we can jump away, it will be right on top of us," Hades said. "And in the *Elysium's* current unprotected state, even a single Tsakali scout ship crew could overtake us." He didn't say we would have no choice but to trigger the *Elysium's* self-destruct. He didn't have to.

"The pirates might distract them," I suggested. "That could buy us some time."

Hades' attention returned to the holoscreen. He tapped the *Elysium's* beacon on the navigation chart, and the view zoomed in to show the area immediately surrounding the ship. Where the pirate fleet had been a moment ago, now there was only empty space.

"They're already gone," Hades said, his words resounding in my bones.

[38]

Hades and I stared at the navigation chart on the holoscreen. Hades drew in a deep breath, preparing to break our stunned silence. "Fiona must install the new processor *before* the Tsakali scout ship emerges from FTL," he said resolutely. "It's our only hope."

Dread knotted in my belly. "I'm not comfortable relying on hope," I murmured. "We need a contingency plan." My voice gained strength as I spoke. "What can we do to buy Fiona some more time if they arrive before she finishes installing the processor? There must be something . . ."

An idea tickled my mind, and I glanced over my shoulder at the balcony overlooking the Bridge from the gephyra chamber one level above. I narrowed my eyes, visualizing the gephyra in the center of the room and the chaos fragments tucked away beneath it, powering the traveling device.

Out of the corner of my eye, I saw Hades look at me, then follow my line of sight up to the gephyra chamber.

A discomfiting sense of déjà vu struck me. "If we removed the chaos stone and hid it in a dampening box," I thought aloud, "the Tsakali wouldn't be able to sense it, right?"

"Correct," Hades said. "Though doing so would shut down both Gertie and the simulation."

I nodded to myself, mentally dismissing those two byproducts of temporarily removing the chaos stone. Yes, this would increase the odds of more of our incorporeal human passengers noticing the lapse in awareness and figuring out the truth about their simulated existence, which would open up many of the uploaded humans to consciousness suicide. But, their chances of survival would still be better than if we self-destructed. Then they would be dead. Full stop.

I stared through the navigation chart to the deceptively peaceful view of the stars on the viewscreen ahead as the pieces of a plan fitted together in my mind. "But the Tsakali would still be able to detect the chaos fragments powering the gephyra," I said, voicing the still forming idea.

"Yes," Hades agreed. "They will most certainly be close enough to detect the energy signature from the chaos fragments. Unless they, too, are placed in a dampening box."

The unsettling sense of déjà vu intensified. Once again, I felt as though I was hurtling toward inevitable doom.

"If we remove the chaos stone and shield it in a dampening box," I said, voicing my plan, "and if we completely power down the *Elysium*, then stow the chaos fragments in a smaller ship and launch it into space like it's trying to flee from the Tsakali . . ." I looked at Hades. "Do you think they would assume that smaller ship was the source of chaos energy they detected from Nykta's system? Would they take the bait and follow that ship?"

Hades' brow furrowed, and the corners of his mouth drew down in a thoughtful frown. "It's possible." He laughed under his breath and slowly shook his head. "That might just be crazy enough to work."

I flashed him a tense, tight-lipped smile and nodded once. "Good enough for me."

[39]

Arms crossed over my chest, I leaned back against the free-standing control panel in the dimly lit gephyra chamber. The red glow of the emergency lighting cast eerie shadows along the walls, like the ghosts of all those stored in the Vault of Souls, silently observing our efforts to save them. I still felt like hell, but the anti-radiation injection Hades had dug out of the emergency kit and jabbed into my thigh was staving off most of the effects of the radiation sickness—for now.

Meg and Hades huddled together, crouched by the base of the circular gephyra platform. Two more Zari psychics flanked them, directing the light from a pair of luminous energy orbs onto the vertical hatch door that would give access to the gut of the machine as Hades worked on the screws holding it shut.

Hades had already placed seven screws beside the small orichalcum box sitting on the step above the hatch door and was working on the eighth and final screw. He raised his head and placed the last screw on the step, then removed the hatch door and handed it to Meg. She twisted, placing it on the floor behind her.

Hades stretched out on his belly on the floor, his neck twisted awkwardly as he peered into the dark hole. He raised one hand

and gestured for the psychics to move their light orbs closer, then said something to Meg, his voice too quiet to reach my ears.

Meg bent down, lying in a child's pose with her arms stretched out in front of her as she also peered into the inner workings of the gephyra. Delicate strands of amethyst psychic energy shot out from her fingertips and reached through the hatch, searching for the chaos fragments.

"Cora," Selene said through a private comms feed. We had agreed she should communicate through me while Hades assisted Meg in removing the chaos fragments. It was a delicate procedure, and we didn't want his focus divided. "The chaos stone is contained in the dampening box," Selene told me.

Anxiety coiled in my belly. Hades had already shut down all secondary and tertiary systems, leaving only the artificial gravity and life support systems online. And Gertie and the simulation, of course. Soon, he would shut those down as well, including Gertie, making the *Elysium* appear to be dead from the outside. We could survive within the ship without life support for a couple of hours, and our hoplon suits—or atmos suits for the non-psychics—would quadruple that time. If life support stayed off-line for too long, it was going to get cold in here, and eventual oxygen deprivation would make our brains fuzzy, but it would buy us more time.

Hopefully, we wouldn't need it. Fiona was fully aware of what was at stake, and she was working as quickly as possible to hook the new processor into the ship's existing array, so we could get the hell out of here *without* a Tsakali tail.

My attention was pulled to the broad, open doorway as Raiden entered the gephyra chamber and headed straight for me. His face was drawn, and his injured arm had been tucked into a sling. He had forgone a session in the asclypos to free up the healing machines for those who had suffered more dire injuries, instead, letting Meg set his dislocated shoulder manually.

I offered him a brief smile as he neared, then returned to watching Meg as she painstakingly removed the first chaos fragment. It floated out from the dark abyss, encased in a cocoon of shimmering amethyst energy. Meg guided the chaos fragment to the small orichalcum box sitting open on the step in front of her. The orichalcum would hold the chaos fragments without burning up, but it wouldn't hide their energy signature like a dampening box would.

Raiden settled in beside me, leaning against the control panel and watching Meg and Hades work.

"How's your mom doing?" I asked quietly.

"Stable," he said, rubbing the back of his neck. "She'll live. Diana, too." He lowered his hand and blew out a breath. "Though for how long?" He stared ahead, despondency seeping into his voice. "I guess we'll find out soon enough."

I reached for his arm, rubbing gently before sliding my hand down his forearm to twine our fingers together. "This will work," I said, pleased that my voice sounded more confident than I actually felt.

Raiden grunted, a soft sound that told me he wasn't so sure.

Giving his hand a squeeze, I returned my attention to the scene at the base of the gephyra. Meg guided the second chaos fragment into the golden orichalcum box. Just one more to go.

"This might not even be necessary," I said, hoping to reassure Raiden. And myself. "Look at how prepared we are—we have a plan A *and* a plan B." I grinned, glancing at him sidelong. "How often does *that* happen?"

A faint laugh rumbled in Raiden's chest. "What can I do to help?" he asked, looking at me with eyes haunted by the ghosts of his fallen comrades.

If I hadn't been drained dry of psychic energy, I likely would have sensed the extreme tumult in Raiden's mind as his PTSD wrestled for control. He didn't just *want* to help. He needed to help. He needed something to focus on—something that would take his mind off his past trauma.

"You can help me pick a ship," I said as we watched Meg

guide the third and final chaos fragment into the orichalcum box. "I'd love the company."

"I can do that," Raiden said, a faint smile softening his mouth.

Meg picked up the orichalcum box and stood, then hurried our way. Hades pushed up off the floor. I wasn't sure if I was seeing things, or if he wavered on his feet. He looked my way and nodded once before heading for the stairs leading down to the Bridge to shut down all remaining systems. I watched him closely but didn't notice any more unsteadiness.

When Meg reached us, she handed me the box with its precious cargo.

"Thanks," I said, flashing Meg a quick smile. I sensed her desire to accompany me down to the transport hangar and shook my head, glancing at Hades once more.

He gripped the railing as he descended the stairs. For support? Or was he always a railing gripper? I narrowed my eyes. I wanted to say no, but I couldn't be sure.

When his head sank below the level of the floor, I looked back at Meg. "Stay with Hades," I told her. "Keep an eye on him. He says he doesn't need a session in the asclypos, but he probably does, and we can't afford to lose him."

His head injury had been significant enough to knock him unconscious for several minutes at least. If there was any bleeding or swelling inside his skull, Meg was the best substitute for an asclypos with her innate affinity for using her psychic gifts for healing. She could at least keep him stable until this was all over and we could force him into an asclypos.

Meg nodded, understanding exactly what I was asking of her. She turned away from us and jogged toward the stairs, following Hades down to the Bridge.

"Let's go," I said, glancing at Raiden.

We hurried down to the transport hangar, heading straight for the *Argo* tucked away in its storage bay near the airlock at the back of the hangar. It was the only ship with a functioning self-contained AI capable of auto-piloting itself—and the chaos frag-ments—away.

As we neared the storage bay and the ship came into view, I slowed from a run to a walk and shook my head. The loading ramp was down. It shouldn't have been down.

I stopped just shy of entering the storage bay and stared at the *Argo*, my hands on my hips and my head cocked to the side.

Raiden stood beside me, alternating between looking at the ship and looking at me. "What? What is it? Is something wrong? Because your face is making me think something's wrong."

"I don't know," I said, frowning. "Meg ran a post-flight systems check when we returned from Nykta. It's an automated process, and the *Argo* should have shut herself up tight when the process completed." I narrowed my eyes, settling into my certainty. "The ramp *shouldn't* be down."

With Gertie totally encumbered by the simulation, we hadn't been able to run a ship-wide scan of the *Elysium* to make sure we had cleared the ship of any remaining pirates, but our psychic sweep should have found the final few stowaways. Had pirates evaded their search and hidden in the *Argo*?

I started toward the ship, my steps cautious and quiet. I reached over my shoulder to draw my doru while deactivating my regulator with my other hand, only remembering I was temporarily out of psychic energy when I was unable to extend the doru to its full combat length. "Damn it," I hissed, stuffing the stubby doru back into its sheath.

Raiden gripped my shoulder, holding me back. "I'll go."

When I looked at him, he released my shoulder and drew his laser pistol. I nodded and crossed my arms over my chest. Despite his shoulder injury, he was still in far better shape than I currently was.

Raiden snuck toward the *Argo*'s loading ramp, his weapon raised and ready to fire. He crept up the ramp and disappeared into the ship.

I held my breath, waiting.

A moment later, he reemerged, scanning the hangar as he jogged down the ramp. "If someone was here, they're not anymore."

I started toward the ramp, chewing on the inside of my cheek. I glanced over my shoulder several times, paranoia and the inability to access my psychic powers making me feel like I was being watched. As soon as Raiden and I were up the ramp and standing within the *Argo,* I hit the button to close the loading ramp with the side of my fist.

Nothing happened.

Brow furrowing, I pressed my palm hard against the button. Maybe I hadn't pressed it all the way?

Again, nothing happened.

"Hold this," I said, handing Raiden the orichalcum box. I ran to the front of the ship and pressed the button that should have powered up the engine.

The control panels remained dark, the engine silent.

"No, no, no . . ." Frantically, I pushed buttons and flipped switches, but the controls remained stubbornly dead. No matter what I did, the *Argo* wouldn't respond. I planted my hands on the control panel and hung my head.

"We got a problem?" Raiden asked from close behind me. He moved to stand at my side.

"Yeah, we've got a problem." I looked at him without raising my head. "I know why the loading ramp was open. And why it wouldn't close." I shook my head and jutted out my jaw, fighting the urge to scream. To cry. "The bastards sabotaged the *Argo,* probably to prevent any of us from escaping. The ship's dead."

"Can we fix it?" Raiden asked.

I shook my head. "Not in time." I straightened and spun around, racing across the cabin of the *Argo* and down the loading ramp. I hightailed it into the next bay over to check the viability of the ship stored there.

I needed to find a functioning ship and seal myself inside with the chaos fragments—and without Raiden—before he realized that any other ship would need to be manually piloted. Meaning, I would need to be on the decoy ship with the chaos fragments, flying it away from the *Elysium* to lead the Tsakali scout ship off the ark ship's trail.

The scout ship would catch me. It wasn't a question of *if*, but a matter of *when*. They would catch me, interrogate me, and kill me. But by the time they were finished with me—by the time they figured out the ploy—the *Elysium* would be long gone, and everyone I loved would be safe. It would be a sacrifice worth making.

Not that Raiden would see it that way. Which was why I needed to find a viable ship *now*.

The ship in the next storage bay had been crippled by the pirates as well, as had the three other ships we had previously repaired to be capable of basic space flight. I stared down the line of storage bays, taking in the string of ships in varying states of repair. Frustration brought tears to my eyes, and I balled my hands into tight fists, digging my nails into my palms.

I turned away from the lineup of useless ships as Raiden approached, the orichalcum box tucked under his arm, and looked at the inner airlock door. My focus shifted to the pirates' shuttle parked in the open space directly in front of the airlock door, and hope surged within me. The pirates wouldn't have sabotaged their own ship. *And* there was a good chance it would have a functioning AI system that could auto-pilot.

I glanced at Raiden and nodded toward the pirate's shuttle. "Come on," I said, launching forward into a run. I could hear Raiden following close behind me.

"Cora," Hades said, opening a private line through my comms patch. "The Tsakali scout ship has emerged from its FTL jump. It's far enough out that they won't have a visual of the *Elysium* yet, but we only have a few minutes until it's within range."

Spurred on by his warning, I ran faster. Once the scout ship spotted the *Elysium*, even apparently dead in space, as it appeared now, the Tsakali would never believe our ruse. We needed the decoy to be flying away from the *Elysium* with the chaos fragments *now*.

"Powering down artificial gravity in five, four, three, two, one," Hades announced. It would take a while to notice a decrease in the pull of the artificial gravity, and almost three full minutes until we were floating in a zero gravity environment. "What's the status on the decoy?"

I pumped my arms, adrenaline enabling me to push my weakened body far beyond the normal limits. I raced up the loading ramp and onto the shuttle.

"Almost ready to launch," I said, crossing the first two fingers of my right hand. "Open the inner airlock door."

I dashed to the helm at the front of the ship and tapped my heels together to magnetize my boots. My last few lunging steps had been a little floatier than usual. I punched the engine start button and let out a semi-hysterical laugh as the engine powered up, making the floor of the ship vibrate beneath my feet.

Raiden's boots clanged on the metal floor as he jogged onto the shuttle.

I sidestepped to the navigation station, waking up the holoscreen to chart a course away from the *Elysium*. I drew a random line across the screen, telling the ship where to go—anywhere that was *away*—then double-tapped the *execute* button near the bottom of the navigation chart.

The screen flashed red, and a warning box appeared in the center of the holoscreen informing me the auto-pilot was off-line.

"No!" I wailed, hope deflating.

Desperate, I looked over at the pilot's station, noting that the flight controls were of the same orb style as the *Cerberus*. At least I knew how to fly this ship. Small mercies.

I closed my eyes and bowed my head, taking deep, even

breaths to slow my suddenly racing heartbeat. I thought of the Titan and what she had said about the fatigue of this endless struggle. Was I tired?

Yeah. I was exhausted. All the time.

Did I want it to end?

So damn badly.

Well, it looked like this was it. My fight was coming to an end. But not my people's fight. They would live on to continue this endless war. They would survive, but part of me felt like I was getting the better deal.

At least now *I* could finally find some peace.

[40]

Raiden's footsteps slowed as he neared. "What's wrong?" he asked, reading the bad news from my defeated posture.

I raised my head, my cheeks wet with tears, and looked through the windshield into the airlock. The inner door was open. All that was left to do now was to propel the decoy ship into the airlock and out into space. To fly it away. To leave everyone I loved.

Should I say goodbye? Or should I just go? I wouldn't be able to risk radioing the *Elysium* once I was through the airlock—there was too great a chance the Tsakali scout ship might pick up on the signal and trace it back to the *Elysium.*

"Don't tell me those dickwads disabled their own ship," Raiden rumbled behind me.

I shook my head, swallowing repeatedly as I grappled with the turbulent emotions muting my voice. "Not—" The attempt to speak came out as little more than a rasp of air. I cleared my throat. "Not exactly," I said. "The auto-pilot isn't working. I—" I swallowed roughly, then cleared my throat again. "I have to fly the ship myself."

Raiden didn't respond right away. For a dozen heartbeats, I

stood cocooned in his silence. In my peripheral vision, I saw him set the orichalcum box on the pilot's seat, and then he slipped out of his sling and his arms were around me, the front of his body flush against the back of mine. He trembled as he held me, each breath shakier than the last.

My resolve wavered. I didn't want this. I didn't want to leave my people. To leave him. I wanted to fight. To suffer. To feel pain and anger and loss and everything that sucked about being alive, because the good things—love and joy and hope—far outweighed the bad. My nostrils flared and my chin quivered. A silent sob quaked in my chest.

And Raiden held me tight. He pressed his lips against my temple, inhaling deeply. "It's going to be all right," he said, his voice huskier than usual.

I squeezed my eyes shut, pushing a fresh batch of tears over the brims of my eyelids and streaming down my cheeks. I would say goodbye soon. Just a few more seconds. Just a few more heartbeats. I wasn't ready to go yet.

Raiden shifted one of his arms higher, closer to my neck, while the other held firm around my ribcage. His hold tightened, choking off my air supply.

My eyelids snapped open, and I writhed in his hold, twisting and bucking. But he was unrelenting. I clawed at his forearm, then reached back for his face, slapping and hitting him blindly. I kicked off from the front of the navigation panel, but Raiden held tight. He was too strong. I couldn't break free.

Spots danced around the edges of my vision, closing in. My lungs spasmed, trying and failing to draw in air.

"I'm sorry, Cora," Raiden said, his voice breaking. His breath was hot against my cheek. His next words whispered through my bones as the dark curtain of unconsciousness slid shut.

"I love you."

[41]

I woke feeling weightless. My hair had escaped from my ponytail and formed a dark halo around my head, and my arms floated at my sides. Only my boots' magnetism kept me tethered to the floor.

I groaned, and my eyes fluttered open. I waved my hands around my head to shift my hair out of my face and blinked several times, slowly and deliberately, processing the shift in my surroundings. I was no longer inside the pirates' shuttle, but outside, anchored by my boots a half-dozen feet from the end of the open loading ramp. Raiden stared out at me from the top of the ramp, his expression grim but determined.

I heard the whine of hydraulics, and then the end of the loading ramp lifted off the floor. Raiden was taking my place, sacrificing himself by piloting the ship, so I wouldn't have to.

I wouldn't let him do this. I couldn't lose him. Not now. Not ever. He was one of the main pillars in my life, and without him, I would crumble.

I dragged my leaden feet toward the ramp, but I was too weak. Too slow.

"Raiden!" I cried out, twin knots of panic and fear cinching around my heart. "No!" I bent my knees, channeling as much strength as I could into my coiled muscles, then tapped my heels together to demagnetize my boots. I launched myself toward the rising loading ramp.

Too late.

The ramp sealed shut, locking me out of the shuttle. I clung to the hull of the ship, dragging myself along the side until I reached a circular porthole, giving me a view of Raiden inside the ship. He turned away from the raised ramp and started toward the helm.

"Raiden!" I screamed as I banged on the hull with one fist while I gripped a service handle with my other hand, my fingers curved into rigid claws. Tears welled anew, and sorrow choked me from the inside. "Raiden! Don't do this!"

Raiden stopped mid-step, paused, then turned toward me and approached the porthole.

"Please, don't do this!" I begged, the words coming out between jerking sobs.

Raiden pressed a hand to the porthole and gazed out at me, his eyes burning with the purest expression of love.

I stilled, unwilling to waste my last moments with him in a fit of blind panic. Sucking in a stuttering breath, I raised my hand and pressed my palm against the glass directly over Raiden's hand.

Raiden touched his fingertips to the comms patch behind his ear. "Cora . . ." He shook his head slowly, his lips parted but voice silent, as though he was waiting for the right words to coalesce on his tongue.

"Thank you," he finally said, his voice gruff. "You brought me back to life . . . gave me something to live for." One corner of his mouth lifted in the barest hint of a smile. "Something worth dying for. I can never thank you for that. But I can do this. For you. For my mom and Diana and everyone else on that ship."

I shook my head, tears streaming down my cheeks and nose running. I sniffled. "Please don't do this."

Raiden's lips curved into a gentle smile. "Promise me something?"

"Anything," I said, my chest convulsing with a barely contained sob.

"This is not your fault," Raiden said, his voice somber, his eyes resolute. "It's *my* choice. Don't blame yourself."

I closed my eyes and leaned my forehead against the porthole.

"Promise me, Cora," Raiden demanded. "Promise me you won't blame yourself."

A sob clawed its way up my throat and burst out of my mouth. I nodded against the glass.

"What's the decoy's status?" Hades asked through my comms patch. "We need to launch the chaos fragments immediately, or the ruse will be pointless."

I dragged my eyelids open and raised my head, staring at Raiden through the porthole. I drew in a shuddering breath and mouthed, "I love you."

And then I wrapped my grief in a stranglehold and cleared my throat to respond to Hades. "The decoy is ready," I said hollowly, all too aware that my next words would expel Raiden from my life forever. "Open the exterior airlock door."

I stared at Raiden through the glass for a heartbeat longer, then maneuvered the soles of my boots flush against the hull of the shuttle and pushed off, launching myself away from the ship. From Raiden.

I caught hold of a post before I flew past it, then tapped my heels together to magnetize my boots. I angled my feet down toward the floor, and my soles attached to the metal grating with a clang. When I looked up, the shuttle was already halfway into the airlock.

An alarm blared, the discordant chimes warning of an impending decompression. The sound muted as the inner airlock doors slid shut, sealing Raiden off from me. I could still see the ship through the viewing pane, but I couldn't see Raiden.

I watched the exterior door slide open, and the shuttle hovered in the airlock for a moment, like a breath held, before flying away. In a blink, the shuttle was too far out to see with the naked eye, but still, I stared out into space. I could feel Raiden out there, dragging the shards of my shattered heart behind him.

I waited until the outer airlock doors slid shut before turning and starting my trek back to the Bridge. Zero gravity sped up the trip, and without even knowing how I made it back there, I suddenly found myself floating toward the navigation console. I tapped the heels of my boots together and anchored myself to the floor as I stared up at the place where the 3D navigation chart would appear as soon as the system was brought back online.

Meg joined me, silently offering support at my side. She was the only person who knew what had happened down in the transport hangar. She was the only one who knew Raiden was gone.

"The new processor is installed and ready," Fiona declared triumphantly through the comms patch. "Fire her up!"

Fiona's words should have unleashed a flood of relief. Instead, a stony fist clenched around my heart.

A hum filled the air as the *Elysium's* systems came back online, breathing new life into the old ship. Lights flickered overhead, then turned on. I could feel the initial pull of artificial gravity. Finally, the holoscreen flashed on over the pedestal in front of me.

I focused on the pair of blinking red beacons racing away from the *Elysium*, the first Raiden's shuttle, the second the Tsakali scout ship. With each blink of those two beacons, the Tsakali ship inched closer to the decoy. To Raiden.

I gripped the edge of the pedestal so hard that my hands and arms shook.

The beacon representing Raiden's shuttle blinked out, and this time, it didn't reappear. Only the Tsakali scout ship remained, suddenly still.

My heart stuttered, and I stood immobile, paralyzed. A wave

of sorrow so heavy washed over me that I had to lock my knees to keep from collapsing.

"All systems are operational," Hades announced. "Brace for FTL jump."

An alarm blared. The ship shook, and we were away.

[42]

I stared at the screen displaying Emi's vitals in the wall behind her reclined recovery chair, watching the line from her heart monitor dip and peak. Zari psychics occupied six of the other chairs, all in varying states of healing. Only the upright recovery chair behind me sat empty. *My* recovery chair. I had abandoned it almost as soon as I woke, and now I perched on the visitor's chair beside Emi's recliner. I would be here for her the second she opened her eyes. I owed her that much.

My psychic energy had replenished, for the most part, but I kept my regulator activated to block all external input. I was having a hard enough time keeping my own tsunami of grief under control. I didn't need to add anyone else's to the mix.

And there was a lot of grief on the *Elysium* these days. Seventeen of the Zari psychics had fallen to the pirate incursion. Nearly one-fifth of their number. I was hardly the only person nursing a shattered heart.

The FTL alarm blared, and I leaned forward, bracing myself against the armrest of Emi's chair. A moment later, the ship shook as it dropped out of FTL.

I glanced down at the consciousness orb nestled in my lap.

Tangerine ribbons swirled under the glassy surface, all that remained of Raiden. He had made his last backup right before I left for Nykta and he entered cryosleep, what felt like a lifetime ago. Before the pirates attacked. Before the Tsakali scout nearly found us. Before Raiden sacrificed himself to save us all.

I recalled how I had felt when I was younger, after Raiden left for the military, so certain he would die fighting abroad. But he hadn't died. He came home. I supposed I should have been grateful for the extra time I had with him.

But I wasn't. All I felt was a bone-deep loss for the time we could have had together but never would.

Part of me wished I had given him less of me, so I wouldn't feel his absence so intensely. But another part of me wished I had given him more. I should have held him tighter and soaked in his steady, grounding presence for as long as possible. But how could I have known we would have so little time together?

Oddly enough, Hades was the one who understood my grief the best. He knew what it was to be the survivor, to watch someone he loved—me—sacrifice herself so he could live on. He had mourned me the same way I now mourned Raiden.

Hades' relentless drive to bring me back no longer seemed so selfish. I could relate. The mission—the hope—staved off the pain. I would have given anything for such hope to see my Raiden again. I would have *done* anything.

I blinked, and a tear snuck free between my lashes and streaked down my cheek. Sniffling, I raised my hand to wipe the tear away. I stared at my damp fingertips for a moment, surprised I had any tears left in me. I felt dried up. Wrung out. Numb.

I gently curled my fingers around Raiden's consciousness orb and reached out to set it on the tray table attached to the side of Emi's recliner, then pulled my legs up onto the seat of my chair and hugged them to me. I rested my cheek against my knee, my stare lingering on the tangerine ribbons of Raiden's consciousness.

I wanted Emi to be there when he was uploaded into the simulation. She was his mother. It was her right.

But also, I was afraid.

Promise me, Cora. Promise me you won't blame yourself.

As Raiden's last words replayed in my mind, I looked away from the orb, averting my gaze to the floor to trace the geometric pattern of the metal grating.

I was struggling hard with keeping that promise.

What if this slightly out-of-date version of Raiden didn't agree? What if he *did* blame me? Because for the past day and a half, other than the periods I had spent unconscious, recovering from sessions in the asclypos, my mind had been taking me on a grand tour through my memories, making pit stops at all the points in time when I could have done something different to change this outcome.

If only I had given Raiden some other job when he came to me in the gephyra chamber. Then he wouldn't have been with me down in the transport hangar. He would still be alive. Still be here.

But I wouldn't.

That was the reality of the situation, and it sickened me. The moment we entered the transport hangar together, our survival had become mutually exclusive. One of us had to fly the decoy away. One of us had to save the two billion souls stored on this ship. One of us had to die.

And one of us had to live. To remember. To grieve.

Why did *that one* have to be me?

Cloth rustled as Emi stirred in her recliner, and my attention snapped to her face. Dread twisted around in my gut. Emi's eyes fluttered open.

My feet slipped off the edge of the chair, and I set them on the floor. I scooted the chair closer to the side of the recliner. "Hey, Em," I whispered, reaching for Emi's hand with both of mine. I waited for her eyes to open fully and focus on me. I attempted a smile, but my heart wasn't in it. "Welcome back. How are you feeling?"

Emi inhaled deeply, then winced and pressed her free hand against her side. The external wound was gone, but her body was still healing from some of the internal damage. "A little sore," she said, her voice a mere wisp of sound. She licked her lips and cleared her throat.

I released her hand to reach for the stainless steel tumbler sitting on her tray table. I handed it to her, and she sipped water from the straw eagerly.

"What happened?" she asked, releasing the straw. She scanned the room, and I knew what she was looking for. Or rather, *who*. "Is Raiden all right?" she asked when she didn't find him here.

My gaze dropped to the tumbler gripped in her hands. "He, um . . ." I took a deep breath, my hands gripping my knees. "He saved us." I flicked my gaze up to Emi's face, but I could only meet her eyes for the briefest moment. I refocused on the steel cup and then I told her what happened.

My cheeks were wet by the time I reached the end of the story of Raiden's sacrifice. I glanced at the consciousness orb resting on the tray table, innocuous and unnoticed by Emi. Until now.

Emi stared at the consciousness orb in silence, tears streaming down her cheeks. Her blank expression told me shock was setting in.

"I'm sorry, Em," I said, ending with a strained squeak. "I'm so sorry. I—it should have been me." I sank deeper into the chair, waiting for Emi to lash out at me. To blame me.

Emi extended her hand, her palm open and inviting.

Hesitantly, I placed my hand in hers, unconsciously holding my breath.

Emi curled her fingers around my hand, her grip firm. She sniffled, then cleared her throat. "If it had been you," she said, her eyes locking with mine, "then I would have lost you both." Her chin quivered and her face crumpled, buried under a mask of agony. Silent sobs shook her body, and her hand squeezed mine spasmodically.

I moved to the edge of the recliner and wrapped my arms around Emi, holding her close in a futile attempt to absorb some of her sorrow. I clung to her, as she did to me. And together, we mourned.

[43]

I clung to Emi, deeply entrenched within the catharsis of crying.

"Cora?" Hades' voice reached me through my comms patch, quiet and tentative. "Meg assures me you're still awake. Can you come to the Bridge? There's something you need to see."

Sighing, I loosened my hold on Emi and pulled away. I flashed her an apologetic smile, then sniffled and wiped under my eyes.

I touched my comms patch behind my ear as I stood and turned away from Emi, one arm hugging my middle. "Can it wait?" I asked Hades.

"No," he said resolutely. "It can't wait."

I closed my eyes and drew in a slow, deep breath. Whatever Hades needed from me, it had to be important. He wouldn't have called me otherwise. On my exhale, I straightened my spine, squared my shoulders, and opened my eyes.

"I have to go," I told Emi as I turned to face her. She looked so small and frail, like the faintest breeze would shatter her into a million tiny pieces. "Do you want me to send my mom over?"

Emi shook her head, her red-rimmed gaze sliding off me to stare at the consciousness orb sitting on the tray table. "Let her rest." She reached for the crystalline orb, tenderly cradling it in both hands as she moved it to her lap. "Besides," she said, gazing down at all that remained of her son, "I'm not alone."

Heart hurting, I gave Emi's ankle a squeeze through the blanket draped over her legs. "I'll come right back," I promised before turning and heading for the doorway.

I hurried to the Bridge, wanting to get whatever this was over with and return to Emi as quickly as possible. I found Hades standing in front of the navigation console, his hands clasped behind his back as he stared at the 3D model of space on display. I joined him, coming to stand at his side, and he glanced at me.

"I don't want to leave Emi alone for long," I said, my voice hollow.

Without a word, Hades pointed to a blinking red beacon near the edge of the holographic model. He had increased the scale of the model to show the vast distance spanning from the solid white beacon representing the *Elysium* and the blinking red dot on the opposite side of the Milky Way.

I shook my head, not sure what I was looking at. "What—" My eyes widened, and the question died on my tongue. The ship's call tag matched that of the shuttle. My heartbeat quickened. "Is that—" I swallowed roughly, my eyes stinging with the threat of even more tears. I cleared my throat. "Is that *Raiden*?"

"It is the shuttle, yes," Hades said.

I felt his stare burning into the side of my face, but I couldn't tear my focus away from the blinking red beacon. My nostrils flared, and I clenched my jaw.

Hades returned his attention to the holographic model, reaching out to tap the tip of his index finger against the star nearest the shuttle's beacon. An info box appeared below the point of light.

"This is *Acheron*." Hades pinched his thumb and forefinger together, then drew them apart, zooming in the entire holographic model on the selected star. The star's name was familiar, though I couldn't place it. Planets appeared, their orbits projected by dashed lines curving around the glowing star. The blinking red beacon shifted to the fourth planet out from the star. Hades tapped on the planet, and again, a small info box appeared.

"*Othrys*?" I blurted, my eyes bulging. I ripped my stare away from the holographic model to look at Hades. "The shuttle is on the Tsakali home planet?"

Hades nodded sagely, once again clasping his hands behind his back. "The planet they abandoned long ago, as the star was growing increasingly unstable and *Othrys* could not sustain life for much longer."

A thousand questions whirled around in my mind. What happened to the shuttle after it vanished from our radar? Had Raiden somehow escaped from the Tsakali scout ship? Or had he been captured? How had his ship come to be on Othrys? Was Raiden there, too? Could he survive on that dying planet? If so, for how long?

But only one question truly mattered. I glanced at the blinking red beacon, then returned to looking at Hades. "How long would it take us to get there?"

"I've already charted the course," Hades said, his focus returning to the holographic model. "As soon as the FTL drive is recharged, we can jump. We should reach Othrys in just under six hours."

Six hours to reach the shuttle. Six hours to find out what happened to Raiden. Six hours to get answers to all those questions spinning around and around and around inside my skull.

I had wished for a mission—some sliver of hope that I might see Raiden again, in the flesh, however slim that sliver might be. Well, there it was, right in front of me.

And yet, I couldn't bring myself to accept it fully, like I feared it was a trick. An illusion. A mirage.

Like I would blink, and the signal from Raiden's ship would disappear.

I looked at the beacon blinking steadily on the holographic

model of Othrys. "It could be a trap," I said, stating the obvious. "We would be risking everything."

Hades nodded. "It could be, but Acheron emits enough gamma rays that it will hide the burst of chaos energy from our arrival. They won't be able to detect us jumping in."

As he spoke, hope swelled within me. We were really going to do this.

"We can scout more once we've arrived," Hades added. "Unless you don't think it's worth the risk."

"I—" I leaned forward, gripping the curved edge of the pedestal. "I have to know. If he's still alive . . ." I squeezed my eyes shut, and a single tear slid down my cheek. "I have to know."

Hades' hand covered mine. "Then let's go find out."

Thanks for reading! You've reached the end of *Song of the Soulless*, but not the end of the Atlantis Legacy. Cora's adventures continue in *Blood of the Broken* (Atlantis Legacy, #5).

Go to www.authorlindseysparks.com/sacrifice to grab a FREE copy of
Sacrifice of the Sinners, the Atlantis Legacy prequel novella.

MORE BOOKS BY LINDSEY SPARKS

ECHO TRILOGY

Echo in Time

Resonance

Time Anomaly

Dissonance

Ricochet Through Time

KAT DUBOIS CHRONICLES

Ink Witch

Outcast

Underground

Soul Eater

Judgement

Afterlife

ATLANTIS LEGACY

Sacrifice of the Sinners

Legacy of the Lost

Fate of the Fallen

Dreams of the Damned

Song of the Soulless

Blood of the Broken

Rise of the Revenants

ALLWORLD ONLINE

AO: Pride & Prejudice

AO: The Wonderful Wizard of Oz

Vertigo

THE ENDING SERIES

The Ending Beginnings: Omnibus Edition

After The Ending

Into The Fire

Out Of The Ashes

Before The Dawn

World Before

THE ENDING LEGACY

World After

For more information on Lindsey and her books:

www.authorlindseysparks.com

Join Lindsey's mailing list to stay up to date on releases

AND to get a FREE copy of *Sacrifice of the Sinners*.

www.authorlindseysparks.com/sacrifice

ABOUT THE AUTHOR

Lindsey Sparks is a bestselling Science Fiction and Fantasy author who lives her life with one foot in a book—so long as that book transports her to a magical world or bends the rules of science. Her novels, from Post-apocalyptic to Time Travel Romance, always offer up a hearty dose of unreality, along  with plenty of history, mystery, adventure, and romance.

When she's not working on her next novel, Lindsey spends her time hanging out with her two little boys, working in her garden, or playing board games with her husband. She lives in the Pacific Northwest with her family and their small pack of cats and dogs.

www.authorlindseysparks.com

Facebook: www.facebook.com/authorlindseysparks
Facebook Reader Group: www.facebook.com/
groups/lovelyreaders
Instagram: @authorlindseysparks
Pinterest: www.pinterest.com/authorlindseysparks
Newsletter: www.authorlindseysparks.com/join-newsletter

www.ingramcontent.com/pod-product-compliance
Lightning Source LLC
Chambersburg PA
CBHW050822190726
48286CB00007B/1960